The Blackmore Collection

CLEAN REGENCY ROMANCE

THE LADY SERIES

DAISY LANDISH

Editing by Rachael Lammie
Cover art by CharmingPixyArt

BEACHES AND TRAILS
PUBLISHING

About the Author

Daisy Landish is a romance and contemporary fiction author living in the UK, whose clean and sweet novellas have tugged at readers' heartstrings across the pond and beyond. When she's not writing love stories, Daisy spends her time reading, hiking at dawn, and riding into the sunset on her horse, Rosebud.

www.daisylandishromance.com

f facebook.com/daisylandishromance

X x.com/daisy_landish

◎ instagram.com/daisylandishbooks

a amazon.com/author/daisylandish

BB bookbub.com/authors/daisy-landish

g goodreads.com/Daisy_Landish

Also by Daisy Landish

Spring Break: Cozy Mysteries for Spring

Missing The Lady

THE LADY SERIES BOOK THIRTEEN

Chapter One

"Give it to me! It's mine, Bea!"

"No, Bri. It isn't yours!"

Releasing an unladylike groan, Emily Blackmore placed the feather quill back in the small cup of ink and rose fluidly from her pedestal table. As the oldest daughter of Lord and Lady Blackmore, the Earl and Countess of Keymouth, it was her duty to intervene when one, two, or all of her four sisters, or younger brother, were on the war path. She walked across the Oriental rug to the door with graceful steps and yanked it open. She crossed the rugged corridor to the room adjacent to hers.

Her identical twin sisters stood in front of their canopied bed in their riding habits, tugging a blue ribbon. Placing her hands on her hips the way her mother did whenever she was cross with them, she clicked her tongue with distaste.

"Beatrice, Bridget, cease this foolishness at once!" she chided the black-haired girls. "Papa and Mama are still abed. Do not disturb them."

If their mother woke up because of the raucous, Emily would receive the blame as the eldest daughter. She glared at her sisters, who returned the angry stare.

"Give me the ribbon," she demanded, stretching forth her hand.

Grudgingly, the twins handed it to her with identical pouting lips.

Emily surveyed the ribbon and sighed. It would be difficult to determine who owned it, as both of them had loved blue accessories that matched the colour of their eyes.

"Why don't we search for the other ribbon?" she suggested and moved towards the chest of drawers in a corner of the room.

"We do not have time for that, Emily. Hastings sent word that he's waiting for us," Bridget pointed out.

"And we do not want him to be cross with us when we're late. His beak-like nose flares, making him look like an angry ostrich," Beatrice inserted with a giggle. Seconds later, Bridget joined in the tittering.

Since their riding instructor awaited their arrival in the stables, Emily stared at her fifteen-year-old sisters, at a loss about what to do. She needed to settle the issue and then return to her letter writing.

"Beatrice, Bridget, why don't you go riding now and then we'll look for the other ribbon together when you get back? I'll hold onto this one." Knowing they would protest because they were a headstrong lot, she quickly added, "Whoever argues with me won't get my share of biscuits during afternoon tea."

The twins shared a mischievous look and smiled. Their heads bobbed in agreement.

"Off you go." She took their hands and led them out the door, down the corridor, and down the rugged stairs before returning to her room.

Hardly had she settled at the table when she heard a soft knock on the door. A tired sigh escaped from her lips. Would she ever finish her letter before it was time for breakfast?

"Come in," she called with exasperation.

Her maid, Mary, entered the room with a beatific smile and dipped a small curtsy. "Begging your pardon, my Lady. I received this letter last night from Mr. Baines."

Emily's sky-blue eyes widened, and she whirled around in her chair with excitement lifting her face. Mr. Baines was a footman in the Duke of Linfield's household. Her beau, Philip Sinclair, had put the onus on the footman to send his letters to her with the utmost secrecy. And it was Mary's duty to receive the letters without Emily's parents any the wiser.

Emily jumped to her feet and took the correspondence from the smiling maid, who speedily exited the room. She hastily broke the envelope's seal and unfolded the letter. With widened eyes, she scanned the contents of the letter.

My Dearest Emily,
I hope this letter meets you in the best of health. I am most
delighted to inform you that I am done with my commission. Yes,
my love. I am coming home to you, at last.

Unable to stop herself, Emily screamed. Quickly, she clamped a hand across her mouth, but she knew it was too late. Her immediate younger sister, a light sleeper, would have heard the scream and would come to investigate the cause. Hopefully, she hadn't woken her parents, whose bed chambers were down the corridor. Her other youngest sister and brother slept like the dead, so she knew they wouldn't have heard her.

Like clockwork, she heard a door open, and footsteps hurried towards her room. A sleepy-faced Olivia opened her door and entered the room. Her eyes travelled across the room as if she expected to see someone else other than her older sister.

"Are you being attacked?" Olivia, her favourite sister, asked, rubbing her right eye.

A bright smile crossed Emily's oval face. "Philip is coming home."

The last vestiges of sleep disappeared from Olivia's blue eyes. She hurried forward and clasped Emily's hands. Together, they jumped happily, cackling like little schoolgirls.

"That's wonderful news, Emily. Did he say when he'll arrive in England?" Olivia enquired when they stopped hopping.

"I haven't finished reading the letter," Emily confessed with a sheepish smile. "I was overcome with joy at the news of his impending return."

"Well, go on then," Olivia requested as she walked towards the bed to lie on it.

Without further prompting, Emily proceeded with reading the rest of the letter.

I have not been told precisely when we'll leave here, but I guarantee it will be soon. Lord knows I won't sleep a wink until I arrive in London to behold your beautiful face. I will count the days until I can hold you in my arms and profess how much I love you. Until then, rest easy, my love, knowing you and I will be together soon and forever.
Yours alone,
Philip.

Emily clasped the letter to her heart and whirled around the room in her pink nightdress while Olivia laughed.

"I can't believe he's finally coming home." Exultant laughter bubbled from her throat. "When he told me he was joining the King's army, I was appalled. But after he explained he had to do it because of his Father, I understood and gave him my blessings, even though I feared I might never see him again. Oh, I'm so happy!"

Olivia sat on the bed with a worried frown wrinkling her forehead. "What about his limp? Does it not bother you?"

Emily waved a dismissing hand in the air. "I do not care if he returns to me crippled. All that matters is our love for each other."

"If you say so, Lady Sinclair."

Emily giggled and twirled to the large wooden dressing mirror where she imagined herself in her mother's wedding gown, walking down the aisle with her arm entwined in Philip's. Her oval face brightened with joy, as she imagined the long veil encasing her blonde hair trailing down the altar. Even though she barely reached his shoulders, she knew that they would make a perfect couple.

"I can't wait," she gleefully exclaimed.

"At last, we can tell Papa and Mama," Olivia put in and clapped her hands with glee.

Emily's heart missed a beat.

Chapter Two

Emily's heart thumped against her chest as her mare pranced majestically across the fields. The wind blew wisps of her blonde hair from her hat, and she reached for them with a shaky hand to put them back in place.

Sweet Mary, I'm as nervous as a cat on a hot tin roof.

Two years! It was two years since she last set her eyes on the man her heart so desperately craved to see. Now that the hour was upon her to gaze into his handsome face again, she was a mass of nerves. She looked down at her velvet riding habit with its tight bodice, high waistline, double cape-collar redingote, and buttoned skirt, hoping that she would appear lovely in his eyes.

Beside her, Olivia also rode regally in similar attire, looking as though she didn't have a care in the world. To her left, was Mary in her black and white maid's uniform.

"Thank you aplenty for agreeing to act as my chaperone, Liv. I know you dislike riding in the mornings," Emily told her sister.

A smile graced Olivia's beautiful face. "Well, I would have said I hope you'd do the same for me, but I do not wish to sneak around with my proposed suitor when the time comes."

Emily laughed. "When the time comes? Liv, you're ten and six and have already been introduced in Court. If it wasn't for..." She paused and gave her sister a conspiratorial wink.

At her behest, Olivia had feigned an illness on the night of her coming-out ball and refused several suitors who showed interest in her when she later attended several soirees. Emily would forever remain grateful to her. For if her sister had found a suitor, their parents would have carried out their threat of finding Emily a husband, since she had rejected many suitors. Unbeknownst to them, she was waiting for Philip.

"Thank goodness for that," Olivia heaved a sigh of relief. "I do not wish to wed anytime soon. So, I'm somewhat fretful that now that your suitor is back, Mama and Papa will focus their attention on me to get married." She wrinkled her pert nose with disapproval. "Why do men get to marry of their own choosing, but women must be rushed into marriage as soon as we have our first flow? Tis unfair."

Emily would have replied to her sister's usual tirade about how unfair females were treated, but she had caught sight of a man on a large stallion a short distance away, just by the gatekeeper's former cottage. Her father had built their gatekeeper a larger cottage for him and his family on the other side of the estate. Her heart raced again, and she tried to focus her attention on Olivia's continued diatribe. But she couldn't.

Everything in her leapt for joy at the sight of the tall, broad-shouldered man of muscular build seated majestically on a brown stallion, attired in all-black riding clothes and boots. His raven black hair blew haphazardly in the wind as his penetrating turquoise blue eyes searched her face with joy. His slightly tanned skin was a testament to his period on the battlefield. He looked just as perfect as he had when she laid eyes on him four years ago at her cousin's birthday party.

Emily's heart lurched in her chest as he slid awkwardly from the horse because of his bad leg, but he managed it well. Like someone in a trance, she watched as he leaned on his black cane and limped towards them. Her lips parted, her cheeks flushed, and her eyes enlarged at the wonderful sight he made.

He's become even more handsome than when I last saw him.

When he reached them, he first turned his attention to her sister and bowed slightly. "Lady Olivia."

"My Lord," Olivia remarked with a smile. "Welcome back."

"Thank you, my Lady."

His focus finally returned to Emily. She feared she might just swoon. Sweet Mary, she had faked swoons just to avoid meeting unwanted suitors who had come calling, but she might actually lose consciousness from the anticipation of Philip holding her in his strong arms.

She regarded him with adoring eyes as if he was the most incredible thing to ever grace the earth.

"My Lady," he proclaimed in a low tone, and she closed her eyes for a breathless moment, enjoying the sound of his voice. When she opened them, he reached for her with one arm, and she gladly slid off the saddle into his welcoming embrace.

Pent-up relief flooded her that the man she loved so much was finally home. Tears she couldn't hold back raced down her beautiful face.

"Please do not cry, my beloved. You will make me think that this is a sad reunion."

She forced a smile through her tears. "You know it is not, my love. I have yearned for this moment for so long that I have thought of nothing else, especially after I received your letter."

"You echo my thoughts and words, my Lady." He cupped her chin and caressed her face. "I know I ought to do this right, but I find I cannot wait any longer."

Emily frowned as she wondered what he was talking about. Her eyes became as huge as dinner plates when he went down on his right knee.

"Pardon me, my Lady, for I cannot bend on my left leg. "I love you, Emily, with every breath in me. Will you do me the honour of becoming my wife, my Lady?"

Emily lifted her head to look at her sister. Olivia beamed from ear to ear. "Would you please give him a reply, Em?"

Philip chuckled. "Thank you, Lady Olivia."

Emily blushed to the roots of her blonde hair before nodding as she stared at Philip with all the love in her heart.

"Yes, Philip. I will marry you."

His throat bobbled as he swallowed thickly. "You accept me, bad leg, and limp, without a title, little money, and all?"

She clasped his clean-shaven chin in her hands. "Yes, Philip. I do not care if you came back to me blind, crippled, deaf, or mute, or even if you were a pauper. I love you just the way you are."

He pushed himself to his feet with a sparkle in his eyes. "Oh, Emily. You've made me the happiest man on earth."

Joyous laughter rumbled from her chest when he lifted her and swung her around, notwithstanding his bad leg. Olivia came forward when he set her down to offer her congratulations. Mary stood afar, smiling.

Feeling as if all her dreams had come true, Olivia hugged her sister and gazed at her betrothed with adoring eyes.

"Walk with me a little, my Lady, if you don't mind," Philip requested, after the two sisters finally pulled apart in their euphoria.

Emily acknowledged that she would do anything for him, irrespective of any request he made. And she fell into step with him. Olivia and Mary walked discreetly behind, leading the horses.

They enjoyed a leisurely walk as Emily filled him in on some interesting happenings in England while he was away. He assured her that he would call on her father to formally seek her hand in marriage after he had spoken to his own father, The Earl of Linfield.

Emily could hardly believe what had just transpired in the fields on the way back home. Now, at last, she could tell her parents about the man she had loved since she was fourteen. How wonderful!

Chapter Three

"I must say, Lady Emily, you look like a breath of fresh air this morning," Mary mentioned two days later as she combed Emily's waist-length tresses.

Emily broke into a short laugh. "Why, Mary, words akin to poetry from you?" Emily stared at her maid's reflection in the mirror.

Mary paused the brush strokes, her face as red as a tomato. "Pardon me, my Lady. I did not mean to be too forward. I am grateful that you taught me to speak well and to read. I do not mean to take it for granted."

"Oh, hush now, Mary. You did nothing of the sort." Gazing in the mirror, Emily's eyes trailed over her oval face, her delicately carved brows, pert nose, and rosebud lips. The soft blush on her cheeks reflected the blossoming of love in her heart for Philip. She accepted that not only was she fine-looking, but she felt good with the knowledge that not only was she in love, but she was also loved in return.

"Thank you for the compliment, Mary. I do feel wonderful," she remarked, as the maid tied her hair in a yellow chignon to match her yellow muslin dress and slippers.

After a brief knock, Sarah, her youngest sister, entered the room in her morning gown, followed by Alexander, the Blackmore family's youngest child and only son.

"Emily, Mama and Papa wish to speak with you in the drawing room," her thirteen-year-old sister informed her while her ten-year-old brother jumped on the canopied bed like he was wont to do whenever he entered her room.

"Alexander!" she admonished with a warning finger at him.

He gave her a toothy grin before climbing down from the bed. She could never be cross with him, smiling back before she could stop herself.

"What did you do wrong?" Emily asked Sarah, who had gone to the window seat to look down at the garden. Her parents never summoned her in unison unless they wanted to talk about marriage, which they hadn't done in a while, or to berate her for not taking good care of her sisters or brother caught in mischief.

Sarah turned around with innocent-looking light blue eyes and shrugged. Her quiet demeanour never failed to intrigue Emily. She never could guess what the young girl was up to.

"I did nothing wrong."

"Then it must be Beatrice and Bridget. Did they fool Mama and Papa again by each pretending to be the other?"

Sarah shook her head.

Emily turned to Alexander. Still grinning, he shook his head. Olivia rarely got into trouble, so it left Emily with dread that her parents wanted to talk about marriage. Mayhap it was for the best. She would tell them about Philip if pushed to, so they would stay their hands about choosing a suitor for her as they had often threatened.

"Very well, then." Emily fluidly rose from the stool and, with one last glance at the mirror, she exited the room while making sure her siblings repaired to their own rooms.

As she walked down the stairs, she felt a trickle of excitement at the thought of telling her parents that she had finally found the man she desired to marry. They would be overjoyed. With the anticipation of the elation they would feel at her long-awaited news, Emily pushed open the double doors of the drawing room after a brief knock. She dipped a perfect curtsy to her parents, who were seated on the sofa, having tea and Cook's millefruit biscuits.

"Emily do take a seat and have some tea," her mother invited with a fond smile.

Too excited about her news, which would cause her teacup to rattle in her hands, Emily refused the offer and chose the green brocade armchair by the French windows. The picture of the scenery made with its green fields, and flourishing colourful flowers, reminded her why Spring was her favourite time of year.

Her mother, whom they all got their looks and blonde hair from—apart from the twins and Alexander, who spotted black hair like their father—delicately dabbed her lips with her handkerchief and studied her daughter's face.

"Should I tell her, or do you prefer to do the honour?" her mother asked her father, which surprised Emily because he rarely spoke. Her mother was the talker.

To drive home her point, her father simply nodded.

"I've got good news, my darling!" Her mother's joyous laughter rang out in the room. "You are to be married come Summer."

Emily's eyes enlarged, and her palms suddenly became clammy. Her heartbeat increased its pace, and she felt faint.

"What?" she croaked when her parents stared at her with expectation.

"It was most fortunate of us to have been at the opera last night. We met an old friend of your Father's. The Duke of Stanbridge. While we conversed, he told us that he is seeking a wife of good breeding for his eldest son, The Marquess of Holton." Still, in her exhilaration and not sensing her daughter's distress, the Countess went on. "Of course, we told him we had a suitable bride for his son. So, my dear, prepare. Lord Holton will call on you in a few days."

Emily jerked to her feet. She couldn't take any more of her mother's words. "Mama, I will not marry him. You can't and won't make me."

Her mother gasped in horror. "Emily, what has gotten into you for you to speak to us in such a disrespectful manner? Apologize at once!"

Emily, seeing her mother's angry face and her father's tightened one, realized that she couldn't take the stubborn route to plead her case, or she would alienate them. Dropping to her knees before them, she placed both palms together.

"Mama, Papa, I'm sorry for speaking rudely to you. But I cannot marry Lord Holton."

Her mother shook her head. "You will. It's hardly our fault that we were forced to choose you a suitor. After all, you've been rejecting eligible men since your first Season for the flimsiest of reasons. Is it your desire to be on the shelf like an old maid?"

Emily shook her head and chewed on her bottom lip. Was this the right time to tell her parents about Philip? Would it make them change their minds about the Duke's son?

"But Mama, I have found a suitor."

Her parents shared a startled look.

Emily smiled. "He returned from the war a week ago. He loves me and wants to marry me, and I love him, too."

With a frown contorting his face, her father asked, "Who is this man you speak of?"

"His name is Philip Sinclair. He's the youngest son of the Earl of Linfield," she blurted out, desperate to be heard.

Her father leaned back in his chair with shock and then rage filled his blue eyes. "You want to choose a penniless and untitled man over a Marquess, a man who would someday become a Duke?"

"I love him!" Emily cried.

"What do you think you know about love?" her father threw at her with a savage bite.

"Be reasonable, Emily," her mother softly put in. "We want a good future for you. This man isn't a good match for you, my dear."

"But he is, Mama. I love him."

"You will grow to love Lord Holton just as I grew to love your Father," her mother gently said, but Emily vigorously shook her head.

"I don't—"

"Linfield's youngest son?" her father interjected. "Isn't he the one I heard returned home from battle, a cripple?"

"He's not a cripple!" Emily yelled. "He was injured in the line of duty and will forever walk with a limp, but that hardly classifies him as a cripple. He's a war hero, Papa. He served his King with honour."

"What do you know about honour?" he snapped.

"I might know nothing about honour, but I know everything about love. Philip and I love each other. I do not care if he doesn't have a title to his name, social standing, or wealth."

"But I do," her father barked. "While I commend him for his bravery and service to his King and country, he is not fit for you. My first daughter will not marry such a fellow. You will marry Lord Holton, and that's final."

"But, Papa, I—"

"Silence!" his voice came out like a whiplash, and Emily shrank back in horror. With tears smarting her eyes, she shot to her feet. "I won't marry him. I won't!"

Sobbing helplessly, she ran to the door. Her mother called her, but she didn't look back as her heart clenched with despair. She fell on her bed in her room and sobs shook her lean frame.

Chapter Four

"They mean for me to be unhappy like more than half of *the Ton* in their arranged marriages," Emily sobbed in Philip's arms the following day.

After crying herself to sleep the previous day, she had woken up and sent word to Philip, requesting that they meet secretly at the gatekeeper's cottage the following morning. She had hardly arrived there with Olivia and Mary in tow when she dismounted from her horse to throw herself in Philip's arms, weeping hysterically.

"Why, just the other day, my friend, Elizabeth, told me that she should have waited like me instead of allowing herself to be coerced into marrying a man of good social standing who is old enough to sire her. She's very unhappy."

"Hush, my love." Philip handed her his snow-white handkerchief. "I do not like to see you like this."

Emily daintily dabbed at her eyes. "Mayhap you should come with me to see my parents. Maybe if you tell them how serious you are about marrying me and tell them how you plan to take care of me, I'm sure they will relent."

Emily's lips parted in alarm when she saw Philip wince and his face furrowed into a frown. "What is it, my love? Has my horrible news made you change your mind about taking me as your wife?"

Philip shook his head, cupped her wet cheek, and solemnly avowed, "Never doubt my love for you, Emily. My intention towards you hasn't and will never change. I will marry you irrespective of these obstacles."

Flicking her tongue across her upper lip in a nervous gesture, she probed further. "Then, what is it? Why do you not want to come with me to see my parents?"

His hand dropped from her face, and he turned slightly away from her. "You're not the only one with bad news regarding our plans to get married, my love."

All the colour drained from Emily's face at his ominous words. Her hand went to her lips involuntarily in horror of what he was about to tell her.

"You mean...," she left the words hanging.

Philip retrieved her hand from her mouth and squeezed it. "Please do not despair, Emily. We'll find a way through these challenges."

Emily shook her head. "Please tell me the truth. Your Father refused you marrying me, didn't he?"

He raked his fingers through his hair and nodded.

"But why?" she went on. "Why? If I'm good enough for a Duke's son, why am I not suitable for you?"

"It's not you, Emily. You're fit for a King. But the truth is, before my return, my Father had already arranged with the Marquess of Harrington. He wants me to wed his oldest daughter on her first Season."

Emily felt as though someone was sucking the air out of her lungs. Anguish filled her, for she knew Philip would never go against his father's wishes. The Earl of Linfield ran his household like the army. Not one of his five sons had ever done anything contrary to his dictates. Like his four older brothers, Philip had joined the army just to please him. She was aware that Philip had always lived in the shadows of his older brothers and had, as a result, developed low self-esteem because of his lack of status. That is, until they met. Emily had made him feel special, like a man in his own right.

"All is lost then," she declared with despondency.

Her parents didn't want them to get married, and now, Philip's father was also against it. What hope did they have of being together?

"No!" Philip vehemently refuted. "All hope is not lost, darling. If I have to speak to my Father every day until his ears become sore from my constant badgering, then I will do it."

Emily stared at him with scepticism. The Earl of Linfield was a formidable man. She was as sure as night followed day that he would disown Philip and cut him off if he dared to marry her without his consent.

"Do not look at me with so much doubt in your eyes, Emily. I know I have never stood up to him before, and I have always done what he ordered of me. But you must know, my love, that this is the first time I have wanted something so desperately." He placed her hand against his chest. "Feel my heart, Emily. It beats for you. If I am ever compelled not to see you again, or marry you, I swear, my heart will stop beating in protest. I cannot begin to imagine my future without you."

"Oh, Philip." More tears dropped from Emily's eyes.

"I beg your pardon, my Lord," Olivia, who had been sitting on the broken stone steps of the cottage, came forward. "I did not mean to eavesdrop, but I do not like seeing my sister so distressed."

Emily sniffed and bestowed on her sister eyes filled with love for her.

"I see the only solution to this problem is for you two to elope," Olivia suggested with a small shrug.

Emily gasped. "Olivia!"

"I speak the truth; Emily and you know it. As both parents want to play God in your lives, you might as well take the role yourselves. Go to Gretna Green and tie the knot."

Emily glanced at Philip to see how he was taking the suggestion. His face was unreadable.

"That's scandalous, Olivia. Have you forgotten? When word gets out about what Philip and I have done, you and our sisters will find it hard to ever find a good suitor."

Olivia clicked her tongue. "Don't you worry about that, Em. It will blow over when another scandal occurs, which most certainly will. You and I both know that us Blackmore sisters don't frighten easily. Besides, with a sizeable dowry, men would practically break down our door seeking for a Blackmore girls' hand in marriage."

Emily could not help but laugh. It was true. But she did not want to take such a drastic measure, one that would hurt her family. Regardless of her parents' stance, she loved them dearly and would not want to bring disgrace upon them. No one liked to be the topic of gossip among *the Ton*.

Philip agreed with her when he shook his head. "I do not think the situation has called for such an action, Olivia. Thank you for the suggestion, though." With a determined look in his eyes, he carried on. "I have decided I will speak to my Father again and tell him I do not wish to marry the Lady he has chosen for me. I will come to the manor tomorrow and tell your Father of my intention to marry you."

Emily's eyes lifted. "You will?"

"Yes, my love. I will. I will do anything for you, even fight the entire Napoleon army alone just for you, my darling. Come what may, we will get married."

Peace settled in Emily's heart at his declaration. They would fight for their love. "Thank you, my Lord. It's you or no one else." And she meant it. She would rather remain a spinster than marry anyone other than the man she loved.

Chapter Five

I t took all the teaching that her parents and instructors had inducted into Emily since she was a little girl for her not to bite and chew on her nails while she waited.

"Would you please stay still, Emily?" Beatrice complained from her position at the window seat.

"Yes, Emily. You're making us dizzy, walking back and forth like that," Bridget inserted with a frown.

Emily paused in her pacing and glared at her sisters. "Do you expect me to sit still, or sing a Ballard while I have no idea what is going on in the drawing room?"

"Well, you sent Olivia to eavesdrop at the door, didn't you?" Bridget asked with a twinkle in her eyes.

Beatrice shrugged. "If you had sent us instead, we would have brought you word by now."

"No," Emily refuted. "You would have started arguing with each other as you're wont to do and Papa and Mama would have caught you."

"At least we would have heard something before being banished from there," Beatrice pointed out.

Bridget concurred with a nod.

Emily ignored them and continued pacing. About half an hour earlier, Mary had hurried to inform her of Philip's arrival at the manor. Her father, out of propriety, had grudgingly given him an audience. He had sent word to her, forbidding her to come anywhere near the drawing room, or he would not give Philip a listening ear. She had diffidently smiled because her father knew her well. She had planned to plead her case with Philip beside her. And now, she awaited news of their fate from Olivia.

Why is it taking so long? Should I be hopeful? Does it mean Philip has convinced Papa that we make a perfect match?

Emily wasn't left waiting any longer when she finally heard hurried footsteps heading towards her door. Shivers of apprehension raced through her as she awaited her sister's arrival.

Olivia slowly pushed open the door. The sadness in her eyes told Emily all she needed to know. Her father had refused Philip's proposal. Her face turned pasty as she quietly walked to her bed, head lowered, and sat.

"Give me the heart-breaking news, Olivia." Emily lifted her head. "Papa refused, didn't he?"

Olivia twirled her hands by the door and nodded. "Philip tried his best to convince him that he can take care of you, but Papa vehemently refused. He said if Philip truly loved you, he ought to allow you to marry a better man."

Aghast, Emily hastily asked, "And Philip agreed with him?"

Olivia shook her head as she moved away from the door to sit beside her. "He pleaded with Papa to consider your feelings, but Papa was adamant. Papa warned him to stay away from you because he had already permitted Lord Holton to court you, and he didn't want any scandal arising from him courting you, too. He left shortly after that."

"Oh, Philip." Tears stung Emily's eyes. "I can't bear the pain he must be going through right now due to Papa's rejection, just because he's without title and not fairly flushed in the pocket." She jumped to her feet with tears streaming down her face. "Why can't Papa see that I do not care about such things? If he truly wants me to be happy, he will agree to Philip and I getting married."

"I'm so sorry, Emily." Olivia rose and put her arm around her sister's shoulders. "There must be something we can do to make Papa change his mind."

The twins moved forward with identical, sorrowful looks. They put their arms around their oldest sister in solidarity.

Beatrice pulled away from the embrace some seconds later with hope in her eyes. "Perhaps when Mama returns from visiting friends, we could all speak to her to talk to Papa on your behalf."

Emily sighed and wiped her tears with the handkerchief she retrieved from her morning dress. "It's no use. Mama is with Papa on this. They believe marrying Lord Holton means I will someday become a Duchess. They do not know I'd rather be a penniless commoner than the wealthiest Duchess in all of England."

"It might not be so bad being a Duchess, you know," Bridget chipped in and got kicked in the chin by her twin for her troubles.

Emily extricated herself from the circle and hurried to her table. "I must write to Philip post-haste."

She brought out writing paper from one of the drawers on the pedestal table, dipped the quill in the ink, and then paused. What could she write? What could she say to the man she loved who was just unfairly rejected by the man he had hoped would be his father-in-law? Her heart clenched with pain. Would Philip and she truly never be together because of their parents? It was all so unfair.

Olivia came forward. "You could do as I suggested the other day."

Her eyes elevated to find Olivia giving her a knowing look. Emily shook her head. Elope? Could they really do that? She couldn't bear to imagine the scandal it would cause. Could she be so selfishly in love to disregard what eloping with Philip would do to her family? But she loved him so much, that the thought of not marrying him left her in despair.

She broke down in tears again and her sisters comforted her. Finally pulling herself together, she wrote to Philip and asked him what they would do now that everything seemed to be against them. Could they surmount the obstacles before them?

She waited on pins and needles for his reply to her letter. She was afraid that, irrespective of his promise to her the day before, he would write to tell her to forget about him and marry Lord Holton.

Her hands shook when his reply, at last, came as she unfolded the letter. The first two sentences she saw made her heart skip a beat.

My love, we elope to Scotland tomorrow night. Are you in accord?

Was she?

Chapter Six

"Surely you must know it is for the best, Emily," the Countess of Blackmore told her daughter.

Emily stared at the black and white swans at the lake as they played in the water. She wished she could be as carefree as those regal birds. They did not have a care in the world. After she and her mother fed them some bread during a walk to the park, the birds had gone about their business, waiting until their next feed from the Blackmore gamekeeper.

Alas, that wasn't the case for her. In a few hours, she would leave England for good with Philip so they could be joined in Scotland without their parents' consent. No respectful family would ever receive them in their homes, even if they returned to England. The *Ton* would consider them outcasts wherever they went, even though some people thought eloping was romantic. Her parents would most likely forbid her siblings from ever speaking to her again. Not that they would listen. Her sisters would correspond with her, notwithstanding.

She held back a sob. How she would miss them! They had been joyous when she divulged the contents of Philip's letter to them. With glee, they had plotted how to keep her absence hidden from their parents so that she and Philip could make haste to reach Scotland, or close to it, before they found out.

"Emily, don't tell me you're so distraught. You're giving me the silent treatment."

Emily's face reddened. Lost in her thoughts, she had forgotten her mother had spoken to her. "Forgive me, Mama. I was miles away."

Her mother let out an audible sigh. "Tis to be expected. That's why I requested you join me for my morning walk. Thinking so much isn't healthy, I must tell you." She reached for her daughter's hand on the bench they sat on and held it. "Darling, your Father and I mean well for you. Someday, when you look back in your respectful position as the Duchess of Stanbridge, you will be pleased you heeded our counsel and married Lord Holton. Just you wait and see."

Emily knew that her mother's enthusiastic words would never come to pass, but she simply nodded.

"I, too, didn't want to marry your Father, at first. I had my sights on my childhood friend. My parents had other ideas, and I'm grateful to them for leading me aright. I have no regrets marrying your Father."

Emily shook her head. "But I may not be so lucky, Mama. Have you thought of that?"

"You will." Her mother patted her hand and smiled. "We've heard wonderful things about Lord Holton."

But not as wonderful as my Philip.

"You will forget about this Philip as soon as you have your first babe."

Emily blushed and looked away, thankful when a footman came to inform her mother that one of her friends had come calling. As they walked back to the manor and her mother complained about early morning callers, Emily looked around the estate. Knowing she might never be allowed to return to the only home she had ever known left a thick knot in her chest.

The rest of the day went by like a blur before Emily. She kept counting the hours until she would have to leave the manor for good. Even when her father called her during the afternoon tea to speak to her about gracefully accepting Lord Holton's proposal, she could hardly answer him. He chalked it up to her sulking and sent her away in anger. She went to the pavilion where she found Olivia engaged in her favourite pastime, reading.

Olivia lowered her book with great annoyance and said, "Good heavens, we shouldn't have told Beatrice and Bridget about your plans. The tittering lot will give it away soon, what with the way they've been going about whispering and giggling like silly little schoolgirls."

Emily laughed, enjoying the fragrance of the flowers in the surrounding garden. "They're only excited. You know they have always been corky."

Staring at her with keen eyes, Olivia asked, "Are you?"

"Yes. No." Her befogged mind could not really say what she was feeling.

"All will be well, Emily. Perhaps, with this act of bravery, Papa and Mama will allow the rest of us to marry men of our choosing. They would be scared of more scandals tied to the Blackmore name."

Emily's lips twitched. "So, I'm the sacrificial lamb of some sort?"

Laughter flowed from Olivia, and she hugged her sister. "I shall miss you dearly."

Teary-eyed, Emily replied, "I'll miss you more."

Emily tried to keep her emotions at bay when she bade her parents a goodnight rest after they retired to the drawing room. The twins would keep them busy by playing the pianoforte and singing. Olivia and Sarah would help her escape. Sarah had misled their parents into thinking that she wanted Emily to help her with her French, as her French tutor planned on giving her a difficult test the following day.

"We aim to study all night without disturbance," Sarah fibbed shamelessly.

Olivia used the excuse of reading, which didn't come as a surprise because everyone knew she loved doing that. Since Alexander wasn't in on it and was an early bird, they had kept him out of it.

With Olivia and Sarah's help, Emily was accompanied by Mary, who would act as her chaperone. They escaped from the manor through the side door.

"Godspeed," Olivia, in tears, told her as they embraced one last time.

Crying silently, Emily and Mary rode to the gamekeeper's old cottage on the horses they had arranged earlier with the stable lad. There, they met Philip, two footmen, two coachmen, and his old governess, Mrs. Lackey, who would act as Emily's formal chaperone until they were wed. They had arrived in two carriages.

"Are you sure about this, my love?" Philip questioned her as soon as she reached them. "It's not too late to change your mind and go back home."

She smiled, trying to hide her nervousness. "It's too late now. Mayhap if I had not met you and fallen in love with you. But as it is now, I cannot go back."

"I will make you the happiest woman in the entire world," he earnestly declared.

She giggled. "I reckon on it, my Lord, else all this will be all for naught. Are you a man of your word, kind Sir? Because I intend to hold you to it."

He drew her in his arms, laughing. "Have no fear, my fair Lady. I told you I would do anything for you, didn't I? So, here I am, at the risk of getting shot by your Father and disowned by mine when they find out what we've done."

She gasped.

"No worries or regrets. You're more than worth it."

Emily glanced back at the imposing manner that the moon cast its shadow upon before she climbed into the coach, where his former governess already waited.

To love, she toasted inwardly.

Chapter Seven

Thoughts of her family filtered through Emily's mind as the night gave way to dawn. She wondered if they had been discovered. Had her mother, in her grief, taken abed and asked for her hartshorn, which she customarily did when she heard scandalous news about anyone close to her? Her mother's theatrics usually made her laugh. Now, she found no humour in her mother's suffering. Her father, most likely, had summoned everyone in his household to question them about her whereabouts and to find out her accomplices. Her sisters would prefer to be stoned with rotten tomatoes in the village square than to divulge her secret.

"Do not look so downcast, my Lady. You will make me feel like I abducted you."

Emily turned and bestowed on her beloved an uplifting smile. "'Tis not so, darling. I am merely wondering if our actions have been revealed, and what of my parents' reaction to it."

His handsome face turned solemn, and he nodded. "Fret not, love. All will be well in the end."

"Well, I certainly hope so. Your Father will never forgive me for what he'll term a betrayal of his trust," Mrs. Lackey, who sat beside her in the coach, chipped in and then smiled. "But I never could say no to you, my favourite ward, could I?"

Philip smiled back and shook his head. "Thank you for your sacrifice. I promise you it will be worthwhile."

The elderly woman curved her body to look at Emily. "I can see that."

Emily reddened and lowered her head. As the travelling chaise had rolled across the countryside, the older woman had questioned her as if she were a prisoner of war before falling asleep hours ago. They had found a common footing and ended up liking each other.

"I have told the coachman to stop at the nearest inn. I reckon we will arrive in half an hour or thereabouts. We'll stop for breakfast and refresh ourselves and the horses. We still have a long way to go," Philip informed them.

Emily nodded and looked out the window at the lush greenery. Blackmore was quite a distance from London and then Scotland. Without drawing attention to her actions, she curved her body slightly in Philip's direction so she could surreptitiously look at him without appearing bold, even though he was her betrothed, and she had a chaperone.

He looked exceptionally handsome in the light of day in his sky-blue shirt, dark blue coat, and trousers. His long legs, stretched out across the large cabin floor, were crossed at the ankles.

Her face turned a rosy hue when she lifted her gaze to study his face and found him watching her. His right eye dimmed in a wink and his face broke into a fond smile. Emily blushed terribly and looked away. The governess's short laugh worsened her embarrassment.

They arrived at the inn a short while later. Although the sun was high in the sky and trickles of sweat beaded her forehead, Emily put on the hood of her cloak to not be recognized by anyone in the bustling inn while the stable lads took the horses away to be fed and groomed. Unfortunately, Philip could not find any spare room or table for them. Even the private parlour had been booked.

"A Marquess sent his footman some thirty minutes ago to book some rooms and a private parlour," the apologetic innkeeper informed them.

As if on cue, a tall, broad-shouldered man and a small travelling party arrived at the common room just then. Emily deduced he was the

Gentleman who had made preparations aforehand. She was certain Philip would have done the same, but for the hastiness of their journey.

To her admiration, Emily watched as Philip conversed with the Marquess about sharing the private parlour and the rooms for the ladies where they could refresh themselves.

After a rather awkward moment, he agreed. With a sigh of relief, Emily followed the innkeeper's wife up the stairs a quarter of an hour later with Mary and Philip's former governess in tow. By the time she returned downstairs, the serving girls had spread a sumptuous meal across the two tables that were put together for their sake.

The men stood as she entered the parlour. Philip helped to pull a chair out for her and Mrs. Lackey. Emily looked from the Lady seated before her to the Gentleman by her side and wondered what their story was. The man had an aura of authority about him and, just like Philip, spoke little as well. She tried conversing with the Lady for the fact that they were sharing a meal, but the former wasn't forthcoming.

"Thank you again for allowing me to share your room," Emily tried again.

The Lady ducked her head and simply nodded. "It's fine."

"We haven't been introduced. I'm..."

"My dear, I hardly think it's an occasion to be throwing names about," Mrs. Lackey interjected.

Emily turned to look at her with horror. It was only right to know with whom one was dining and who to direct thanks for their benevolence. Surely, with all her years of training others, the older woman ought to know that.

Leaning sideways in the pretence of trying to arrange the wisps of hair that had escaped from Emily's tortoiseshell comb after she pulled back her hood, the older woman whispered, "Don't be so naïve, you sweet child. Can you not see that they have the same intention as you and my dear boy?"

Emily, coloured to the roots of her hair, darted a glance at the Gentleman and Lady. With swiftness, she lowered her gaze in order not to embarrass them. Little wonder Philip had not made the introductions when they met. It made Emily speculate if the inn was like a pathway for all those heading to Gretna Green. Possibly.

Emily ate the delicious food, barely able to conceal her curiosity about the couple. Philip and the Lord discussed the weather, the war, amongst other things, while Emily had long given up on drawing a conversation with the woman.

After they had dined and rested long enough for the journey ahead, Philip suggested they depart. A message was sent to the coachmen to get the chaises ready.

"Good luck," the Lady croaked when Emily bade her goodbye.

Did I just see a sparkle in her brown eyes? Emily pondered as she walked out of the parlour and the inn with her arm nestled in the crook of Philip's arm. So intent on deliberating if they would still encounter the other couple in their journey to be wed, she didn't at first notice when Philip had stiffened beside her. She lifted her eyes to his face, thinking it might be his bad leg aching him. When she saw anger in his eyes, not pain, she followed the direction of his gaze and inhaled sharply. Standing a few feet from them beside two black-lacquered coaches were five armed men. The Earl of Blackmore's emblem shone on the doors of the coaches.

How did they find us so soon?

"Lady Emily, your Father has requested us to take you back to Blackmore. Would you please come with us with no hassles?"

In that moment, darkness enveloped Emily.

Chapter Eight

Propped against an astonishing heap of pillows, Emily noisily blew into her handkerchief.

"Emily, you cannot continue like this," Olivia stated with a worried frown.

Her red-faced and puffy-eyed sister eyed her with annoyance. 'Why ever not? Isn't it obvious that my life is ruined? What am I without the man I love?" She wrinkled her nose, red from constant sniffling. "A bag of nothingness."

Olivia's eyes watered. "Please do not speak in such a manner, Emily. I hate to see you so desolate."

Emily shrugged. "I think you're the only one who does. Papa and Mama hate me enough to not wish me happiness."

Olivia shook her head. "It might look as if they don't mean well to you, but I know they love you, Emily. Mama was almost hysterical when Alex told her you were gone. Papa was at his wit's end. They feared more for your safety than your reputation. Highwaymen have become quite intrepid of late, coming out at any given time of the day."

"They didn't trust Philip, a former soldier, to take good care of me because they see him as a cripple and unfit to be their son-in-law," she spat out with bitterness. "Well, congratulations to them, here I am." She spread her arms wide. "Back home, unharmed."

"Only unharmed?" Olivia asked tentatively, and Emily understood what she meant. She hadn't given her sister details of the journey till the time they captured her like a common thief.

She nodded and blew her nose again. Yes, she had returned home unmarried and uncompromised, kicking and screaming until she lost consciousness from fatigue. When she had come to in Philip's strong arms, the men had warned him to stay his hand when he reached for his pistol to prevent them from taking her. Afraid they might hurt him, she had agreed to go with them. But it dawned on her that they would take her home to her parents and she would never be allowed to see Philip again because of what they did; she had been panic-stricken and acted like a bedevilled girl. And it had been all for naught. They had deposited her unceremoniously at the manor and went about their business as if they hadn't just crushed the dreams of two people in love.

And to her disappointment, her parents had managed the situation in such a way that word never got out. In her growing depression, she was tempted her to go to the dailies to tell them her story of eloping with the man she loved, just so she could force her parents' hands and make Lord Holton cry off marrying her. Knowing it was selfish, she had thrown away the idea.

A soft knock sounded on the door, so soft that the distraught sisters didn't hear it at first. When it became louder, Emily exhaled audibly. Possibly it was her mother, there to coerce her to eat her meals. Ever since she returned...no, was dragged back, to the manor two days ago, she had refused to eat anything. Pleas for her to take even a bite from an apple by her mother and sisters had fallen on deaf ears. Her furious father hadn't joined in the attempted coercion.

"You ought to be ashamed of yourself for almost bringing disrepute to this family because of a stranger."

His words had cut into her heart like a sharp knife into ham. And she had sobbed nonstop for hours on end. She was weak from lack of food and constant weeping. She wouldn't give in until they allowed her to marry Philip, even though they forbade her to ever see or speak to him again.

"Come in," Olivia called.

A timid-looking Alexander with tears welled in his eyes walked into the room.

"Emily, please say you forgive me for telling on you." He wound his hands together. "I was afraid for you when I saw you riding out from my bedroom window. I thought you would come to harm. I heard Mama and Papa talking about highwaymen attacking people anywhere and anytime."

Emily stretched her arms, and her brother ran into them, sobbing. "I forgive you, Alex. I could never stay mad at you. Thank you for caring enough about me to tell Mama and Papa about it."

He pulled away and stared into her wet eyes. "But you have been so sad. And you refused to eat. I saved some scones for you, but Sarah told me not to bother because you won't take anything until Papa changes his mind." With hopeful eyes, he asked, "Should I get them?"

She had never denied him anything before, but she needed to make a stand, or her parents would never take her seriously. "Maybe later."

His face fell. "Are you still mad at me?"

"I was never mad at you." She kissed his wet cheek. "All is forgotten. What have you been up to?"

He grinned and talked about his lessons, which she listened to half-heartedly. Her mother came into her bed chamber, and her other sisters, a quarter of an hour later.

Lady Blackmore sat on the bed and regarded her daughter with worried eyes. "Do you wish to lose your beauty, Emily? Your eyes are sunken, your skin is sallow, and your cheeks are gaunt. All because of a man. What manner of foolishness is this?"

Defiantly, Emily said, "I do not care if I lose my beauty, Mama. Of what use is it to me when the one my heart craves for will never be allowed to see it again?"

"Cease this idiocy at once, Emily. He is not the only man in England. Lord Holton will make you happy and help you to forget about this man who had no regard for us by taking you away in such a scandalous manner."

"You forced his hand. You forced us. He came here like an honourable man to talk to Papa. But what did he do? He rejected him."

"For the best reasons."

"No. For your own reasons. You think I care about wealth and titles and opulence? I do not." She sniffed. "I am prepared to waste away until you and Papa understand that it's either Philip or no one else. And if you force me to marry that man, I swear I will visit an apothecary for the appropriate poisons."

Her mother shot to her feet, aghast. "Desist from saying such things, Emily. It is not profitable."

Emily held onto her defiance. "I have spoken my mind. Can a human live without its heart? You have wrenched my heart from my body by forbidding me to marry Philip."

"I see we're at a stalemate. Your father won't give in, and neither will you. Stubborn lots! I shall have a talk with him again, but know this, he's more obstinate than you. The sooner you accept your fate with Lord Holton, the better for you."

With that, she left the room. Her siblings straggled after her, all talking at once, pleading with her to reconsider.

Emily was left alone in her misery. Never would she accept what they wanted for her. "Oh, Philip. How I miss you!"

Chapter Nine

Although her parents forbade her from seeing Philip again, they said nothing about exchanging correspondence with him. And so, Emily and Philip continued to exchange letters with the help of her sisters. Because of her role in the elopement, Mary was banished to the kitchen. Another maid had been assigned to Emily, one who was charged not to speak to her, only see to her needs. Thankfully, her sisters had feigned innocence in the whole ordeal.

Consequently, their parents had instructed them to watch over her. Furthermore, they had even gone as far as enticing them with their favourite things just so they would inform them about her activities. Given such breathing room, Philip and Emily carried on writing to each other daily.

Only Philip's immediate older brother had known about his plans, as fate would have it. And so, they joined heads together for success this time around. Philip had written to her the previous day to tell her of the new plan. They would hire someone of their stature to head for Scotland while they would head for the Colonies. By the time their parents discovered the deceit, they would be long gone.

Emily acknowledged that it was a brilliant idea, which she kept up her sleeves to prevent anyone from knowing, divulging her secret, and throwing a rub in the way. She trusted her sisters with her life, but she couldn't tell what their parents might have enticed them with, what might be too much for them to resist. Or be ridden with guilt, should they be found out. And then there was Alexander.

"Best I keep it close to my chest, Olivia," she informed her sister, who had pressed her for details as they took a leisurely stroll in the Blackmore Park. Their parasols hung above them to keep their porcelain skin from the sun's harshness. "The less you know, the better for you. I wouldn't want our parents to think you betrayed their trust. Why, they might just force you to marry Lord Holton."

Olivia cringed with revulsion. "I dare say this whole incident has taught them a lesson—the Blackmore sisters have ounces of steel in them and can't be forced to do what they don't want."

Emily let out loose laughter, her first in days. Only Philip's letters brought a smile to her lips these days, and her sisters' attempts to make her smile. Oh, she would miss them dearly.

"He is here!" a scream rent the air.

Emily's face fell. She knew who her twin sisters were referring to as they ran towards them. Her mother had informed her that the Marquess of Holton would visit her that afternoon and impressed on her to behave well.

Breathlessly, the twins reached them. "Mama said you should return to the house post-haste. Lord Holton is here."

Emily groaned perceptibly.

Bridget gave her a smile filled with mischief. "Do you wish for us to make utter nuisances of ourselves? Beatrice and I could act like lunatics fit for Bedlam. That ought to make him run with his shirttails flapping behind him."

Emily placed a hand across her mouth as laughter shook her slim frame.

"Mayhap, Olivia could declare her love for him," Beatrice suggested.

"I will do no such thing." Olivia, affronted and looking scandalised, stamped a slippered foot on the ground.

The twins observed her with disappointment.

"We could pretend to be one person. Frightened old Sir Wesley to smithereens the other day. He was near to having a heart attack. Mama had to send for her smelling salts to revive him."

"Didn't that earn you two being reprimanded to your rooms for two days?" Olivia reminded them.

"Ah. But it was worth it."

"So, what will it be?"

Emily beamed at them. "Thank you for your suggestions and desire to help. I will handle it on my own. I will simply tell him I do not wish to marry him."

"Oh, la, how boring!" the twins cried in unison and walked away with displeasure.

"Those two might just be the death of our parents when it's time for them to get married."

"It would serve them right," Emily laughed and then sobered up as they arrived at the manor.

"Good luck," Olivia clasped her sister in a tight embrace before walking away.

Emily slowly walked to the drawing room. She closed her eyes, took in a deep breath, and released it slowly. She pushed open the double doors and stopped short when she saw the man standing by the fireplace, looking out the French windows.

"You!"

The man with whom they had shared the private parlour at the inn moved slightly to confer on her a rueful smile. "For my sins."

With her eyes still as huge as dinner plates, she queried, "What are you doing here?" Then she gasped. "Were you sent by my parents to spy on us that day? Were you the one who sent word to them regarding where to find us?"

"Please come, and take a seat. I'll explain everything,"

Emily was about to do his bidding, but then remembered that she had told herself she would be so disagreeable to him. He wouldn't wish to remain in the same room with her, let alone want to marry her.

"Do not deign to tell me what to do in my Father's house."

Surprise entered his grey eyes at first, then amusement. "Forgive me, my Lady. I did not mean to be so...forward." He settled himself on a wingback chair by the fireplace. "Please come in. I have something to tell you."

Even though it was traditionally wrong for a Gentleman to sit before a Lady, she knew he had done so to make her come into the room. She hoped with all her heart that whatever he wanted to tell her ended with the sentiment that he did not wish for them to be wed. Emily, with light steps, walked into the drawing-room and sat a few paces from him on the settee. She didn't close the door for propriety's sake, but she wouldn't put it past her sisters to eavesdrop. The twins might just carry out their devious but hilarious plans if they reckoned things weren't going so well for her.

"Lady Emily, I had nothing to do with you returning home to your parents in...in such a manner." He rubbed his hand across his bearded chin as if he was trying to hide laughter. She peered at him intensely so she could accuse him of mocking her. He dropped his hand and looked serious again. "Truth be told, I did not know who you were until I saw the coaches and heard the man you were with calling your name when you were taken away. Then, I realized who you were, and I was blown away by the turn of events. Coincidence had brought us to the same place with the same intention."

Emily frowned because she was yet to ascertain where the talk was heading. All she wanted to hear from him was that he would not seek her hand in marriage. But what about the Lady he had been travelling with? Perhaps he was a rake who led women astray by promising them marriage and running away with them just to have his wicked way with them.

"You will have to do better, my Lord," Emily leaned back in the chair. "For, I do not understand."

He nodded. "Right. Do you want to marry me?"

Shock reverberated in Emily's body at the direct question. She had come there intending to act so terribly; he wouldn't ask her such a question.

She answered truthfully, elevating her chin, and looking him directly in the eye. "No, my Lord. I do not want to marry you."

Her lips parted when she saw his face soften with relief. Hope rose in her chest.

"I do not wish to marry you, either."

Emily found it hard to sit still after his blunt confession. Was this really happening, or had she fainted from exhaustion on the walk back to the manor and was now having the sweetest dream ever?

"I love Miss Anna Wallace, the second daughter of the Baronet of Herbyshire. I have loved her since I was sixteen. Yes, she's merely a Baronet's daughter, and I'm to be a Duke someday. But she means more to me than the title and all the wealth and prestige that comes with it."

He rose and paced the room. "It's only unfortunate that my Father didn't understand that which forced my hand to flee from England so I could marry the one I truly loved."

Emily pinched herself to be sure she wasn't watching a play, or someone was playing a cruel trick on her.

"Seeing you being taken away that day with your beau struggling to get to you despite his limp made me realise what a coward I had been. The knowledge that you didn't want to marry me gave me the courage to stand up to my Father and reject being coerced into marrying you when I loved another Lady. I threatened to abdicate the title and my position and he reluctantly relented." A smile lifted his grey eyes. "You see, I'm the only son eligible to become his heir. My brothers have scandals trailing them till even the West Indies." He fluidly rose. "In conclusion, I apologise for my cowardice. If I had spoken to my Father earlier, I dare say you and your beau wouldn't have thought of leaving England for Scotland. I will speak to your Father at once and apologise profusely. Luckily, they haven't yet announced the marriage banns."

Only the thought of being forcefully made to marry him, if they were caught in such a compromising position, stopped Emily from rising and throwing her arms around him.

"Thank you," she whispered, with tears in her eyes. Maybe now her parents would allow her to marry the only man who had captured her heart forever.

Chapter Ten

"Pinch me, my love. Lest I be dreaming."

Philip chuckled as he twirled her slowly around the vast ballroom floor in his manor. "Do you not realise your Father still looks at me as if I'll still flee with you from England? If I were to cause you any form of pain right now, he might have me arrested on the spot by Bow Street Runners."

Held in the arms of the man who was now her husband, attired in her mother's lace wedding gown and being watched by family and friends on her wedding day, Emily laughed softly. "Papa has forgiven you for that. Pray tell, wasn't it the two of you who went for a long walk this past week?"

Philip grinned. "Believe me, my love, you do not want to know how that conversation went."

"Oh," she raised her head to adoringly gaze into his eyes filled with amusement. "I thought it went well. Papa came back home smiling."

"Yes. I agreed with him that if I ever hurt you, he would have me shipped to parts unknown."

Laughter shook her body. "He didn't!"

"He sure did. But he need not ever make such plans because as long as I live, as long as there's breath within me, I will never cause you pain."

She nodded with a beatific smile. "I believe you."

Philip drew her closer, not minding his limp and she leaned into him, finally able to enjoy his embrace without feeling sinfully wicked about it. Her eyes moved around the beautifully decorated ballroom with wreaths, ribbons, and flowers, and the people dancing beside them. She caught Philip's father smiling at her, and she forced a smile back. She had never met a more intimidating man. As fate would have it, he had admired the way his youngest son had stood up to him and insisted he wanted to marry the woman his heart desired. Fortunately, he hadn't yet approached his friend about his interest in their families' joining together in marriage.

Philip's brothers, who were all in attendance, had to intervene though. Their intercession had prompted the Earl of Linfield not to only bequeath Philip one of his manors, but a small business for him to manage as well. Now, Emily's parents' minds were at rest that her husband would be able to take care of her. Not that she had ever been in doubt of that. Philip was a brilliant man who had already thought of some investments he wanted to venture into with his friends. With the money from the business his father bequeathed him, he planned on putting his personal business ideas into fruition. He hadn't planned to hang on his father's sleeve.

Emily glanced at her parents, who were dancing a few feet away. Given Lord Holton's disinterest in marrying her, her parents had reluctantly accepted Philip to avoid a scandal. Whispers had already begun about their aborted elopement. Someone from the inn must have recognized her. She didn't care about that anymore. All her dreams had come true, and that was all that mattered.

At last, it was time for them to depart for their honeymoon. She went upstairs to change. Mary and Olivia helped her.

"Get prepared, Olivia. It's your turn next."

Olivia put a hand up in protest. "Not if I have anything to do about it."

"You can't escape it. I bet they already have plans for who they want you to marry."

Olivia's lips twitched with mischief. "If anything, your ordeal has taught me, it's to be one step ahead of our parents."

Emily tsked her tongue. "Godsend you with your plotting. Let me know if I can help."

"I most assuredly will."

Outside the manor, Emily gave her teary-eyed mother a long hug. Her father stood beside her with pride in his eyes. He kissed her cheeks and bid her a happy married life. Emily hugged her sisters and Alexander before Philip helped her into the travelling chaise. She dabbed at her eyes with her handkerchief as she waved her family goodbye. Her husband comforted her until she pulled herself together. Now that they could be together without a chaperone, she leaned into him. She was comforted by the fact that she could come to visit her childhood home as she pleased.

"Where are we going?" she asked as she was not familiar with the terrain.

He evaded her gaze. "Didn't I tell you?"

"No, you didn't." She wrinkled her nose, her eyes narrowing with suspicion. "You have kept it a secret."

His eyes twinkled. "Scotland."

Emily put her hand across her mouth as laughter quaked her shoulders. "I hope Papa never gets to find out."

"It doesn't matter now that you're finally mine." He drew her into his arms and kissed her.

"I'm yours forever," she affirmed with exultation.

The End

Falling for The Lady

THE LADY SERIES BOOK FOURTEEN

Chapter One

"Olivia! Papa and Mama want to see you in the drawing room."

A gasp escaped from Olivia's lips as she whirled around from the floor mirror she had been staring at. Her shock came not from her youngest sister, Sarah, and her younger brother, Alexander, who entered her room without being summoned. It came from the news. Surely, she should have expected it. But certainly not on her birthday. She just turned seventeen a few hours ago. Couldn't they have given her a little time to adjust to being a year older? She eyed her siblings, who, regardless of the many servants in the Manor, were always the ones their parents sent to fetch someone. Did they always hang around the drawing room whenever their parents were in residence?

"Don't look so miserable, Liv," Sarah encouraged with a small smile. "Maybe they want to give you another birthday present."

Olivia shook her head in refutation at the words. Customarily, her parents presented their six children with only one set of gifts per birthday. The gorgeous pearls lying in her dresser drawer were a testament that she would not receive more gifts from them.

"I'd sure love it if they told Cook to bake you another lemon cake," Alexander mentioned with a grin.

"But of course. So you can make yourself fat like a pig," Sarah chided in her usual sharp tongue.

"Better than looking as thin as a rake," Alexander retorted with an equal bite.

"Enough!" Olivia snapped. "The fact that Emily married and left doesn't give you the right to speak to each other like that in my presence. By God, I will take a switch to both of you."

Their young faces paled, and Olivia felt terrible for pouring her frustrations on them. Quickly, she moved forward to draw them into her embrace. She missed Emily dearly. Her older sister would have handled the situation better. As she was now the oldest child in the house, it was her duty to put her younger siblings in line; a task she didn't enjoy because she would rather stay in her room to read her books.

"Am I forgiven?"

Both adorable faces nodded with small smiles. Olivia took in a deep breath and exhaled lightly. She could only hope that her parents were summoning her for something her mischievous twin sisters did, something Sarah or Alexander did. They did so frequently. Particularly, since Emily married her sweetheart and left Keymouth to live with him.

Olivia thought of feigning illness, perhaps claiming it was from eating too much cake at her small birthday party earlier in the day. But she knew that wouldn't fly with her parents. After Emily's stunt of almost eloping with her beau, her parents were now wary of their children and what they were capable of.

"Come along," she said as she lifted the skirts of her purple lace gown. "No point delaying the evil hour."

Muttering a prayer that she might be wrong regarding her parents' reason for requesting her presence, she exited her room, strode down the rugged corridor, and descended the carpeted stairs.

"Help me," she told the several portraits of her ancestors hanging on the walls.

"Good luck," Sarah whispered as she and Alexander turned in the direction of the side door leading to the garden.

Olivia almost called them back for Dutch courage, without the alcohol, of course. Acknowledging their presence wouldn't help her, she knocked briefly on the doors and threw them open.

"Olivia! I thought you would have changed out of your party dress by now. 'Tis almost dinnertime."

The early reprimand by her mother almost made Olivia lift her skirts, turn around, and run back to her room.

She curtsied to the Earl and Countess of Keymouth who sat regally on the sofa overlooking the French windows, enjoying a bottle of sherry before dinner. With nervous fingers, she pushed a strand of her blonde hair behind her ear. For once, she hadn't tied it in a chignon but allowed it to flow down her shoulders to her back. She sat on the armchair before the fireplace.

"I was just admiring the dress one last time when Sarah and Alexander came to deliver your message."

"Emily chose well. It complements your eyes," her mother praised. The dress was a birthday gift from Emily.

"You know I'm not one to dwell on preambles," her father abruptly cut in. "Today, you became seventeen, more than ripe for marriage. So, Olivia, my darling, you either attend the coming London Season and find a suitor, or we'll do so for you."

Olivia's lips parted company. It was worse than she had envisaged.

"But Papa, it's Beatrice's and Bridget's Coming Out Season," she protested firmly.

"Correction. It's *your* second Season. They will have theirs next year."

"But, Papa—"

He put a hand up. "No, buts, my dear. I will not have you or any of your sisters put us through what Emily did," he explained tightly.

Her mother, looking sympathetic, concurred with her husband. "Yes, darling. We do not wish to be held ransom again simply because you fancy yourself in love and then go against our dictates. So, before the end of the Season, bring us a man or else we'll find one for you and by God, you will marry him."

"No eloping either," her father grimly added. "And need I remind you to bring a man befitting your status as the daughter of an Earl?"

Olivia gritted her teeth until they almost turned to powder. Her face turned a rosy hue as she tried to come to terms with all her parents just said.

"That's unladylike, Olivia," her mother pointed out.

Forcing me into marriage when I'm not ready is unladylike, Olivia almost shouted, but she put a rein on her flailing emotions.

It was all Edward's fault. If only her cousin hadn't reneged on their agreement. Witnessing the whole drama that ensued before Emily's marriage to her husband, she had taken matters into her hands. She had clearly deduced that as soon as her older sister was married, her parents would focus their attention on her. She had written to her mother's brother's son to pretend an interest in her, so her parents would leave her be about the marriage issue for a while. Edward had agreed until he fell in love with a friend's sister and wrote back to tell her he could not go through with it for the sake of the Lady he loved.

"Sulking will get you nowhere, my love. What say you about our proposal? The ball is in your court now. Play it wisely," her mother gently advised.

With a resigned sigh, Olivia rose to her feet. "Very well, Papa and Mama. I will do as you have requested. I will attend the ball and find a man worthy of my hand."

"Excellent."

"Brilliant."

"May I be excused?"

To plot. She silently added.

"Yes."

She dipped a curtsey and departed from the room as her mind raced to form a new plan. Her parents thought they had won because she acquiesced so easily. Oh, they had no idea what she was capable of. There was no way that was she getting married soon.

Chapter Two

Still seething from the news of the newest staff member in the Blackmore family, *a companion*, who sat beside her, Olivia glanced out the window as her father's carriage made its way down the long drive towards the rumbling Manor ahead.

'Tis all Edward's fault. She repeated the words that had become a litany over the past few days since her parents gave her the marriage ultimatum. As if that wasn't bad enough, when she announced that she wished to visit her cousin's family a few miles from Keymouth, her parents had surprised her by hiring a companion to go everywhere with her. She had argued that her three sisters and brother could act as her chaperones, but they refused.

"You're too intelligent for your own good, Olivia. We refuse to take chances. Miss Fitzroy will accompany you wherever you go," her mother had told her and then patted her cheek when she saw how furious she was. "Not that we don't trust you, my dear. Circumstances have forced our hands. You and Emily are quite alike. Bold, spirited, and very much fond of having your own way."

And her own way, she would certainly get.

"You don't have to look as though someone stuck a stick up your back, Olivia. It's only marriage, not like we're sending you to the gallows."

Olivia gave her younger sister a quelling look. "Oh, hush. I don't expect you to tell me anything intelligible about it. What do you know about marriage?"

Bridget clicked her tongue as she cut in. "I know if it weren't for you, Bea and I would be preparing for our first Season."

"No one is stopping you two since you're so desperate to get married. In fact, why don't you tell Papa you want to take my place?"

Both twins stuck their tongues out at her. Incapable of letting it go, not in the mood she was in, Olivia did the same. And they all burst into laughter, except her companion.

"Now, children, behave!" the middle-aged woman told them as the carriage approached the Manor and made a stop.

"Me first!" Bridget exclaimed and scrambled out of the carriage, the way she always did when they travelled.

Olivia shook her head. "For shame, Bridget. Mama will have apoplexy if she could only see you."

Bridget laughed. "You're only upset because I won."

Giggling, Olivia stepped down from the coach with the help of the footman. Normally, she would take time to enjoy her surroundings before entering the building. Not today. Serious business brought her here. Lifting the skirts of her blue travelling gown, she climbed up the stone steps where a red-liveried butler was waiting to thrust open the door.

"Welcome, Lady Blackmore."

"Thank you. Pray tell, where is Edward?"

"Mr. Barton is taking a walk in the garden with a companion."

It was on the tip of Olivia's tongue to ask the identity of her cousin's companion, but she managed to quell it. Servants knew practically everything that went on in a household, so she was sure the butler would know who the person was.

However, she brushed past him into the house and headed for the garden, not waiting for the rest of her travelling party. She had already told her sisters what to do so she could have some privacy with Edward in order to tell him to find someone else to take his place in her pretend courtship plan.

On cue, she heard Beatrice scream behind her. "Sweet Lord, my head. An entire fleet of ships must be sailing through it."

"I fear she will swoon!" Bridget cried.

"Beatrice!" Miss Fitzroy shouted.

Giggling at her younger sisters' theatrics to distract the older woman, Olivia hurried through the side door without a backward glance.

"Thank goodness," she whispered when she discovered her cousin's companion was a man and not the Lady he was in love with, as she had feared it would be. She drew closer to the men who had their backs to her. She recognized the tall, broad-shouldered man with dark brown hair and well-fitted clothes as her cousin's best friend—Thomas, the Viscount Corley of Stenford.

"Where does he expect me to find a bride? I find the thought of attending balls surrounded by silly blushing debutantes with their eager mothers and guardians nauseating. He means to cut me off from my position as his heir and my inheritance of the title and his estates if I do not find a bride this coming Season to produce an heir of my own. Does he not realise that I'm only three and twenty? I'm not ready for all that baggage. Tell me, Edward, where do I find a woman who will be willing to pretend to be my betrothed just so I may have a year of respite?"

Olivia could hardly believe her ears. Had she fallen asleep on the ride here or was this real? She tried to remember what she knew about Thomas Corley. His father was the Earl of Livingston and he was the oldest son; next in line for the Earldom. What a perfect match! Not only was he pleasing to the eye, but he was also a known acquaintance, and could possibly be called a friend.

"Forgive me for being too forward, My Lord. I believe I'm the bride you're looking for."

"Good God, Olivia! Where did you come from?" Edward's blue eyes widened. Before she could reply, he went on. "Please do not start with that nonsense plan of yours. We're discussing serious matters here."

Affronted, Olivia raised a warning finger in the air towards her irate cousin. "Don't you dare speak to me. You broke your promise to me and so, you can no longer tell me what's serious or not." She turned her attention back to Lord Stenford who gazed at her, amusement filled his brown eyes. "My Lord, let me tell you why I'll make a wonderful fake betrothed to you. Not only do I speak three languages, but I also have a vast knowledge of the arts, math, and science. I assure you that I won't bore you to tears when we're out in polite company. I'm not a henwit like most debutants. You will never regret having a fake courtship with me because we have the same cause. We do not wish to marry—yet."

Olivia smiled disarmingly because she could clearly see that she had astounded the young Viscount.

"Lady Olivia?" he called as if he just realised that she was the one standing before him.

Olivia laughed. "Come now, Thomas. Let's not stand by such formalities. You and I have been friends since I've gotten to know you through this obnoxious cousin of mine."

"I know. I'm merely flabbergasted at your proposal."

"My parents wish to force me to wed, but I'm not yet ready."

He rubbed a hand across his chin-strap beard. "May I ask why?"

"Let's just say I'm not ready to be caged and spend the rest of my life popping babies like it's going out of fashion."

Thomas threw back his head and gave a sharp bark of laughter.

"And you, if I may ask?"

He grinned. "Well, I haven't finished sowing my wild oats."

Olivia laughed softly.

"And he loves another, which means this won't end well by the time you fall in love with him."

"Cease your yapping, Edward." She turned to the Viscount, "Kind Sir, you're in no danger of me falling in love with you. We'll have a serious business arrangement and nothing else. When the Season is over, our contract will expire and then, we can do as we please."

He shrugged, still looking amused. "That sounds plausible."

"Then do we have a deal?"

"We sure do." He took her outstretched gloved hand and shook it.

"There you are!" Miss Fitzroy's voice rang out in the distance.

Olivia, smiling brightly like the shining sun above, whirled around and hurried towards the harried woman. Nothing could take away her joy at that moment, not even when Edward again proclaimed in an ominous tone, "This will not end well."

Chapter Three

He's late!

Only the rule of decorum instilled in her since she was a baby had stopped Olivia from gritting her teeth in public. She was certain that the four hundred people in the enormous ballroom would hear her above the din if she dared to try it. Her Grace, the Dowager Duchess of Stockham, always threw the first ball of the Season, and everyone who was everyone attended. Well, everyone looking for a husband or a wife, that is.

Her dance partner led her back to where her mother and Miss Fitzroy were seated on the sidelines, watching the dancing couples. Olivia chanced another glance towards the impressive stairs decked with the most exquisite gold rug where men and women who had been announced by the Duchess' butler descended into the crowded, candle-lit ballroom. Her gaze drifted across the beautifully dressed men and women waiting to be announced, but she didn't see the Viscount Corley of Stenford amongst them.

That pesky man! Had he simply been toying with her when he agreed to her proposal? Or when he sent her a note informing her they would meet at the ball to begin the first phase of their plan? Or had Edward the meddler talked him out of it? Thomas didn't look like a man who allowed other people's opinions to sway him, except that of his father, of course.

"Permit me to say again, my Lady, that you look absolutely stunning. Just like a rose budding in spring."

Olivia almost rolled her eyes as they passed through the throng of people. For every compliment she had gotten from every man that had danced with her, she ought to be prepared for callers almost breaking down her door the following morning. But she wouldn't because she had shut them down repeatedly.

"The exquisite blue dress you have on does you much justice. It brings out the colour of your eyes and makes them look even more captivating."

"Why, thank you, Lord Appleton."

"May I call on you tomorrow?"

Thankful that her mother and Miss Fitzroy were a short distance away, she bestowed on him the fondest of smiles and replied, "No, you may not."

The tall and handsome man blinked. "I beg your pardon?"

"No, you may not call on me, My Lord, because it would be an utter waste of time," she sweetly said. "You see, my heart belongs to another. I merely await his arrival."

Tight-lipped, he replied, "I see. Little wonder you've been glancing at the stairs all evening. I thought you were just being shy."

"How wrong of you." She playfully tapped him with her fan as she had oft seen women do. "I'm never shy."

"I see that now."

Olivia didn't know if it was her imagination or if Lord Appleton actually hastened his footsteps. He delivered her back to her mother without saying a word. He simply bowed and left. She heard a loud sigh beside her and knew her mother was about to complain again that no one had said glowing remarks to her. She had no idea what Olivia had been saying to them. She was about to beg her mother not to waste her breath when she heard the name she had been waiting for all evening.

"Viscount Corley of Stenford."

Her eyes immediately flew to the stairs. There he was. The man who would make her plans a success. For some reason she couldn't understand, her heart raced as she watched him descend the stairs with a rather bored expression on his face. Had he always looked this handsome or was it his evening clothes that made him look taller? Is his angular face more stunning? His aristocratic features, the aquiline nose, firm lips, and jaw more pronounced? His cream neckcloth, black jacket, and trousers were tailored to perfection. Suddenly, she felt so hot in the crowded space, that she opened her fan and waved it across her heated face.

Gently flapping the fan to hide her nervousness, she surreptitiously surveyed him as he went about the noisy room, exchanging pleasantries with friends. With chagrin, she watched as he stood with a group of men. Had he not yet seen her? Granted, the ballroom was crowded but she was in his direct line of sight. Did she need to wave her fan or handkerchief in the air? He stayed where he was; conversing, laughing, and drinking champagne with the men. It took everything in her not to march over to him to give him the length and breadth of her tongue.

When it appeared as though he would not seek her, and Olivia was about to take permission from her mother to go to the retiring room for a few minutes, the blasted man finally disengaged from his friends and sauntered over in leisurely strides. Her heart pounded and then her eyes darkened with anger when she saw amusement in his brown eyes as he drew closer. She waited patiently as he greeted her mother and all the women in their small party before he turned his attention to her.

"Lady Blackmore. You look ravishing. May I have this dance?"

Olivia nodded, even though she felt like giving him the cut for keeping her waiting. Holding her tongue, she allowed him to lead her to the dance floor.

"You're easily the most beautiful Lady here tonight. That dress is very becoming."

"Are you trying to sweeten me, so I do not chop off your head for coming late or ignoring me?"

He chuckled.

"Do you know not that it's ungentlemanly to keep a Lady waiting?"

With his eyes still twinkling with humour, he remarked, "Mayhap you could teach me a thing or two about etiquettes. I fear I may be lacking in such areas, seeing that I have never really cared for the whims of Society."

Her lips twitched. "And what have you been doing with your time all these years?"

He shrugged and put on a bored expression. "Being a libertine, as my father puts it."

"Little wonder he's about to cut you off."

"Yes, but you're here to save me from a life of penury, aren't you?" He smiled. "If the looks we're receiving are anything to go by, I think our plan is working."

"*My* plan, you mean. Why do you say so?"

"For one, the old biddies in the corner have been smiling affectionately at us. And then, some of my mates, probably the ones who have an interest in you, are glaring at me as if they'd love nothing better than to invite me outside for a duel."

Olivia giggled helplessly. She glanced around her and discovered he was right. Her mother and her friends nodded at her with approval.

"Or maybe it's your dress. I don't think I've ever come across such a style before."

"Oh. Have you been much accustomed to the styles of women's dresses?"

He grinned. "I have female cousins who talk of nothing else but the latest fashion in London and Paris. I have had to withstand them changing dresses to seek my approval."

Olivia looked down at her dress and had to agree with him that the modiste who delivered the gown, and the others, had outdone herself. The high-waisted, sky-blue silk dress was held together by white lace ribbons at her shoulders. It flowed to her blue glass slippers and paired with white gloves that reached her elbows. Her blonde hair had been done up in a chignon with tendrils bordering her oval face. She had on her ears and neck the pearls her parents had given her for her birthday. Her parents had spared no expense in her Season wardrobe just to make sure she hitched a husband. Her sisters had also fawned over her before they left their London townhouse on Jenkins Street.

"You look like a princess, Liv. If you don't find a husband tonight, then all the men in England must be blinder than bats," Sarah had told her, which had elicited laughter from her.

Olivia struggled with the knowledge that she had chosen the prettiest dress in the collection for his benefit.

No! I didn't.

"No comeback? You must be tired from swirling around the dance floor all evening. My apologies."

She wanted to tell him that wasn't it, but she decided not to bother. She didn't want him asking what she had been thinking to render her silent. She could hardly tell him she had carefully dressed for his benefit.

"I better hand you over to your mother before our plans get ruined."

She frowned. "How so?"

"For one, the music has ended. Secondly, I wish to dance with only you tonight, but then, that would be frowned upon, right? I must brush up on my book of decorum now that I'm to be seen in Polite Society."

Olivia wondered why her pulse raced. Simply because he desired to dance only with her? It was only natural since he detested balls and didn't fancy being placed on the auctioning block of the popular 'marriage mart'.

"I see."

They moved through the throng of people where an old woman told them they made a perfect couple, causing Olivia to blush.

"May I call on you tomorrow, my Lady? Perhaps we could take a ride through the park?" Thomas asked after handing her over to her mother.

"Very well, my Lord."

"Shall we say noon?"

"Noon is fine, my Lord."

He bowed to the women before leaving their presence. Olivia couldn't help showing the happiness she felt in her eyes, signifying that her plan was working.

"Tis not right for you to wear your heart on your sleeve, my dear," her mother softly chided. "I take it he has caught your fancy?"

"Very much so, Mama."

"Splendid. We will have someone look into his family for any skeletons."

Olivia didn't care whatever her parents intended to do. All she knew was that her plan had been set in motion and was rolling along just fine. She feigned a slight headache half an hour later so she could go home to write to a pregnant Emily about her plans. And also, to stop herself from looking all over the packed ballroom for Thomas, which her mother cautioned her twice to refrain from doing.

Chapter Four

"What a lovely day," Olivia stated with glee as she arranged the skirts of her morning dress on the seat of the curricle.

"It is, isn't it? But not as lovely as you," Thomas mentioned with a glance in her direction.

Blushing a little, Olivia looked away and watched the pedestrians strolling along the street. She lowered her voice when she replied, "You don't have to say such things when we are alone, my Lord."

"I merely speak the truth. Besides, are we truly alone?"

They both stared pointedly at the stiff back of Miss Fitzroy in the high seat of the phaeton in front of them, which he had been forced to hire when she insisted on coming along with them.

Olivia smiled. Still speaking in a low tone, she said, "Propriety doesn't permit me to go anywhere with a man without a companion, even if the man and I are in a pretend courtship."

He guffawed. "Propriety is overrated."

Olivia let out a pretend gasp. "I presume you're trying to make me throw caution to the wind, my Lord."

"Is it working?"

"No. I do enjoy reading about scandals, but not with my name entwined in it."

Laughter rose in his throat. "A minor scandal hurts no one."

Her delicately carved brows shot up. "Oh, really?"

"I've been caught in a scandal myself."

She inhaled sharply and curved her body towards him, her eyes filled with astonishment and fixed on him. "I beg your pardon?"

He shrugged as if he was discussing something as trivial as the weather. "It wasn't a big deal. Let's just say 'Polite Society' thinks that I cried off my promise of marriage to a Lady."

"And you're just telling me this now?"

His lips curled into a smile. "Well, pardon me, my Lady. But you did not give me much time to exchange life stories with you when you came to me with your proposal."

She stabbed a finger in the air at him. "Don't you dare pin this on me!"

He shrugged again as if he didn't have a care in the world. Olivia wished there was a crane handy to remove his shoulders in order to stop him from repeatedly making the annoying movement.

"I'm not. Hence the reason for this outing. We should, in the least, get to know a little about each other."

"I'm afraid that's out of the question." She reclined back in the seat.

"Why?" he frowned.

"Because my parents are probably using a fine-tooth comb to go through all your ancestors as we speak."

The odious man thought this to be funny as he roared with laughter. Incapable of stopping herself, Olivia hit him with her parasol, only to meet Miss Fitzroy's frowning gaze.

"Such an unladylike display, my Lady!" she called in her most reproachful tone, drawing the attention of pedestrians enjoying a stroll.

Still grinning, Thomas concurred. "Yes, my Lady, acts of violence are not welcome upon my person. For there might be consequences." He scratched his beard. "Say, recanting my interest in you."

Pursing her lips into a thin line, Olivia looked away. She pretended to wave at someone who was obviously waving at someone else on the other side of the street.

This too elicited laughter from Thomas. "Olivia, I did not mean to annoy you. Even if your parents were to hire the finest Bow Street runners, I doubt they'll find any ugly-looking, cobweb-filled skeletons in my closet."

"Apart from you breaking a Lady's heart."

"It was hardly that."

"Then tell me everything."

He shook his head. "I'm sorry, Olivia. It's a sore topic for me and I do not wish to discuss it. Suffice it to say, it's in the past and that's all that matters. It hardly made ballroom news, so you need not worry about anything."

She gazed at him with scepticism. "I wish I could believe that. I know my parents."

"We'll cross that bridge *if* it comes up. Now, could we please take a walk? Apparently, half of the men at the ball last night chose to take their intended to the Regent's Park. We'll be here for at least an hour before we get there."

Olivia sighed. She had noticed the unusual number of carriages heading towards their intended destination. "Very well then. Although, I know this is just an excuse. You not been inclined to take me to the park in the first place."

He chortled. "You know me so well already, my Lady."

He pulled the curricle to the side of the road and helped Olivia down from it. He held her hand for a moment longer than necessary before he dropped it. Olivia's heart thumped at the simple gesture, and she wondered why. They informed Miss Fitzroy of the change of plans, much to her annoyance. She alighted from the phaeton, frowning, and walked behind them.

"I hardly know anything about you, my Lord. Perhaps you could tell me more about your odious father."

He groaned. "The Earl of Livingston is a force to be reckoned with. Talking about him rubs me off wrongly, so I'd rather talk about my mother. Even though she's sickly, she's the sweetest mother ever. She never fully recovered after the birth of my younger brother, William. It was a difficult birth. I thought I had lost her until by some miracle she survived some days later."

As Thomas spoke about his mother, Olivia sensed how much he

loved her, and it warmed her heart. It showed he was capable of being a good husband and father. How wonderful.

She stopped herself short. What did it matter to her if Thomas ended up being a terrible father? It was nothing to her. She blinked as she tried to concentrate on what he was saying while nodding at passersby who gave them enquiring looks.

"Tell me more about your family. I know you have four sisters and a brother," he probed. "Your elder sister is married. What are your likes, dislikes, and daily interests?"

She told him about how bothersome yet enjoyable it was growing up with five siblings and how she was finding it hard to exact authority over her younger ones. He laughed through it all.

"I enjoy reading."

"Really?" His brows arched. "I also enjoy reading. What do you read? Romantic novels and poems by Lord Byron?"

"Goodness, no. I enjoy intellectual books."

They spent the next hour talking about books until Miss Fitzroy told them she was tired. They turned back to their waiting conveyances and headed to the Blackmore's townhouse. Thomas bade her goodbye, "I hope to call on you soon."

As her maid, Sally, helped remove her gown, Olivia decided that it had been a delightful day. She had enjoyed Thomas's company as well.

Chapter Five

"Olivia!"

Groaning inwardly, Olivia lifted her head from the blanket she had placed on the floor of the attic. She had stayed there all morning after breakfast to hide from her family so she could read one of the books Thomas had sent her. So engrossed in the book, Olivia hadn't heard her mother coming up the stairs. If her mother found her, it meant that her siblings wouldn't be far behind. True to her thoughts, she heard the twins arguing a short distance away. This was obviously the end of her interlude away from her family. Oh, how dearly she missed Emily.

Her mother stood by the door with her hands on her hips, looking displeased.

What now? Had the twins 'mistakenly' poured a vase of water on their unsuspecting London butler through the window again?

"Olivia, why, everyone has been searching for you," her mother stated with a scowl.

"Afraid I eloped with Lord Stenford?" she tried to joke, but it fell flat on her peeved mother.

"If Sarah hadn't recalled you going up the stairs, I wouldn't have remembered how you enjoy going to odd places to read."

Sarah! Traitor!

"I wish to speak to you at once! Rise immediately from the ground like a proper Lady and come down to the salon posthaste."

"Yes, Mama."

Whirling around, her mother walked out the door, leaving her daughter to scramble to her feet in the most undignified manner. Olivia smiled, knowing it would have dismayed her mother had she seen her. Still holding onto her book, she suppressed the urge to sniff it like she had done when it was first delivered to her. Of course, it smelled like dust. But then she had caught the distinct, faint scent of tangy lemon, which was characteristic of Thomas, she had noticed from the few times she had been with him. It brought a smile to her lips, which was quickly wiped away when she came into contact with her twin sisters.

"Thinking about Lord Stenford?" Bridget sweetly asked.

"I could have sworn that three weeks ago, you did not wish to be wed." Beatrice peered at her keenly. "Did the sight of the handsome Viscount have you change your mind?"

Olivia hastily brushed past them. "Mama and Papa should have left you lot back in Keymouth."

She ignored the snickers behind her and hurried down the stairs to the salon. Her mother was already seated on a wing-backed chair by the fireplace. It had rained earlier, so there was a chill in the air.

"Sit down, Olivia."

Olivia did her bidding, choosing a brocaded armchair a few paces from her mother. "I will not beat around the bush, for I wish this discussion to be over before your father returns from White's."

Her daughter swallowed tightly as she guessed what the discussion would be about. Alas, she would have to find someone else to take Thomas's place. Who would it be? Something squeezed her heart at the thought of not seeing Thomas again, smiling with him, discussing with him, and...

Good heavens! What am I doing? Thomas is only a friend. An accomplice.

"Do not look so distraught before you hear what I have to say." Her mother exhaled audibly. "I have to tell you the decision your father and I came to after our findings. Lord Stenford must marry you as soon as propriety permits without eyebrows raising at the cause of the haste."

Olivia didn't know when she rose from her chair, but she suddenly found herself on her feet. "What?"

Her mother sighed with regret. "Yes. It has to be so. A few years ago, he repudiated from marrying a Lady he offered for. We cannot take chances of that happening again, not when he has blatantly made his interest in you known to all of London." Frowning a little, she added, "Couldn't you have declined at least one of his invitations? Played a little hard to get? You've spent almost every day of this week together. Tongues have waged over how happy the two of you are together— always smiling, laughing, and talking in whispers."

"That was the pl..." She bit her lip to keep from divulging that being seen together in parks, balls, and soirees was all part of the plot. She took the last part of her mother's words as a mere exaggeration. True, she and Thomas enjoyed each other's company, but they didn't always do those things. Did they? Thomas made her laugh a lot, but...

"Pardon?"

"Em...I meant we like each other, so naturally, we'd want to be together."

"Marvellous. Then you won't argue about wanting to be together officially and forever. Your father has sent word to him to present himself here tomorrow to fix a date for your wedding. It would have been today, but your father is otherwise engaged."

"But, Mama, you're rushing us. We do not want to wed now. We want to get to know each other better."

Smiling amiably, her mother replied, "You can do that after your wedding. Lord Stenford has proven to be fickle. Why, some people have described him as a rake."

"It wasn't his fault he had to call off his engagement with the Lady."

Her mother's jaw dropped. "You mean you're aware of it?"

"Yes," she reluctantly said. "He told me...they ...they" she tried to come up with a plausible story to exonerate him. "They were ill-suited."

"Bah!" She waved a hand in the air. "That's not an excuse to break a woman's heart."

"But he didn't. Even if he did, he won't break mine." She fell to her knees. "Mama, please do not hurry us into marriage. I do not want to marry now and be tied down for life. I want to travel and see the world."

Her mother patted her cheek. "You can still do that with your husband."

"No! All married men want are heirs. As soon as I'm with child, I won't be allowed to do a lot of things."

Her mother shook her head. "Dear Olivia, it's already obvious to all and sundry that you and Thomas are in love. When a man loves a woman, he will do anything for her, to make her happy. Keep that in mind, my darling, and you will have your way."

Olivia didn't hear anything past her mother saying she and Thomas were in love. Were they such talented actors to have successfully deceived the *Ton*?

"You shouldn't be worried about getting married, Olivia. What you should be worried about is Thomas rejecting our proposal. If that happens, other men might not want to marry you, thinking you're 'used goods.' Or your father might want to force a duel for your honour."

Horror filled Olivia at her mother's last words. Dear God, what had she done? Thomas would never agree to marry her. And her father, who had also threatened to fight a duel with Emily's husband when they tried to elope, would certainly not hold back in this case. Despite his brash nature, she knew that her father loved his daughters very much and would do anything for them.

Oh, no. How do I fix this?

Chapter Six

"I'm afraid I'm here to bring bad news, my Lady."

"More terrible news than mine?" Olivia asked as she and Thomas took a leisurely stroll in the cool of the evening.

Distraught by the turn of events earlier in the day, she had sent word to his townhouse that she wished to see him urgently. He had sent a message back—much to her chagrin—that he couldn't make it until later in the evening as he had pressing matters. She had paced her room all day, waiting for his arrival, and praying her parents would allow her to see him. Fortunately, her father left the house immediately after lunch and her mother had taken to bed with a slight headache. Only the pesky Miss Fitzroy had been awake and maintained coming with her when she suggested taking a walk with Thomas when he arrived.

He frowned. "Do you have bad news as well?"

"Yes. You would have known about it before now had you arrived earlier." She couldn't help the note of displeasure in her voice.

When Thomas didn't immediately respond, she glanced at him. She had expected him to smile and throw her a teasing reply, but his face was rigid. Good God. Was he about to beg off from their plan?

She rubbed a hand across her nape in a nervous gesture. "Is anything amiss, my Lord?"

Keeping his gaze straight ahead, he said, "My mother's illness took a turn for the worse this morning. I received your note just as I was about to leave after receiving the news."

"Oh." Shame flooded her for being so insensitive to his plight, knowing how much he loved his mother. "I'm sorry."

"There's no need to apologise."

"Is she alright?"

He shook his head. "The doctor said she has a short time to live."

"Oh, Thomas. I'm so sorry." She couldn't imagine the pain going through him. She couldn't bear to think of life without her mother.

He raked his fingers through his groomed hair, dishevelling it. "I love my mother and will do anything for her."

"Of course."

He stopped walking and turned to look at her with intense eyes as if trying to stare into her soul. Her heart thumped as she scrutinised him. She had never noticed the golden flecks in his brown eyes until now. Her eyes widened when right there on the sidewalk, he went down on a bended knee.

"Would you do me the honour of becoming my wife?"

Olivia, with her face as red as a tomato, looked around her at the few people that were about. She saw a couple on the other side of the street who stopped walking and smiled.

"What are you doing?" she whispered fiercely, conscious of Miss Fitzroy a few feet away, whose eyes were almost popping out from their sockets.

Olivia was ready to give him the cut and warn him never to come calling again for defaulting on their plan when his next words left her dumbfounded.

"Fulfilling my dying mother's last wish of me," he answered shortly. "She has heard about you and assumed we're very much in love. And so, she wishes to see me wed before her demise."

Tears instantly stung Olivia's eyes. It would have been the sweetest thing she ever heard if it didn't involve her. How could she say no to such a proposal? He wasn't doing it for himself but for the love of his dying mother. Could she reject a dying woman's request—the one thing that would make her happy before her death? What if it were her mother?

"Oh, love, get him out of his misery and tell him yes," an old woman who was passing by said. Another one clapped her hands.

Miss Fitzroy came forward. "What's stopping you, Lady Blackmore? You two are obviously in love. It's fashionable these days to marry for love. Why won't you say yes?"

"It's not that simple, Miss Fitzroy."

"Love is simple. Human beings make it complicated."

Olivia wanted to yell at her that they weren't in love, but she swallowed her words. "Could you please give us a minute?"

Miss Fitzroy grudgingly went away, grumbling about stubborn ladies.

"My parents have the intention of summoning you tomorrow to force you into fixing a date for our wedding."

His forehead wrinkled in a frown.

"They heard about your *little* scandal."

"Oh."

"Before I give you a reply to your proposal, I need to know what happened."

"It's—"

"And don't you dare tell me it's not a big deal. I might just kick you in the shin."

"I'm on my knees."

"It doesn't matter."

"May I stand up?"

"No, you may not! You will remain in that position until you explain what happened, and I give you a reply."

He sighed. "Alright. Three years ago, I fell in love with Susan Whitfield. She reciprocated my love until the wealthy Earl of Cornerstone took an interest in her. She chose wealth over love and jilted me to marry a man old enough to be her father because she couldn't wait for when I'd become an Earl. In the foolishness of my love for her, I told everyone who asked about me withdrawing my offer that it was all my idea—just to protect her. Love can make one do foolish things, which is why I do not wish to marry for love. Believe it or not, or as foolish as it might sound, I still have feelings for her. We Corleys love only once and for life."

Olivia felt his pain. Sadness flooded her that he would never give his love to another when he was such a warm and loving man.

He went on, "And so, it is the intense love for my mother that has pushed me into asking for your hand in marriage. I know this wasn't the plan but seeing as your parents want us to get married shortly and my mother does too, then I think we no longer have a choice in the matter. Our trying to outsmart our parents has backfired."

She nodded. Circumstances had proven that things could turn around in the twinkling of an eye, even if they were going so well earlier.

"You need not worry. I'll be the kind of husband that you desire. I will give you the freedom to do as you please. And whenever you're ready, be it five or ten years from now, you will give me an heir and I'll let you be. So, what do you say?"

Olivia bowed her head and whispered, "Do we really have a choice? The die is cast, and we have to go with it."

"Since we're the cynosure for all eyes, could you please not look like I'm about to send you to the gallows?"

Olivia's eyes flashed fire at him. "This was not my plan."

"Please."

The emotion-laden word melted her stony heart. "Very well, then. I'll marry you. But you must keep to your promise."

He whistled with relief. "May I stand up now?"

She shrugged. "I guess so."

He stood and gently dragged her into his arms. She stiffened and looked at him with questioning eyes.

His eyes twinkled with jollity. "It's required, Olivia. I thought you knew everything about etiquette."

Olivia relaxed in his arms and was startled when they heard a round of applause.

"Congratulations!" the people chorused, and Olivia blushed to the roots of her hair. It was left to see now if she wasn't making the biggest mistake of her life.

Chapter Seven

Olivia stared at her reflection in the wooden floor mirror with carvings on its side. The elegant yellow silk skimmed her body, highlighting her slender waist and slightly rounded hips. Her curls were bound up her hair with a white ribbon. Thomas had told her he loved her hair up because it showed her lovely neck. Her face flushed as she remembered.

"Daydreaming again about your betrothed, aren't you? I say, Olivia, for someone who didn't want to get married, you sure have a funny way of showing it," Beatrice mentioned with a sneer, swinging her leg by the window seat.

"You're forever in a daze these days," Bridget, of course, added. "Thomas did this. Thomas said that," she mimicked with a smile.

Olivia, laughing, took one of the pillows from the bed and threw it at her sisters by the window.

"I do not have the time to banter words with you two." She twirled around. "How do I look?"

"Like a girl in love," Sarah proclaimed as she entered the room with a bouquet of red roses.

Olivia jumped and placed her hands on her hips. "Why does everyone keep saying that?"

"Because it's the truth," Sarah answered and handed her the bouquet. "This just arrived for you. No need to ask who it's from."

Olivia's eyes lit up. Thomas was really taking this engagement thing too far. He bestowed on her gifts at the drop of a hat. Truly, he acted the part of a besotted fiancé. But she knew it was only for the benefit of his mother who had arrived in London for their wedding. She positioned the roses on her bed and retrieved the small envelope attached to it.

These beautiful roses don't do you justice, but they are the closest I could find to describe how stunning you are to me. Thinking of you.

Love,

Thomas.

She wasn't surprised when Beatrice snatched the note from her hand and ran to her twin by the window. Both of them read the letter and giggled helplessly.

"Liv, I must say that things have worked out well for you. We know this started as a fake courtship but now, it's real and you and Thomas have fallen in love."

"Cease your mindless chatter, Bridget." She stamped her feet on the ground. "Thomas and I are not in love. It's simply a charade. We have to act the part for his dying mother's sake."

"Um," Sarah drew closer to her older sister. "Were you acting the part just now when your eyes lit up as you read his letter and a blush crept up your cheek? You looked as if you wanted to dance the waltz in joy."

The twins clapped their hands with glee at Sarah's astute assessment. Struck dumb by what her youngest sister just said, Olivia took her cloak from the bed and hurried out of the room amidst giggles.

As she descended the spiral staircase, her mind went over the words. So what if she reacted that way to Thomas's gift and letter? It was expected of her to be pleased. After all, she had never received gifts from men before him. And truth be told, she did like receiving gifts. It made her feel special. Thomas, admittedly, made her feel special.

Ever since she accepted his proposal, he had been the perfect fiancé. There was nothing else she could do. She didn't have the heart not to grant a dying woman her last wish. When the announcement of their engagement came out in the *Times*, the *Ton* had flooded them with invitations to balls, soirees, jousts, and races. She and Thomas had attended them as they prepared for their wedding in two weeks. Thomas had adorned her with attention wherever they went, and she lapped it up like a dog. Assuredly, in the eyes of everyone, they were in love. But only they knew the truth. She liked Thomas and enjoyed his company, and that was all. He was still in love with the Countess of Cornerstone, so there was no danger of him falling in love with her. They had spent the last two weeks together after he had signed the betrothal contract, and she had got to know him better, liked him some more, and yearned for his company. That couldn't be love, could it?

"I'll have to write to Emily to ask her what it means for one to be in love," Olivia said to herself. And for crying out loud, she had only known him for a short while. Was it possible?

"Hmm. Such deep musings frighten me."

Olivia's heart skipped a beat when she bumped into Thomas, and he held her to stop her from falling.

"You!"

"Yes, me!"

"What are you doing here?"

"Have you forgotten we're to attend the Grisham's ball?"

"Yes. I didn't know you were already here. Sarah didn't tell me."

"I told her not to. I wanted to take delight in watching you come down the stairs, looking like an angel." He sighed with disappointment. "Alas, you didn't even see me. Tell me, my Lady, what were you thinking? Still find the thought of marrying me distasteful?"

Olivia quickly shook her head. Over the past two weeks of being with him, enjoying his company, and looking forward to seeing him had made her realise that it might not be so bad getting married to him, all together.

"As long as you do not renege on the promises you made when you proposed to me. I desire to see the world. So, soon after we're married, I will go to the Colonies, and maybe the West Indies next."

An unreadable expression crossed his face, which he swiftly masked.

"What is it?"

"Nothing. I only wondered if it wouldn't be awkward that soon after our wedding, you leave. We've worked so hard to keep the image of a besotted couple. It would be a shame to spoil it."

"But no one will know I'm gone. They will assume I'm in one of your country homes."

"We're supposed to be seen in public for a while after our marriage."

"Sweet Jesus! Fine. Six months. And then I travel."

He grinned and took her gloved hand to kiss it. "Your wish is my command, my Lady."

A smile curved her lips. "Now that's what I'm talking about."

Rich laughter bubbled from his throat. He reached out to cup her chin. Olivia felt as if her heart would jump out of her chest from the rapid way it was pounding. But why?

"Lord Stenford! Olivia! You're standing too close to each other."

Olivia gasped and turned to see her mother standing by the salon door with a stern look on her face. Flushing, she pulled away from Thomas's hold.

"I know how wonderful it is to be in love, but you two must observe some level of decorum."

"But, Mama, we did nothing wrong. He merely held me from falling when I bumped into him. And before you ask why I did, I was lost in thought and didn't see him there."

Her mother smiled. "Pray tell, what were you thinking about?"

Olivia ducked her head to hide her flushed face from her mother and her betrothed. Those bothersome sisters of hers! They had put the thoughts in her head and now she could hardly think of anything else.

On the way to the ball with Thomas, her mother, and Miss Fitzroy in the carriage, she could think of nothing except what her sisters had said. Was she really in love with Thomas?

Half an hour later at the ball, Olivia came to a conclusion. He held her in his arms, and she now found it hard to breathe properly because she was too conscious of the strength of his masculinity and his lovely scent, which hadn't bothered her in the past. When her eyes blazed with jealousy as he danced with other ladies and laughed with them, she knew the truth.

Sweet Mary, I'm in love with Thomas.

Chapter Eight

Yawning, Thomas turned in his seat and asked as the thick curtains closed, "Is it over?"

"No," Olivia laughed. "Only a change of scenery."

"Good heavens. I don't think I can withstand any more of that loud singing," he complained with a frown.

Puzzlement filled Olivia's eyes. "Why are you here if you do not enjoy the opera?"

"I came here to be with you. As it appears that you obviously love the opera, I didn't want you to be bored."

Olivia changed the focus of her gaze to the heavy curtains as she waved the fan across her heated face. Thomas always told her the sweetest of words lately. She reckoned it was because they were in public. Even though they were seated in a private box in the theatre, she believed people in surrounding boxes could hear them. She surmised that he said it for the profit of those who might be eavesdropping.

"Why, thank you, gallant Sir. You need not have bothered. Now you're being bored to sleep."

He shook his head. "Not with you by my side. I enjoy your company a mite too much, I'm afraid. So, I can withstand not being somnolent throughout the entire performance—just like Lord Wentworth over there—as long as you're by my side."

Her face lifted in a bright smile. "You say the most heart-warming things, my Lord."

"I aim to please. Am I succeeding?" He winked at her.

She beamed. "Know you not, my Lord, that winking in the Bible is considered an act of evil intention towards the person being winked at?"

Thomas's shoulders shook with mirth. "Pardon me, my Lady. All my intentions towards you are pure."

"I certainly hope so. And to answer your question. Yes, you've succeeded in pleasing me and I do enjoy your company. We've become good friends, haven't we?"

He nodded. "Yes, we have. I hope it continues whilst we're married."

"I hope so, too." Desiring to change the topic as it was getting too intimate, she asked, "How is your mother faring?"

A frown contorted his face. "She's surprisingly doing well for someone who was at death's door a few weeks ago."

"Isn't that good news?"

"It should be if I didn't smell foul play."

She frowned. "How so?"

"The doctors gave my mother only a few weeks to live. Granted, she has always been frail, but now, she appears to be as strong as a horse. She attends soirees with my father, something she hasn't done in years."

Olivia winked at him. "Maybe she has a new lease on life now that you've finally left your libertine ways to wed."

A grin softened his features. "You'd make excuses even for Hades."

Hilarity bubbled from Olivia's throat. There wasn't room for more conversation as the curtains drew open at that moment. Olivia had been actively enjoying the music but after her brief discussion with Thomas during the interlude, she became lost in thought. Was it wise to tell Thomas about the change in her feelings for him, or would it be considered too forward? She wished now that she had read romantic novels instead of casting them aside after going through only one. She had found the swooning heroine silly and had put the novel away to read about the constellation of stars. Well, no star would help her now.

Conscious of Thomas beside her, shifting in his seat now and again, Olivia could barely concentrate on the magnificently dressed men and women performing spectacularly. When at last it was over, she heaved a sigh of relief.

Thomas helped her with her cloak, as it was chilly outside, and took her hand. Olivia knew Miss Fitzroy might complain later about them holding hands. She was about to crack a joke about it with Thomas when he suddenly stiffened. Her eyes flew to his face, and it slightly alarmed her to see how taut it was, as though someone had carved it from stone. She followed the direction of his gaze and frowned. Heading towards them was one of the most stunning women she had ever seen. Her raven black hair ran in riotous curls across her shoulders. Her round face appeared as if God had paid extra attention to it upon its creation. When she drew closer, Olivia noted her almond-shaped green eyes, rosy cheeks, slightly pointed nose, and full lips with a little trepidation. Even in her black bombazine gown that accentuated her robust figure, she looked pleasing to the eye.

"Lord Stenford. My! It's been a while, I must say. You look as handsome as ever. I was mighty glad when I received your note as soon as I arrived in London." She thrust her hand out for him to take.

Some seconds passed before Thomas released Olivia's hand to take that of the Countess' and kiss it. Olivia felt the tension in him, like that of a snake waiting to strike.

"Lady Cornerstone, may I present my fiancée, Lady Olivia Blackmore?"

Cold eyes turned towards Olivia to glare at her as if she was something disgusting found stuck to the bottom of her slipper.

"Oh, the supposed wife-to-be." She returned her focus to Thomas. "Surely, you should have done better. It feels as though you've snatched a babe from the cradle, unlike when we were together."

Olivia inhaled sharply. Thomas took her hand and squeezed it as if begging her not to respond.

"Thomas, love, I don't mean to be too forward, but you know you need a real woman like me." Her chest puffed out, and she smiled in a way that irritated Olivia. "I'm a widow now and very much available. Remember what you told me when I was about to get married to that old fart? You told me you'd always love me, and you'd wait for me. Well, here I am, my love. I never stopped loving you, too."

To Olivia's dismay, the Countess stood on tiptoe and whispered something into Thomas's ear, causing his face to harden even more.

"Excuse me, Lady Cornerstone. I must get *my fiancée* home." With that curt reply, he sidestepped the older woman and led Olivia out of the box.

"I'm sorry about that," Thomas spoke into the thick silence that enveloped the coach on their way back to her residence.

Looking out the window at the dimly lit street, Olivia said, "It doesn't matter."

"It does to me. She's the Lady I told you about. The one who jilted me for a wealthy Earl."

"I gathered."

"I owe you an explanation."

"No, you don't."

"Please, Olivia, I do."

She refused to look at him. From the corner of her eye, she saw him rake his fingers through his hair, the way he did when he was nervous.

"Contrary to what you might think, the note I sent to Lady Cornerstone was a reply to the one she had first sent to me. She failed to mention that so anyone within earshot would assume that I alone sent her one. In her note, she wished to come calling. I sent back a reply asking her not to, which I now regret. I should not have answered her at all."

Olivia surmised that he was saying all this to cover his true feelings for his former betrothed. By his own confession, he had announced he still had feelings for her and likely always would.

Olivia remained silent for the rest of the journey. Hardly had the carriage pulled to a stop when she scrambled down and almost fell but for the footman who opened the door and assisted her. She ignored Thomas calling her name and ran up the steps. She did not bother to wait for Miss Fitzroy.

Up the spiral stairs, she ran to her room and flung herself onto her bed. Sobs shook her body as she wept at her love that would never be reciprocated. And now, to worsen matters, the love of his life had not only returned but wanted him back as well.

Her cousin Edward's ominous words came back to mock her. "This will not end well."

Truly, it has ended dreadfully. For her, anyway. Thomas could finally be with the love of his life while she would be in a loveless marriage of convenience. More tears flowed down her face.

Chapter Nine

Dear Thomas,

 I do not know where to begin. Last night opened my eyes to a lot of things. I realize I have been unfair to you. I should never have started this charade. I had no idea how many people would be hurt by it. Please forgive me. I never meant any harm. And so, I release you from the betrothal contract. I will tell my parents everything and make sure they know it isn't and was never your fault. I can't bear to keep lying to them.

 By the time you read this letter, I'll be long gone from London. Please don't look for me to tell me things you don't mean. I wish you well with Lady Cornerstone. I'm delighted that you will finally be with the woman you love. Thank you for everything. I apologize if this paints you in a bad light, given how convincing we have been to the Ton. I shall endeavour to take the whole blame since it was my idea in the first place. I'm sorry if this affects your mother's health. Nevertheless, she will still gain a daughter-in-law, even though not the one she initially expected. It was wonderful knowing you and being your friend. I hope we can remain friends, if our paths ever cross again.

 Olivia.

Olivia reread the letter, her heart breaking into a thousand pieces.

"This will do." She need not squeeze it and throw it in the bin like she had done countless others.

She dabbed at her puffy eyes with her handkerchief. She ought to write to Edward, too, to curse him to perdition for jinxing her arrangement with Thomas. If he hadn't forebode that it wouldn't end well if she fell in love with his friend, perhaps she would be having the final fittings of her lovely lace wedding dress.

Unfortunately, that would never be. Mayhap she would never marry, as the scandal was sure to hit the whole of England; she would be seen as 'used goods' by the Ton.

She sniffed. *What sort of devil entered me to devise such a plan in the first place?* If only her parents had allowed her to get married in her own time as she had always wanted; perhaps she wouldn't have come up with such a dastardly plan.

After a brief knock on her door, a dour-faced Sarah entered the room. Eyeing the trunks by the foot of the bed, she said, "Please do not go, Olivia. Do not leave me at the mercy of Beatrice and Bridget."

Olivia shrugged. "I'm sorry, Sarah. I have to go."

"Things are not as bad as you think, you know. You could talk to Lord Stenford and sort out your differences."

Olivia shook her head. She could never work out her differences with Thomas. She could never play second fiddle to the woman he loved. If she hadn't fallen in love with him, mayhap she would have overlooked his indiscretion with the widow. But she couldn't bear to think of him with another woman. Love was indeed an emotion filled with so much pain, she wondered why people still engaged in it.

Just then, her mother came into the room. She paused by the door when she saw the trunks. "Do not tell me you still wish to leave."

Dipping her head, she replied. "I do indeed, Mama. I have already told Mr. Andrews to send a runner to Emily, informing her of my impending arrival."

Her mother took graceful steps into the room. "I do not know why I birthed daughters who are so stubborn and always do things in the extreme. Couples in love quarrel and have differences in opinions. That's not enough reason for you to call off the betrothal."

Staring at her hands, Olivia replied. "It's more than that, Mama."

The older woman's eyes narrowed. "He didn't take liberties with you, did he?"

Her daughter's head snapped up, and she hastily shook her head. "Good God, no. He was the perfect gentleman with me. Miss Fitzroy can testify to that."

"Then why the sudden change of heart? Last night, both of you could hardly keep your eyes off each other on your way to the theatre. Only for you to return, and I found you in tears. As if that wasn't bad enough, you called off the wedding and want to leave London. Olivia darling, why won't you tell me what's going on? Your father is anxious, too. He means to go over to Thomas's townhouse, and you know what he will do when he gets there, don't you?"

"Please stop him, Mama. Thomas did no wrong. It's all on me. I cannot explain now. I just need to get away from here. I just need some time alone to think things through. I promise I'll write to you and Papa to explain everything."

Her mother put her arms around her, and Olivia felt like a little girl again. "Oh, darling. I'll stay the announcement of your broken engagement for now until you write to us. We will halt preparations for your wedding next week until you tell us to continue or cancel all arrangements. Regardless of all that we said to you weeks ago, we will never force you into a marriage you obviously don't want. Your father and I want nothing but your happiness and that of our other children."

"Oh, Mama." Olivia held on to her mother and wept in her arms until she was spent.

Half an hour later, her father also tried to convince her to stay and sort out whatever quarrel she had with Thomas, but she refused. Her father almost lost his cool with Thomas, but she begged him not to, absolving him of every blame.

Olivia sent a footman to deliver the letter to Thomas just as she finished saying goodbye to her family and climbed the travelling chaise. She did not want an occasion where he would reply before she had the chance to leave. Neither did she want him to come after her nor in his chivalry, claim he would still marry her when they both knew his heart belonged to another.

"Am I doing the right thing?" she whispered after bidding a teary farewell to her sisters. She had refused for anyone to come with her. She was riding with only her personal maid, Sally, and some outriders for protection in another carriage.

Couldn't she be content with him coming home to her every once in a while, even though he had been with his mistress? Was she about to give him up and hand him to the widow on a platter of gold without a fight? Wasn't love worth fighting for? Her shoulders slumped. Not when it would end in misery. Thomas had confessed that he still loved the Countess. She would only be making a huge cake of herself trying to win his love.

"No. This is best. I still have my dignity intact even though my heart is hollow now." She pressed her handkerchief to her lips to keep from sobbing out loud.

Chapter Ten

An hour later, the carriage came to an abrupt halt, jolting Olivia from her troubled slumber and almost throwing her onto the floor of the coach.

Sally was already on her knees, praying to God to save her mistress from the daredevil men.

"What is it, Sally?" Olivia questioned the robust girl.

"Highwaymen, my Lady. They be stopping the carriage to rob us."

Olivia's heart jumped to her throat. But where were the outriders who had been positioned in the other carriage for her protection? Had they been waylaid? Suddenly, she heard voices and knew Sally must be right. Something must have happened to the men.

Her eyes dashed around the coach for anything to protect herself. She grimaced with dissatisfaction when she remembered she had left her small case containing the derringer that her father gave her for protection in her bedroom dresser. How would she show the deadly men that she wasn't a shrinking violet waiting to be robbed? And all her trunks were in the other carriage. She thought of opening the door and bolting for it, but since she didn't know what was going on out there, she didn't want to end up like a mouse caught in a trap.

Without warning, the coach door thrust open, and a man stood there. With his back to the sun, she couldn't make out his face.

Screaming, she raised her hand and punched him square on the nose. The man grunted and held his nose. Seeing that she was at an advantage, she elevated her leg to position a well-placed kick in his midriff. But the man was too fast for her. He grabbed her hand and jerked her towards him. Still screaming like a banshee, she struggled to be free.

"Stop it, my little hellion. It's me!"

Olivia instantly stopped moving at the sound of the voice that had tormented her thoughts.

"Thomas?"

"At your service, my Lady," he said jeeringly, still holding her in his arms.

"Why are you acting like a highwayman? Was your aim to frighten me? You did a pretty good job of it!"

He sighed and gently let her go. "I wasn't trying to frighten you, my Lady. I merely came here to stop your idiotic trip."

Her eyebrows lifted. "Idiotic?"

"Yes." He climbed into the coach and glared at Sally, who was still on her knees, looking amused. "Please leave us."

The maid bowed and hurried out of the coach. Olivia, now calm and seated, was still trying to make sense of Thomas's presence there.

"Do you know what it has taken me to find you, you silly girl?"

She blinked, trying to put her mumbled thoughts together. "Why are you here?"

"Why am I here, she asks." With exasperation, he cupped her chin. "To stop you from leaving me. I thought we were friends. Friends who could tell each other anything and could talk things out if there was a misunderstanding. Yet you sent me that blasted letter and couldn't wait for my reply before fleeing like a coward."

Olivia bit her bottom lip. "I'm not a coward."

"You sure acted like one."

Angered by his astute assessment of her, she shouted, "I didn't want to stand in the way of true love."

He snorted. "What true love?"

She folded her arms across her chest and looked away. "You know what I'm talking about."

"No, I don't. I knew you erroneously judged the situation of things last night, but I didn't expect you to act so foolishly and selfishly."

"Stop insulting me! I only acted in your best interest. I simply wanted what was best for you."

He laughed mockingly. "Ha! What was best for me?"

"Yes. I know you—"

Olivia's words were cut short when Thomas unexpectedly dragged her into his arms and kissed her deeply. "That's what's best for me. *You* are what best is for me. Dear God, could any woman be so blind?"

Olivia, her lips tingling from his intense kiss, could only stare at him nonplussed.

"What must I do to show you how much I love you, Olivia?"

Her heart skipped a beat, and she found her voice. "But what about Lady Cornerstone?"

"To Hades with her! I didn't know I stopped loving her until you came into my life. With every moment I spent with you and yearned to be with you when we were apart, I knew what I had ever felt for her was fake."

She looked at him with doubt in her eyes, afraid to believe him.

He sighed. "Olivia, how many ladies do you think I've been to the theatre with? None, that is. Do you think I attended balls with Lady Cornerstone? Why do you think there wasn't an uproar when we didn't get married? Because we were hardly seen together." He cupped her chin. "Spending time with you made me realise how wonderful you are, and I couldn't help falling in love with you. I wanted to tell you my feelings for you had changed, but I felt you might not want to hear it since that wasn't among the terms of our arrangement. So, I decided to show you, hoping you would get to read my actions for what they truly were —acts by a man desperately in love and seeking permanence with the woman he loves."

Tears glistened in her eyes.

"The engagements, the gifts, going anywhere and everywhere with you were my way of showing how much I loved you and wanted to be with you, but you kept on thinking it was only a part of the act. When my mother came with her supposed dying wish, I was filled with so much joy that I didn't stop to think but ran to propose to you, hoping against hope that you would accept me for me and not because we didn't have a choice."

"I thought you were not ready for all the baggage of wife and heir; Corleys loved only once and for life," she couldn't help throwing his words back at him.

He grinned. "I'm ready for marriage and everything that comes with it as long as you're my bride. You are my one true love, to be loved forever. We'll travel the world together, my love. You need not think I'll stop you from achieving your dreams, as long as we do them together."

Olivia pinched her hand. "I must have fallen asleep, and I'm dreaming."

"You aren't dreaming, my love. I love you, Olivia Blackmore. And from your puffy eyes and the fact that you wrote me that letter, dare I hope you feel the same for me. Even if it's just an inch?"

"What do you think?" Her wet eyes twinkled.

"Your letter, taking all the blame and leaving me because you wanted me to be with the woman you thought I loved, gave me hope. You see, I did the same for Susan back then, all in the name of love. So, I assumed that you must feel the same way for me, to be ready to brave a scandal just so I'd be happy. Was I wrong, my love?"

Olivia shook her head. "You weren't wrong. I fell in love with you, too. That was why I was leaving. I felt I had no right to demand faithfulness from you when I had broken our arrangement by falling in love with you. I couldn't bear to see you with another woman."

He caressed her cheek. "Oh, my love. We've been so foolish. Permit me to make it right." With that, he went on a bended knee on the floor of the coach. "Will you marry me, Olivia Blackmore? For love, this time around."

She beamed from ear to ear. "Yes, I will marry you, Thomas Corley. For love."

He rose, drew her in his arms, and kissed her. Olivia's heart bubbled with joy.

"I don't think we should return to London."

She frowned. "Why not?"

"I think your father is choosing his second as we speak."

Olivia burst into a fit of giggles and clung to him. He held her closer, engulfed by the humour of it too. Peace stole Olivia's heart, for she knew it would always be like this with Thomas. Their love life would be filled with joy and laughter. Olivia would marry her friend turned lover, and her marriage of convenience would be real now because she had found love; and love had found her in the wonderful Viscount Corley of Stenford.

The End

Competing for The Lady

THE LADY SERIES BOOK FIFTEEN

Chapter One

"I trust that you two have put your mischievous ways behind you," Lady Keymouth scolded her twin daughters as she took a sip from her cup of tea.

Beatrice shared a conspiratorial smile with her sister, Bridget, who sat beside her on the brocade armchair by the French windows. Born identical twins, they were fond of deceiving people, since very few could tell them apart. They were of average height and had a slim build. They had midnight black curly hair, round faces, button noses, and rosebud lips. The only visible difference between them was the shape of their eyes. Beatrice's eyes were up-turned while Bridget's were almond-shaped; a subtle difference that most people barely noticed. Bridget, however, had a birthmark on her stomach.

Beatrice placed her cup of tea on the small stool beside her chair and smiled at her mother.

"Mama, we have grown past that. We are ladies now," she refuted with a sweet smile. "Childish behaviours are behind us now that we will soon be wed."

"Oh, really? Just two days ago in Keymouth, you pretended to be each other and deceived Sir Wesley into thinking he was addle-brained. You kept on going to the study within seconds of each other and terrified the poor old man."

Beatrice and Bridget giggled behind their palms.

"'Tis hardly our fault that he fell for our silly pranks," Bridget put in. "Besides, it's not our fault he's addle-brained."

Their mother wasn't placated. "If the two of you carry on with such tricks, believe me when I say our stay here in London will be fruitless. No right-thinking man will marry a silly girl."

"Aww, Mama," Beatrice pouted. "We won't do that to our suitors. Would we?" Her blue eyes twinkled as she glanced at her twin.

Bridget's round face broke into a smile. "It depends."

Her mother's face reddened. "You will do no such thing." She raised a warning finger at both her daughters and said, "Your father and I have spent a fortune to make your first Season a success. You will not ruin it. We expect both of you to make good matches."

"Do not worry, Mama. We won't disappoint you and Papa," Beatrice promised.

"You better heed my warning and be well-behaved like Abigail here." She turned her attention to the young girl seated beside her on the sofa.

Abigail, their mother's late sister's daughter, beamed with joy. Bridget rolled her eyes and Beatrice sipped her tea to hide her laughter. Their cousin was there with them in London for her first Season too. Since the girl's mother had passed, the Countess of Keymouth had the responsibility of introducing her into Society, along with her twin hellions.

"Thank you, Aunt Caroline. I shan't disappoint you and Uncle Albert. I cannot thank you enough for inviting me along. Father is most grateful, too."

Beatrice laughed when Bridget pulled a face. She and her twin found Abigail terribly boring because she acted like a goody two-shoes. She never wanted to join them in their shenanigans because she never wanted to get into trouble.

"It is my pleasure, my dear Abigail. It is what your mother would have wanted, God rest her sweet soul. I trust you will make a good match, even if my rambunctious daughters do not." With that, she gracefully rose to her feet. "I'm going to my bed chamber to take a nap. I suggest you all do the same after tea. You must be well rested for your forthcoming ball."

"Yes, Mother."

"Yes, Aunt Caroline."

The Countess swept out of the room in a flurry of silk while the young girls sipped from their cups and took dainty bites from their biscuits.

"I do not see why it is such a big deal for us to make a good match," Beatrice grumbled. "I'm only interested in attending balls and soirees and meeting people."

Abigail glared at her as if she had committed sacrilege. "What do you mean by that, Beatrice? This is the most important event of the year! We must make good impressions to find suitable husbands."

"That's for those who wish to marry now," Beatrice corrected shortly.

Bridget frowned. "What are you saying, Bea? You do not wish to find a husband? Then why have you come to London with us?"

Beatrice wrinkled her nose like she oft did when she was thinking. When she and Bridget turned seventeen a few months ago, they had both talked of little else but their first ball and getting married. But as the time drew closer, Beatrice discovered that she wasn't keen on getting married just yet. She realised that she wanted to see the world and explore like their older sister Olivia.

"To enjoy myself," she offered with a shrug. "Reading Olivia's letters of the places she and Thomas had visited in their first year of marriage, I cannot help but long for such an exciting life."

"You can do all that with your husband," Bridget pointed out.

Beatrice shook her head. "Not every man is as understanding as Olivia's husband. I might not find a man who would allow me to travel all over the world after our wedding."

"You never can tell if you don't search," Abigail cut in. "You might find a man who might have similar interests as you."

Beatrice snorted. "I do not think so. Most men are only interested in having an heir to continue their lineage."

Abigail let out a sharp breath. "That's an unfair thing to say about men."

Bridget gave her sister a worried frown. "When I'm married, what will you do with yourself? That's assuming you don't find a man who shares your dreams."

Beatrice shrugged. "I might go and visit Emily. I could help with baby Christopher."

Bridget's face lit up at the mention of their nephew. "Oh, Christopher. Bea, you amaze me. Carrying Christopher when Emily visited a few months ago showed me I was ready to have a family. I look forward to having an adorable son like Christopher."

Abigail's head bobbed with enthusiasm. "I, too, long to get married and have a baby. I cannot wait to leave home. If my husband is agreeable, I wish to have lots of children. I do so adore them."

Beatrice sighed. "Well, I wish you both God's speed in your search for worthy husbands. I will merely enjoy myself at such gatherings."

"What would Mama and Papa say if they found out that you do not wish to marry now?" Bridget questioned with concern.

Her shoulders elevated in a shrug. "They need not know." Seeing the worry in her twin's eyes, she shook her head. "Bri, please, do not trouble yourself over me. Mayhap I might find a man to my liking before the Season is over. If I don't, I shall simply return next Season when I might be ready to get married."

Her twin knew her well, for the worry didn't disappear from her eyes. Beatrice had no intention of returning to London the following year. She had a plan to join Olivia in the colonies where she was at present with her husband. Who knew when she would return to England?

The only obstacle to her plans was her parents. If they knew what she was about, they would stop her. She had to find a way to outsmart them just the way her older sisters both did.

Chapter Two

With a frown scrunching her face, Beatrice eyed the spoon of chicken soup her personal maid, Mabel, thrust towards her mouth.

"For the love of God Mabel, haven't I had enough of this ghastly soup?" she complained bitterly in a voice hoarse from coughing continuously.

"No, you haven't," her mother, who stood by the bed, firmly stated. "No one told you to play in the rain."

"But Mama, I wasn't playing in the rain. How was I to know the heavens would suddenly open when I went for a walk? Besides, I wasn't the only one who got wet."

Her mother smiled sweetly. "That's true. Your accomplices are getting ready for their first ball, but here you are, sick with a cold. I dare say you deserve what you got for sneaking out of the house without your companion."

Beatrice bit her tongue from making a cryptic remark about the woman whose duty was to follow her and her sister about. "We thought you hired Miss Fitzroy for Olivia only. We didn't know she was to act as our chaperone, too."

"Given how boisterous you and your sisters are, your father and I decided to keep her on."

"Sarah will inherit her too?" She sneezed and winced from the ache in her head.

Her mother's forehead wrinkled in thought for some seconds. "I don't know yet. Of all our children, our youngest daughter appears to be the most docile. Even Alexander gets into more trouble than her."

Beatrice snorted. "Sarah never gets into any trouble. I miss her, though. I wish she had come with us. Alexander, too." She longed for her younger sister and brother, who kept her company most of the time.

"She's better off in Keymouth with her teachers. She still has two more years before she will come back to London for her own Season. Enough about her. For someone who is sick, you are surprisingly chatty. But I know it's only a ploy not to finish your soup." She nodded at the maid who thrust the filled spoon into Beatrice's mouth.

Since the choice was either to swallow or choke, Beatrice grudgingly swallowed it and grimaced. The soup wasn't that bad tasting, she just hated being abed with sickness. Coughing, sneezing, and feeling as if all the diseases in the world had taken refuge in her body made her cantankerous. Because of the chill outside, her mother had instructed that the fire in the fireplace never went out, to keep her warm always, which led Beatrice to feel as though she was on hell's doorstep. Furthermore, she would miss the ball—an event she had looked forward to all week. Even though she didn't want to get married yet, she wanted very much to experience her first ball.

As if to remind her of what she would be missing that night, a soft knock sounded on the door and Bridget came into the room looking like a princess. "Oh! This room is stifling!"

Her maid had swept her mass of black curls up with combs and tendrils framing her round face. The sky-blue chiffon gown, which matched the colour of her eyes and complemented her pale skin, wrapped around her upper body in a high cut and fleshed out from her tiny waist to her ankles. Pearl earrings and necklaces graced her ears and neck, and satin slippers adorned her feet.

Longing filled Beatrice because she knew this was exactly how she would have looked had she been well enough to attend the ball. The only difference between them would have been the colour of her gown. She had chosen yellow as a contrast.

"My, don't you look fetching," she announced with genuine joy at the sight of her sister.

Their mother clapped her hands. "We will keep Madam Gould-smith for years. She's worth every expensive penny she charged us for both your trousseaus."

"I feel beautiful," Bridget confirmed and gave a twirl, which made her twin laugh and resulted in a bout of coughing.

"I must prepare," her mother announced. "Do get better, my darling." After giving her sick daughter a look filled with love, she exited the room.

Lifting the skirts of her gown, Bridget approached the bed with worry in her eyes. "Is it true you won't attend the ball with us?"

"I fear that's the case unless I want to infect all of England with the flu." A twinkle lit up her dull eyes. "That wouldn't be a bad idea, though. Imagine, everyone, coughing and sneezing all over the place."

Bridget laughed heartily. "Mama will hear nothing of it, though." And then she mimicked her mother. "You must maintain a good impression at all times."

Beatrice giggled until she started coughing again. Bridget drew closer to the bed and held her hand.

"I feel so dreadful about this. I was the reason we tarried this morning when we went for a walk because I wanted to feel the breeze in my hair. I'm so sorry about this."

Beatrice smiled through her weak state. "'Tis not your fault, Bri."

"As penance, I shall stay home and take care of you."

Beatrice shook her aching head. "You will do no such thing." She shrugged, "Maybe this is fate. Recall that I was only going to the ball to have a pleasant time. But you intend to go there to find a beau. So, I think it has worked out well for both of us. Besides, the Season is just starting. I shall attend many other balls."

"Are you sure?" Bridget looked at her with scepticism.

"Very sure. Go and have a good time for both of us. And you will tell me all about it in the morning. Hopefully, I'll be better then."

"Bridget! Why are you standing so close to her? You will catch her disease!"

Both girls turned towards the door to see Abigail standing at the threshold with horror in her eyes.

"Oh, hush Abigail. We would have caught whatever she has by now. After all, we all took the walk together."

"Yes, but she's the only one who is sick. So, we should stay away from her."

Beatrice eyed her cousin. If she had been strong enough, she would have risen to run after her, coughing. However, seeing how lovely Abigail looked in her yellow gown, which complemented her honey-brown hair and eyes, she could only smile at her and ask, "Then why are you here? Pray tell."

"Aunt Caroline sent me to fetch Bridget."

Bridget turned to her and reached for her hand to squeeze it. "I'll see you in the morning. Get better soon."

"Do not touch her!" Abigail exclaimed. "You must wash your hand before we leave."

Beatrice and Bridget shared a knowing smile, for they both knew that not only would Bridget not wash her hand, but she would also rub it all over Abigail's face.

"Thank you, Bri. Have a pleasant time and find the most handsome and wealthiest man at the ball."

Bridget cackled and whirled around. Abigail, probably sensing the mischief in her cousin's eyes, screamed and ran away with Bridget hot on her heels. Beatrice burst into laughter, and as usual, ended up coughing. She could not blame Abigail, though. Their cousin could not understand the unbreakable bond she shared with her twin. Besides, Bridget never fell sick. For a moment, she closed her eyes and prayed that all of the desires of her twin's heart would come to pass.

When she opened her eyes, it was to see a spoonful of chicken soup a few inches from her mouth. She groaned loudly.

Chapter Three

"Oh, Mabel. Whatever Cook put in that dreadful soup last night worked like magic." Beatrice stretched her arms above her head and yawned. "I feel as if I wasn't sick only a few hours ago."

She laughed joyously and pushed aside the beddings. "I must see Bridget and hear what happened at the ball last night."

"I'm afraid she's still sleeping, my Lady. Everyone is still abed."

"Oh," disappointment flooded her. She had forgotten that Bridget wasn't an early bird, particularly after a ball no doubt. "Could you please open the windows? It feels as though I'm in a cooking pot."

Her maid chuckled, pulled the red drapes, and threw open the windows. "You must surely be feeling better, my Lady. Yesterday, it wasn't warm enough for you."

Beatrice beamed. "I sure am, which is why I shall take a walk. It's such a beautiful day." Her eyes lit up at the sight of the rays of the sun streaming into her bed chamber.

"Is that wise, my Lady? You were very ill only a short while ago. You might have a relapse."

Beatrice shook her head. "I won't, Mabel. Now, we must hurry before Mama wakes up and stops me from leaving the house." She sighed because her co-conspirator wasn't awake to help her sneak out of their London townhouse.

Half an hour later, Beatrice, garbed in a lilac morning dress, quietly descended the rugged stairs with her maid in tow. If she hurried, she would be back before her mother woke up. She looked forward to hearing all the details about the ball when Bridget awakened.

"Isn't it a beautiful day, Mabel?" Beatrice said as she opened her parasol and stood for a moment, basking in the warmth of the sun's rays.

"It sure is, my Lady," Mabel concurred with a small smile.

As was customary after the first ball of the Season, very few people were around that morning. Most were probably still in bed, sleeping off the late night. By afternoon, she reckoned carriages would fill the streets with men calling on the ladies they had met at the ball or perhaps taking them for rides to the park.

She sighed with disappointment because she had missed all of that. She had wanted to meet not only men but ladies who would become life-long friends. She couldn't boast of having many from Keymouth. But having a twin made up for a lot in the friendship stakes.

She was about to turn around after the short walk, so her mother wouldn't have apoplexy because she left the house without Miss Fitzroy, when she saw a gentleman on a horse raise his hand as he rode towards her. Self-conscious that he might be referring to someone else, she slightly turned around, but no one was close by.

"Lady Blackmore." The man tipped his black hat when he reached her.

Shielding her eyes from the sun with her hand, she lifted her head to stare at the stranger. Her heart caught in her throat when she took in the magnificence of the man. The wind swept back his raven black hair when he removed his hat and his angular face broke into a smile as he gracefully dismounted from his horse. Stormy grey eyes stared at her with amusement. Beatrice felt like a dwarf before the tall, broad-shouldered, and muscular man dressed in a red coat and black riding breeches that showed the strength of his figure. A small scar on his firm jaw was the only thing that made his handsome face imperfect. She itched to ask how he got it but held her tongue as she didn't know who he was, and he might consider it rude.

"I didn't expect to see you about so early in the day. I may be wrong, but I think I remember you telling me that you do not stir until about noon. After attending a soiree, that is."

Only then did Beatrice realise that he thought she was Bridget. Good God! Was he the suitor that she hitched for herself the previous night? Her sister had done well. Not only was he very pleasing to the eyes, but she could also bet all her pin money that he was a peer of the realm. He attracted aristocracy in droves.

"I...um..." What would she say? Truly, Bridget slept like the dead after an event.

The wise thing to do would be to correct him and tell him that she was Bridget's twin. But for some reason she couldn't understand, probably because they had done this several times in the past, she didn't correct him. What if Bridget never got a chance to see the man again? They had heard of instances where men never called on ladies again when they found others more beautiful, willing, and with larger dowries. Men, some said, were such fickle creatures and this one happened to be interested in her sister. After all, he had stopped just to converse with her. Bridget would never forgive her if she didn't do anything to keep his interest in her.

Think like Bridget, Beatrice.

Even though she and her sister were identical twins who shared many interests and had carried out successful mischiefs in the past, they were dissimilar in several ways.

"It was too lovely a day to waste abed," she finally replied.

A great fib! Bridget wouldn't be caught dead out in the sun. She preferred the wet season because she claimed the sun gave her freckles.

"Truly, it is. I, too, decided it would be a shame to stay indoors," he mentioned with a grin, jerking the scar on his chin.

Unable to stop herself and hoping it wouldn't spoil her sister's chances with such a handsome man, she asked, "How did you come by that scar?"

Her face turned a rosy hue when the man threw back his head and laughed throatily.

"Forgive me for being too forward."

He shook his head. "I like inquisitiveness in a Lady. Besides, I told you when you asked last night that I would tell you someday."

Fudge! Bridget had already asked. She should have known her sister wouldn't have been able to hold her tongue. Their mother had always told them that their tongues would put them into trouble someday.

"It's just that it's quite distinct," she stated and flushed again when he laughed. Although he had the mien of someone whose favourite pastime might be brooding, he sure laughed a lot.

"I will take that as a compliment."

Beatrice turned around to hide her flushed face. "Pardon me..." *Fudge! Was he titled? If he was, what was it?*

She was saved from embarrassment and from confessing who she truly was when a man riding by called to them and tipped his hat.

"Lord Northbridge. My Lady."

Sighing inwardly with relief, she hastily said, "Pardon me, my Lord, but I must return home before my mother sends Bow Street runners in search of me."

He chuckled. "May I walk with you, my Lady?"

She shrugged. "It's a free world, isn't it?" She bit her tongue after her question. Bridget would have readily agreed.

The man didn't appear offended. He smiled. "Is it?"

"Some people think so."

"Then I will walk with you."

She nodded, and he fell in step with her while Mabel walked behind them with a disapproving frown on her face. Her and Bridget's maids never approved of it whenever they deceived anyone. In their entire staff, both in Keymouth and London, only their two maids could tell the difference between them.

Beatrice's nose wrinkled as she caught a whiff of his musky scent. Most men she had come in contact with—not that she knew many— usually smelt of horseflesh, cigars, or ciders.

"I had feared you might be unwell this morning with the way you complained of the heat last night in the crowded ballroom as we danced. But I must say it is a delightful surprise to find you hale and hearty."

Bridget had danced with him? She could not help wondering how it would have been to be held in those strong arms of his, staring into his stormy grey eyes.

Beatrice! What am I doing?

"Um... the ball was stifling, to say the least."

From the corner of her eye, she saw him frowning and her heart dropped. She had obviously put her foot in her mouth.

"You gave the impression that you were having a wonderful time, regardless of the heat."

She quickly recovered. "You didn't allow me to finish, my Lord. Even though it seemed as if all of England was there and made the ballroom feel like we were next door to hell, I still had a pleasant time."

She released a low breath when he laughed. "Yes. You just reminded me that conversing with you had been, and still is, rather entertaining."

Thankfully, they arrived in front of her house just then. Beatrice was keen to get away from him so that she could stop pretending to be her twin. But, at the same time, she realised that she had enjoyed his company rather a lot. Usually, it wasn't hard impersonating her twin, but they had only done that for pranks and not serious business like gaining the interest of a man.

He tapped his aquiline nose. "I hope it isn't too forward of me to ask for permission to call on you tomorrow."

Beatrice stopped in front of the stone steps. "Certainly not, my Lord."

He smiled. "Perhaps we could take a ride to the park."

"That would be delightful."

"Until then, my Lady." He bowed as he took her gloved hand. She curtsied and forced her legs to move away from him when he released her hand. Sweet Mary, if she didn't move slowly, she might fall flat on the steps.

The butler opened the door just when she reached the top step, and she could have hugged him for making her escape faster. Immediately the door shut behind Mabel, and Beatrice let out a heavy breath. Now, she had to see Bridget and fill her in on the exciting yet terrifying thing that just happened.

Chapter Four

"What do you mean I cannot see Bridget?" Beatrice crossly questioned her sister's maid who was heading towards her sister's room with a bowl of water and a towel.

Looking as if she was about to burst into tears, the maid replied, "Lady Bridget has taken ill, too. Your mother has forbidden anyone to see her so it wouldn't spread."

"Bridget? Sick! I find that hard to believe."

"I tell you no lies, my Lady. Your mother doesn't want anyone else catching it."

"But I've already been sick, so whatever is spreading won't affect me," she fiercely countered.

"I'm only following your mother's orders, my Lady."

"I understand but I must see her immediately. Something happened..." She trailed off as she realised it was none of the maid's business. "I must see her at once, even if I have to stand by the door to speak to her."

Without waiting for the maid to respond, Beatrice strode ahead of her towards her sister's room. In Keymouth, they had shared a room until their sixteenth birthday when their parents had insisted they have separate rooms now that they were young ladies.

"Bridget," Beatrice softly called and knocked on the door.

"Please do not come closer, Bea," Bridget, in an unrecognisable weak voice, called as soon as her twin opened the door to the highly heated room, just like hers had been the previous night.

"Oh, Bri." Beatrice said with distress on her face. "Abigail was right, after all. You shouldn't have come close to me last night."

Bridget, propped on the bed with at least twelve pillows, shook her head. The towel on it slipped a little and her maid rushed into the room to right it. "Do not say that again. Abigail will gloat about it until her dying day."

Beatrice couldn't help the smile that curled the corners of her lips. "How do you feel?"

"Terrible." She coughed a little. "How are you feeling? You look better."

"Yes, I feel much better. And that's why I'm hopeful that you will be hale and hearty come the morrow."

"I hope so. I hate being sick. Do you think we caught something in the rain?"

Still standing by the door, Beatrice shrugged. "Most probably."

"You have something to tell me. I can see it in your eyes."

Beatrice giggled because she and her sister had always been able to read each other.

"By the way, you owe me all your scones for the next three weeks," she said with a gleam in her eyes.

"Why is that?"

"Because I just pretended to be you to someone called Lord Northbridge while I went for a walk," she smugly told her.

Bridget's eyes widened. "You met Nicholas?"

Beatrice nodded. "Not shocking. He mistook me for you, and I just had to keep the charade going for your sake as he appeared quite interested in you." Then she frowned. "Wait. Are you already on a first-name basis with him?"

Even though her face was pale from her sickness, Bridget blushed. "He insisted on it. Told me he wasn't too keen on formalities. He found them excessively boring."

"Hump! Is he a rake or what? Mama will not approve."

"Oh, no. He isn't at all. He returned from the colonies a few weeks ago. His cousin, Edward's friend, introduced us at the ball. We got talking, and I quickly realised he wasn't like the other men I had met at the party. So, I relaxed and regaled him with tales of our mischief, but I made it seem like I was referring to our younger (non-existent) twin sisters."

Beatrice frowned. "Why did you do that?"

"I was only trying to be careful. He enjoyed the stories, but I wasn't sure he would fancy being married to someone as mischievous as us."

"Oh. Well, you have the opportunity of correcting that tomorrow because you apparently impressed him."

"Tomorrow?"

"Yes. I agreed for him to take you to the park for a ride."

Bridget shook her head and winced. "But I am so sick! I cannot make it."

"Do not trouble yourself about that, Bri. I believe you will be fine come tomorrow just like me."

After a bout of spontaneous sneezing, Bridget flushed and said, "I cannot go out in this state, Bea. You will have to take my place again."

Beatrice's face contorted into a frown. "I cannot do that, Bri."

She noisily blew her nose in the handkerchief her maid offered her. "Why? We've pretended to be each other many times."

"Yes, when we are playing tricks. But this is different."

"How so?"

"This is a man who might be interested in *marrying* you. We cannot deceive him."

"I do not see why we cannot do that. And it won't be a deception, per se. You will only act like me."

"But Bri, you know we have different interests. I already made blunders while speaking to him earlier about you and I hardly know anything about him."

"I do not know much about him either. All I know is that he is Nicholas Webb, the Marquess of Northbridge in search of a wife."

"A Marquess!" Beatrice exclaimed.

Bridget smiled. "Yes, Bea. A Marquess. If I... no, if *we* play our cards right, I might be a Marchioness someday."

Beatrice shook her head. "No, I'm sorry I cannot do it, Bri. It doesn't feel right."

Her sister stared at her with suspicion in her eyes. "Is there something you aren't telling me, Beatrice?"

Beatrice instantly deflated the level of her gaze. "I don't know, Bri. I don't feel comfortable with this. I might continue making a faux pas that might make him lose interest in you."

"Is that all?"

Fortunately, her sister would attribute the beads of sweat on her forehead to the heated room. How could she tell Bridget that she had not only found Lord Northbridge very handsome, but she had enjoyed the short time she spent with him? Was she supposed to feel that way over a handsome man her sister was interested in?

"Please do this for me, Bea. You aren't interested in getting married soon but I am. Lord Northbridge was the best catch at the ball last night. You should have seen the way ladies flooded him and sought for him to be introduced. It was hilarious. Mama didn't even bother. I was standing with Edward and his friend, Lord Northbridge's cousin, when he walked up to us. I found him quite handsome but seeing how he was out of my league I didn't quite acknowledge him. I think that was what piqued his interest. He asked me to dance, and we had an enjoyable time conversing."

Beatrice remained in her thoughts. She couldn't admit that she was looking forward to seeing him again.

"Please, Bea. You know had the situation been reversed, I would have done the same for you."

Beatrice nodded. Indeed, Bridget would have gladly taken her place.

"You can have all my scones, cakes, and biscuits until I'm wed."

A soft gurgle of laughter burst from Beatrice's throat. "Bribery, too, Bridget?"

Her sister sniffed into her handkerchief. "Anything to get you to do this for me."

"Alright then."

Bridget coughed and laughed. "You never could resist cakes, you sweet-toothed girl."

Beatrice laughed and wrinkled her nose.

I hope I don't regret this.

Chapter Five

"How are your twin sisters?"

Beatrice ducked her head so Lord Northbridge wouldn't notice the grimace on her face. The outing was starting as badly as she had expected. This was what she had been afraid of.

Why did I agree to this? I'll mess everything up and ruin Bridget's chances with him.

She had hoped Bridget would be better when she woke up this morning, but her sister's condition had worsened overnight. And so, Beatrice had to take her place for the chaise ride to the park. Again, her heart skipped a beat at the sight of the handsome Marquess who was garbed in a dark blue coat and black trousers. Tingles had shot through her body when he took her hand and helped her into the chaise. Miss Fitzroy and Mabel were riding in another chaise Lord Northbridge had hired to accompany theirs.

"Um... they are doing fine, my Lord."

He grinned. "I thought we agreed you could call me by my first name."

Fudge! She had forgotten.

"My apologies, my... um... Nicholas."

He chuckled. "Why do I feel as if I'm talking to someone else other than the brazen girl I met two nights ago? Why do you suddenly seem so shy?"

Beatrice closed her eyes at the sight of the well-dressed men and women walking down the street and riding past them in carriages. Wasn't this the right moment to tell Nicholas the truth? She was failing badly at pretending to be her sister, and he was intelligent enough to have noticed. But what would it mean? Wouldn't it ruin his interest in her sister? Bridget would be very cross with her for saying the truth and spoiling things for her. Undoubtedly, Nicholas would be angry at the deception and would most likely call off the outing and never want to see Bridget again. Beatrice had to carry on at all costs.

At that moment, she decided acting like herself would be best for the situation. If she continued trying to behave like her sister, she would muddle things.

And so, opening her eyes and throwing him a radiant smile, she said, "If I appear shy, Nicholas, perhaps it's because I'm trying to correct my barefaced behaviour at the ball."

He shook his head. "Please don't do that. It was what attracted me to you in the first place."

"Oh, really? I had wondered."

"After being bombarded by eager to please debutantes all night, it was a refreshing change to meet someone who appeared not to give a fig about who I was."

"But it was to be expected. You went to the ball to find a wife, didn't you?"

He sighed with exasperation as he expertly controlled the horse's reins. "I did, but I hadn't expected to be flooded by so many young girls who wished to be introduced to me. You see, in the past year, I've been in America, overseeing my shipping business. I believe I told you that."

She nodded, grateful that Bridget had mentioned it, otherwise she would have thought he was testing her.

"Immediately after I returned home, my grandfather, the Duke of Davenshire, requested I get married as my father had wished before his demise. That's according to him, anyway. I wouldn't put anything past him just to get me to do his wish."

She giggled.

"So, I grudgingly went to the ball to find a wife."

Her eyebrows arched. "Do you mean you do not want to marry now?"

He curved his body slightly on the seat and fixed his eyes on her. "If I had the choice, I would hold it back for two or three years. But I must confess that meeting you has somewhat changed my thoughts."

Beatrice's heart pounded in her chest, and she feared that it might jump out and hit him right across the face if he didn't stop staring at her like that.

"I'm a very straightforward person, my Lady. When I see what I like and want, I go for it. I do not mean to be too forward or demanding but I must tell you the truth because I do not like playing games. Of all the girls and women I was introduced to at the ball, only you caught my fancy."

Beatrice suddenly found it very hard to breathe. Despite the cool nature of the day, as it had showered lightly that morning, she opened her fan and waved it across her heated face. Never had a man spoken directly to her in such a manner before. What did he expect her to say to that? She was delighted she had garnered his interest. *No, not mine. Bridget's.*

"So, my Lady, if you do not welcome my attention or you have someone else in mind, please tell me now so I won't waste my time wooing you. I do not enjoy fruitless ventures."

Her heart sang with joy. This was what she had desired. No, Bridget. This was what her sister had wanted and now, she would get it.

"I do not have any other suitor, my Lord. I danced with other men at the ball, but none of them made my heart flip."

"And I did?"

She bowed her head and looked away. "Maybe."

He laughed. "I hope I'll make more than your heart flip in the future."

With a twinkle in her blue eyes, she said, "We'll see."

"May I call you by your first name to distinguish you from other ladies?"

She presented him with a sweet smile. "You certainly can call me Beatrice."

"What a beautiful name. Beatrice it is, then."

Only just realising the mistake she had made, Beatrice lost all the colour on her face. How could she possibly correct the error?

"Is anything amiss? You look like you've seen a ghost." His eyes darted about them, seemingly looking for the cause of her sudden distress.

"I...um..." Oh well. Bridget would have to correct the mistake at a later date when she took her rightful place beside him. "I just wondered how my mother would react if she knew we were already calling each other by our first names. She might send for her hartshorn."

Laughter bubbled from his throat. "It will be between us." And then he gave her a conspiratorial wink. "Our little secret until we deem it fit to tell everyone."

"Agreed."

Putting aside the thought that she was only acting on Bridget's behalf, Beatrice resolved to enjoy herself. And she did. By the time they arrived at the park, it was filled with people with a similar idea of having a pleasant day. Conscious of the eyes darting their way, Beatrice took a stroll with Nicholas across the park while Miss Fitzroy walked behind them, keeping a watchful eye on them. Beatrice laughed inwardly. She would definitely be on her best behaviour in the company of such a man that made her pulse race so rapidly. Quite a few people stopped them to converse a little before they moved on.

Beatrice got to know him; he had a married elder sister and two younger sisters. His mother died after the birth of his youngest sister while his father met his demise during a boat mishap. He had to take over his father's businesses even before he was ready. Presently, at twenty and five years old, he had successfully turned their dwindling finances around. She found it endearing that he doted on his younger sisters.

"They are not as high-spirited as your younger sisters, but they keep me guessing what mischievous thing they would do next," he said with vexation borne out of love for his sisters.

Beatrice laughed softly behind her hand as she recalled when they were much younger and had their parents and the entire staff of Keymouth searching for her and Bridget when they had explored the vast Estate grounds.

By the time Nicholas returned her home an hour later, Beatrice was sorry the outing was over. She wished it would go on for much longer.

"I must thank you, Beatrice, for such an enjoyable day," Nicholas said as he walked her to the door.

"I, too, had a splendid time."

His eyes twinkled. "Does that mean you will attend a musicale with me two days from today?"

Beatrice lowered her eyes so he wouldn't see the disappointment in her eyes. Bridget would be better then and would attend, not her.

"You mentioned you played the pianoforte," he said when she remained silent.

"No, I..." Beatrice bit her lip to keep from blurting out that she sang while Bridget played the instrument. "I mean, I'd love to go with you."

"Superb. I'll send word regarding the time. And mayhap we could go riding one morning."

Beatrice could only nod because Bridget was keener on riding than her.

"Then I must bid you farewell now, my Lady," he stated and took her gloved hand, conscious of Miss Fitzroy's presence who would frown if he were to call her by her first name.

"Thank you for the outing, my Lord."

Beatrice would have loved to watch him leave but Miss Fitzroy hurried her into the house.

"You must never show a man how much you care for him," the older woman chided her as soon as they entered the foyer. "The fact that you have an interest in him must be kept a secret until he offers for you."

Beatrice's face paled at her companion's words. That couldn't be right. She didn't have an interest in Nicholas, did she? Remembering how much she enjoyed his company, her chest tightened.

Oh, no!

Chapter Six

"Have I told you how stunning you look?"

Tried as she might not to blush, Beatrice failed. Compliments from Nicholas always sent a blush to her cheeks.

"Why, thank you, my Lord," she replied, conscious of Miss Fitzroy walking closely behind them. Whenever they were dancing in balls or seated side by side in a box at the opera, she had leave to call him by his given name and vice versa. But as etiquettes allowed for only betrothed couples to call each other by name, they desisted from doing so when they were in the company of others.

Beatrice's head elevated when she heard a low groan from Nicholas. She followed the direction of his gaze and placed a hand across her mouth to hide her laughter. Standing at the other side of the street, waving at them with a dazzling smile on her face, was Lady Melport. Wherever they went, they encountered the older woman who never failed to come over to say hello to them.

"If I didn't know better, I'd say she was stalking us," Nicholas muttered and nodded at the woman who was looking to cross the busy street towards them.

"I think she's a harmless romantic."

"My, my, isn't it the couple of the Season," the woman said immediately she reached them and acknowledged their bow and curtsy with a nod.

Beatrice frowned at the caption. The older woman noticed and laughed.

"Oh, do come now. Don't tell me you do not know you've caught the interest of a lot of people. Why, some daring people have placed bets at White's that you two would be married before the end of the Season."

Beatrice's head bowed as a blush crept across her face.

"I'm rooting for you two as well," she nodded at Nicholas. "Do not tarry in offering for her as I hear a great number of men are ready to take your place at the drop of a hat. The Blackmore family has a good reputation and so does yours. Five daughters with no scandal yet; that is something they ought to be proud of. Perhaps, it's the only son that might put their name in the black book. Who knows? Mayhap they will settle for your twin sister, Lady Blackmore when you marry Lord Northbridge. Where is she anyway? I saw her on the night of the debutante ball. Has she gone back to Keymouth?"

Horror filled Beatrice's eyes at the Countess' question. How was she supposed to answer that when she hadn't told Nicholas the truth? It still amazed her that with the several places they had been to together, no one had yet mentioned her twin sister. It was most likely because they were free from scandals and kept mostly to their country home in Keymouth. So, many people didn't know she was a twin. Lady Melport obviously did.

"Oh. That's Lady Wentworth waving at me. I must join my friends for a game of bridge. See you some other time, my darlings."

Beatrice sighed with relief when she hurried away.

"I've always known her to be nosy, but I didn't know she was senile as well," Nicholas mentioned with a chuckle as they walked on.

Beatrice acknowledged this was the right time to tell him Lady Melport wasn't losing her senses. But when she opened her mouth, she recalled the awesome time she had had with Nicholas these past two weeks, and she saw it going up in flames if she told him the truth.

Bridget's illness had deteriorated to where her parents had prohibited everyone from seeing her lest they catch it. Beatrice had protested since she worried about her twin's health and had to tell her about her outing with Nicholas, but she could not see her. They had exchanged brief notes through their maids, but nothing detailed. And so, she hadn't been able to tell her about her ride to the park with Nicholas. Bridget had simply told her to carry on.

The doctor had arrived and diagnosed Bridget with a severe case of the flu and prescribed that she stay in bed until she got better. As it was too late for Beatrice to confess her true identity to Nicholas, she had had to carry on with the falsehood.

Nicholas had taken her to the musicale, which had been very entertaining. They had attended a dinner party of his friend a few days later. He had also invited her to the opera and presented himself as her escort to two balls.

With every minute she spent with Nicholas, she knew she had been wrong when she said she wasn't ready to get married. She should have said she would get married if the right man came along. But Nicholas wasn't for her. Sadly, he was spoken for.

"Are you alright? You weren't embarrassed by what she said, were you?"

She wrinkled her nose. "Not at all. Like I said earlier, she's simply a harmless romantic."

"Are you?"

"Am I what?"

"A harmless romantic?"

She shrugged. "I don't know. Maybe." She dashed a glance at him. "You?"

He chuckled. "I think I am."

Her eyes grew wide to hold his intense gaze as he stopped walking. Time stood still for a moment while they stared at each other as if they were the only ones in the world. Only the sound of Miss Fitzroy loudly clearing her throat punctuated the highly charged atmosphere.

"You?" She stared at him in disbelief when she found her voice again.

"Why do you find it hard to believe?"

"Most men aren't. They only get married to fulfil their duties and have an heir."

His eyes gleamed with an emotion she didn't recognise. "Then pray tell if I'm not a harmless romantic, why I have fallen in love with a beautiful young Lady I met only two weeks ago?"

The breath ceased from Beatrice's lungs for a minute. Her eyes widened like dinner plates.

"When my brother-in-law told me it took him spending only a few hours with my sister to fall in love with her, I thought he was a candidate for Bedlam. When my best mate declared his love for a Lady he met in less than a week, I thought it was ridiculous. I knew love existed, but I'd never experienced it or believed it could happen so fast. But believe me, my dear, when I say these past two weeks with you have been nothing but blissful. Whenever I'm away from you I spend every moment thinking about you and yearning to be with you again. They say it's love."

Dear God, am I about to swoon? She had faked so many swoons in the past that she didn't know what it actually felt like. The tightening of her chest and her heated face must mean she was about to lose consciousness. *Why now?*

"Forgive me for carrying on and on. What I simply want to say is that I have fallen in love with you, Lady Beatrice Blackmore. May I have permission to officially court you? That is if you feel the same way about me or think you might come to care for me in the future?"

Beatrice was overjoyed. She opened her mouth to tell him she felt the same about him, but then she remembered that she didn't have the right to do that. These past weeks weren't supposed to be about her but her sick twin sister who thought she was only spending time with Nicholas on her behalf.

"I see I have robbed you of words. My apologies, my Lady. Maybe you need some time to think about it, or maybe I need to show you how much you have come to mean to me."

Words eluded Beatrice. She so desperately wanted to tell him that her heart beat for him too, but she needed to speak to Bridget about it first.

"May I walk you back home as I see that I have ruined our outing?" Nicholas said in a rueful tone.

She shook her head. She couldn't bear for him to think he had displeased her with his avowal of love.

"Not at all, my Lord. Your declaration was just unexpected."

"Then I beg your pardon. Mayhap I still need more lessons from my married friend and brother-in-law." His lips twitched in a smile.

She returned his smile. "Perhaps."

He laughed with gusto as they turned around to head back home. Part of her wanted her to sing until her throat became hoarse, and another part of her wanted to crawl into a hole and hide. How would she ever tell Bridget that she had fallen in love with Nicholas?

She was still wondering how she would tell her twin sister as Nicholas walked her to the front door.

"Thank you for yet another beautiful day, my Lady." He took her hand and kissed it.

Desiring to spend more time with him, she said, "Now that you have declared how you feel about me, isn't it time for me to know how you got that scar?"

Surprise lifted his eyes at the unexpected question. His face then relaxed in a smile. "I'll allow you a guess. If you guess wrongly, then you will be forced to tell me how you feel about me."

She nodded, enjoying the light banter. "And if I guess right?"

"Then I will tell you the source of the scar and you can demand anything of me."

Could she demand his forgiveness if she told him the truth? She had to make a good guess first.

She said the obvious thing. "You got it during the war."

He raised his hand and rubbed the scar with a smile brightening his eyes. "You're wrong, my Lady. And now, you must tell me if my feelings are reciprocated."

"You cheated!"

He blinked with stupefaction. "How?"

She laughed. "I don't know. I'm not wrong. It was definitely when you were in battle."

He laughed. "No, it really wasn't. Now tell me the truth." He drew himself to his full height and inched closer to her, ignoring Miss Fitzroy's frown.

With Nicholas this close to her and watching her intently, Beatrice knew there was no way she could lie to him. She would rather have cut off her tongue than hurt his feelings.

"Your feelings are reciprocated, Lord Northbridge. I, too, have fallen in love with you and you have my permission to officially court me."

Chapter Seven

"**B**ridget, I'm so sorry but you will have to give up on your hopes of marrying Lord Northbridge because not only has he fallen in love with me, I, too, can't bear to think of life without him. He wishes to come to see Papa and that's that."

No. That's too blunt. Beatrice paced on the Axminster floor covering in her room as she practised how she would tell Bridget she was in love with her suitor. Although the weather was cool, she wiped the sweat from her forehead with her handkerchief.

Am I being selfish? Why can't I give him up? Bridget could easily take her place without him noticing. She would fill her sister in on all they had discussed and all that had transpired between them.

She sat on her bed and tears stung her eyes. Could she really put into words how she had felt when she first danced with him? How could she describe the enjoyable horse ride they had together a few days ago? And what about their conversations? She and Nicholas had spent long hours talking while they took walks, rides to the park, or danced together. Even at the musicale, they had discussed several musical instruments and then the performance at the opera.

Bridget was bound to suspect something wasn't right if she started talking about Nicholas to her. Her sister could read her like a book. The reason she didn't know how she felt was because of her illness, which had made them unable to spend some time together. But just the previous morning at breakfast, before she went on a walk with Nicholas, her mother had announced that Bridget's fever was gone, and she would join them soon. She had been overjoyed. But now, she didn't know if she wanted to see her sister. Truly, she was glad the worst was over, and that Bridget was hale again. She had honestly feared for her sister's life. But she could not bear having to tell her sister the truth that was in her heart.

A knock on the door jerked her from her thoughts. Her face broke into a smile when Abigail entered the room carrying a bouquet of her favourite flowers, daises. She rose from the bed and hurried to take the flowers from her, knowing only one person would send them to her.

"Lord Northbridge seems quite taken with you," Abigail alleged as she strode towards the window.

Beatrice, after inhaling the lovely fragrance of the flowers, turned to her cousin, who also had been unwell until a few days ago. "How do you feel now, Abigail?"

Abigail reeled around. "Marvellous, even though I've missed a lot this Season. It's ironic that you who weren't interested in getting married are the one who has a suitor."

Beatrice bit her lip to keep from telling her the truth. Abigail couldn't keep a secret, and would no doubt tell their mother that she and Bridget were up to their old tricks again. All this while, her mother had thought she had met Nicholas before now through Abigail's brother, Edward, who also lived with them in the townhouse. Consequently, she and her father had approved of Nicholas's attention on her.

"I'm sure you will find someone suitable before the end of the Season," Beatrice comforted her.

"But not a Duke or a Marquess," Abigail grumbled.

Before Beatrice could reply, another knock sounded on the door, and it opened to admit a smiling Bridget. Beatrice screamed, placed the flowers on the bed, and rushed into the outstretched arms of her sister. They hugged each other as if they would never let go.

"I'm so happy to see you, Bri. I've missed you dearly." Tears glistened in her eyes. It felt so good to be with her sister again, even though she had a tremendous secret to tell her.

Bridget smiled happily. "Me, too."

"How do you feel now?"

"So much better. That blasted fever nearly did me in."

"I'm so glad you're okay now."

"Me too." Bridget tugged at her hand and dragged her towards the bed. She eyed the flowers with mischief. "Tell me all that I missed. How is Lord Northbridge and what progress have you made with him so far?"

Beatrice gave Abigail a pointed stare. Bridget got the message and put a hand across her mouth.

"Maybe when's gone," Bridget whispered naughtily at her.

Beatrice fought to hide her relief as she prayed inwardly that Abigail wouldn't leave them alone anytime soon. When she heard another knock on the door, she exhaled loudly. Who was that now?

"I have the most exciting news, my darlings!" Her mother said immediately she breezed into the room.

The three young ladies turned to stare at the older woman.

"What is it, Mama?" Bridget asked as she drew closer to her.

Lady Keymouth stared at Beatrice. "Lord Northbridge just asked your father for your hand in marriage and he accepted."

"What?"

Bridget clapped her hands with glee. "That's marvellous! Oh, Beatrice, you did it. You're the best sister ever." In her excitement, Bridget forgot that her mother and cousin weren't supposed to be privy to the plan. She exclaimed, "I can't believe it! Someday I'll become a Marchioness."

"Bridget!" Beatrice stared at her, horrified.

Bridget laughed. "It doesn't matter anymore, Bea. They're bound to know in the long run."

Their mother's face scrunched in a frown. "What are you talking about?"

Still grinning like a ninny, she answered, "I'm the one Lord Northbridge wishes to marry."

Lady Keymouth shook her head. "No, not you. Beatrice. He specifically said Beatrice Anne Blackmore."

Beatrice knew the hour she had dreaded was upon her when Bridget swivelled around to fix accusing eyes on her. "You told him your real name? *Why?*"

With pleading in her eyes for her twin to understand, she replied, "It was done in error and then it was too late for me to correct him."

"You devious conniving lout!"

"Bridget, please."

"This was your plan all along, wasn't it? To steal my suitor from right under my nose."

Beatrice reddened. "That's unfair and you know it. I didn't want to go along with the plan, but you insisted. How was I to know I would fall in love with him?"

"That's no excuse! You were supposed to be pretending to be *me* and build his interest in *me* and not you. Sweet Jesus, I feel so betrayed. And by my own twin."

Beatrice put both palms together in a pleading gesture. "It's not like that, Bridget. I tried, I tried to fight it but being with him these past weeks has been wonderful and I couldn't help it."

"*Couldn't help it?* There I was at death's door thinking how you're the most selfless person in the world to be securing a suitor for me. I didn't know you intended to steal him so you would someday become a Marchioness!"

"That's enough, both of you!" their mother shouted while Abigail giggled helplessly by the window. "I can't tell you how ashamed I am of the two of you. How could you have done that to Lord Northbridge? If it wasn't that it would cause a scandal since he intends to go to the dailies to announce your betrothal, I would have told him to call off the wedding. Neither of you deserves him. I warned you not to do this, didn't I?"

"Mark my words, Beatrice, you will never have him," Bridget proclaimed ominously and stormed out of the room.

"Bridget!" Her mother rushed after her.

Abigail, still laughing, went after them. Beatrice crumpled on the floor beside her bed and wept pitifully.

Chapter Eight

My dearest Beatrice,

    I cannot tell you how lonely the days have been without seeing your beautiful face and your heart-warming smile. Why my grandfather summoned me at a time like this remains baffling to me when he knows my heart is in London with you. Words cannot express how much I miss you and long to be with you. I'll count every second until we meet again.

    Love,

    Nicholas.

Beatrice clasped the letter to her heart and sighed while tears glistened in her eyes.

"Why do you look so sad? He'll be back in London before you know it?" Edward, her cousin, who was seated beside her on the sofa in the salon, softly told her.

"I know," she sniffed. "I miss him dearly."

He smiled. "I understand what you mean, my dear. Had Annabel's father agreed to our union, I would have been married by now."

"I'm so sorry about that," Beatrice recalled Edward had a beau once, but her father had rejected the idea of them being together and forced her to marry someone else.

Beatrice didn't tell him that the other source of sadness she felt was the feud between her and Bridget. Her twin sister had refused to speak to her since she discovered a week ago that Nicholas wanted to marry her. She had tried everything she could to make peace with her, but Bridget was adamant that she was a vile person.

"As I was saying, Abigail, I..."

Beatrice's head lifted when the salon doors opened, and Bridget strolled in with Abigail. Upon sighting her, Bridget froze.

"Come, Abigail, let us find another place to discuss. I find one of the present companies here detestable."

"Bridget!" Beatrice jolted to her feet as her twin sister turned away. "Please, we cannot carry on like this. Yes, I agree I was wrong. But you're the one who told me love is such a powerful emotion, it cannot be controlled. God's truth, I didn't mean to fall in love with him. It just happened. I'm sorry about it but I love him and I will marry him."

Bridget spun on her heels, her blue eyes darkening with anger. "Stop lying. You meant to seize him from me from the onset. Otherwise, why didn't you tell him your name was Bridget?"

Beatrice's face paled. "It was a mistake."

Bridget snorted. "How convenient!"

Angered by the condescending tone, Beatrice snapped, "Need I remind you it wasn't my idea in the first place? I repeatedly told you that I wasn't comfortable with the deception."

"Lies! Then you should have maintained you wouldn't go through with it."

"I was trying to help you."

"Such help I can do without! And who did you help at the end of the day?"

Beatrice didn't have a comeback to that.

"Bridget, Beatrice, what's going on? I have never seen the two of you at loggerheads before." Edward cut in with alarm in his voice.

"Dear brother, please do not interfere. It's a matter between two sisters," Abigail cautioned with a glint in her eyes.

"No." Edward shot up from the chair. "Disagreements are bound to occur between siblings. Come now, let's sort things out."

"Fine," Bridget recapitulated. "The only way I will forgive Beatrice is if she refuses to marry Lord Northbridge."

Beatrice gasped. "I cannot do that. I love him."

"Then we're done talking here." Spinning on her heels, Bridget stormed out of the room. Abigail followed her while Edward put his arms around Beatrice as tears poured down her face.

Over the next few days, Beatrice tried to make peace with Bridget to no avail. Although her sister and Abigail attended several balls, they didn't find anyone who caught their fancy, which made Bridget all the angrier.

Beatrice not only missed Nicholas, but she also missed her twin sister. Had circumstances been the way they used to be, she would have shared her feelings for Nicholas with her twin. It broke her heart that her love for her betrothed was costing her the bond she had with her sister. At times, she contemplated calling off the wedding so things could go back to the way they used to be before Nicholas came into the picture. But she found it gravely unfair to herself and him. It was no fault of anyone that they had fallen in love. In one of her letters to Nicholas, she was tempted to tell him the truth and to seek his counsel but she felt doing so face to face was better so she could apologise for her role in the whole debacle. She, however, wrote to Emily and Olivia to offer help with the situation.

A week after Nicholas left London for Davenshire to see his grandfather, her parents summoned her to the salon to glumly tell her Nicholas had called off the wedding, giving no reason at all.

"But... but... he can't do that. Something must be wrong. I received his letter two days ago, and he gave no indication that he was displeased about anything."

"Don't you worry, my darling. He will pay for this disgrace. I have sent a message to him to choose his second," Lord Albert quipped.

Beatrice shook her head. "Papa, please, it hasn't come to that. I just need to speak to him. Something must be wrong somewhere."

"He has obviously seen someone that has caught his fancy, and he means to do away with you like a used dishrag. I won't stand for it."

Bridget looked at him perplexed. It didn't make sense. They had exchanged love letters only two days ago. So why the sudden ending of their betrothal?

"My dear," her mother put in gently. "We'll get to the bottom of the matter."

A memory ran through her mind. *Mark my words, Beatrice, you will never have him.*

"Bridget!"

Lifting the skirts of her gown, Beatrice hurried out of the room and raced up the stairs to her sister's room.

"What have you done?" she asked without preamble to her sister, who sat by her desk writing letters.

Bridget glanced at her with surprise and then returned to her letter. "Leave my room at once. I do now wish to speak to you ever again."

Incensed at the dismissing tone, Beatrice strode to the table. "You won't speak to me again after you have done your worst?"

"What are you talking about?"

"You made good on your threat of me never marrying Nicholas, didn't you? What did you tell him for him to have called off our engagement?"

Bridget stared at her with shock. "I don't know what you're talking about."

"Stop lying, you vengeful wench. You couldn't just bear to see me happy, could you? Undo whatever you did this minute, or you will not like the consequences of your actions."

Bridget rose from the chair and folded her arms across her chest, tilting her chin in defiance. "I didn't do anything, even though I wish now that I *had* done it. Maybe your Nicholas found out what a lying cheat you are and decided he couldn't marry such a person."

"Liar! You told him everything, didn't you? You couldn't just let him go and be happy for me. What kind of a sister are you?" Tears streamed down her face. "I did what I did out of love for you. I repeat, I never envisaged I would fall in love with him. The least you could have done was to accept my apology and wished me well. Instead, you went behind my back to ruin things for me. You will rue this day. I promise you."

Bridget's face turned pasty. "Beatrice, I swear I had nothing to do with his reneging. If I did, I would own it with my chest. Serves you right, though, for falling in love with such a fickle and cowardly man who couldn't tell you to your face that he didn't want you anymore."

Beatrice elevated her hand to slap her sister for daring to insult the man she loved, but her mother entered the room just then.

"Stop this nonsense at once! Shamefully fighting over a man. I thought I taught you two better."

"But Mama, she tore my heart to shreds with her actions," Beatrice protested with tears still rolling down her eyes.

"And you didn't do the same?" Bridget threw at her with an equal bite.

Beatrice, with her face like a storm cloud, poked a finger in the air at her. "If you know what's good for you, Bridget, go and undo what you did, or I'll never forgive you and we'll cease being sisters forever."

With that, she strode out of the room with purposeful steps. If she had to go to Davenshire to explain everything to Nicholas, she would. She couldn't bear to think of life without him.

Chapter Nine

"Edward, please this is crazy!" Beatrice held her cousin's hand to stop him from loading his pistol further.

"Beatrice, please, this is something I have to do. Your honour is at stake here. How dare Lord Northbridge do this to you?"

"'Tis not his fault. I deceived him. Had I told him the truth from the beginning, he wouldn't have called off the wedding," Beatrice pleaded.

"For a man who proclaimed to love you, ending your betrothal contract simply because he found out you're a twin and not the initial one he met is very flimsy."

Beatrice sighed. "We all react differently to what we term as a betrayal of trust. I believe if I see him and talk to him, he will understand why I didn't tell him the truth."

Edward shook his head and placed the pistol in its box and lifted the second weapon to examine it. "It's too late for that, Beatrice. He should have asked to speak to you before ending it. The whole of London is agog at the news. Everyone thinks he found out you're already 'ruined'; hence his reason for crying off."

Although she was alarmed, Beatrice hid it well. "I do not care about the *Ton*. I only care about Nicholas. I can't stop thinking of how betrayed he must feel. He would surely think I intentionally deceived him and made a fool out of him. Initially, he suspected something was wrong when I kept on trying to pretend to be Bridget but when I decided to be myself, he relaxed. Imagine how he must feel upon discovering the truth."

Edward clicked his tongue. "Love is indeed a foolish emotion. Look at you still defending him. Anyway, as I said, it's too late. With your father's approval, I, too, sent a message to him where to meet me for the duel so we could settle this man to man."

Beatrice gasped. "I don't want to lose any of you, Edward. He, too, was in the army."

The door to Beatrice's father's study unexpectedly burst open and Abigail and Bridget rushed into the room.

"Edward, what's this I hear of you going to fight a duel with Lord Northbridge," Abigail sharply queried.

Her brother offered her a solemn smile. "It's not something you should bother yourself about, Abigail. Since Alexander is too young for such a task, I mean to take his place to right the wrong done to his sister."

"This is madness!" Beatrice exclaimed and fixing accusing eyes on her sister said, "You put him up to this, didn't you?"

Bridget inhaled sharply. "Why would I do that?"

"Because this is all your fault," Beatrice hotly remarked. "You made him break off the engagement. And afraid he might change his mind after I speak to him, you poisoned Edwards's mind. If you can't have him, no one else should, right?"

"Your misery must be driving you crazy," Bridget retorted ardently. "You keep throwing false accusations at me."

Beatrice wrinkled her nose. "Says an unforgiving, vengeful girl!"

"Why, you—"

"Cut it out, you two!" Edward bellowed. "No one put me up to this. It is simply my duty."

Abigail stepped forward to take her brother's hand. "Edward, please don't do this. You may not come back alive or unscathed from it. I heard the Marquess is a crack shot."

Edward grinned. "So am I." He placed the second pistol in the wooden box and snapped it shut. "Now, I'll have to wait for Lord Keymouth to return home so we can head out to the fields."

"Edward, please!" Abigail begged when her brother strode towards the door with the box of pistols.

He shook his head. "Have faith in me, dear sister." When he turned away again to open the door, she fell on her knees.

"He's not to blame. I am!"

He spun around. "What are you talking about?"

Beatrice and Bridget shared confusing looks and stared at the sobbing girl on her knees.

With her head bowed, she went on. "I sent word to Nicholas telling him how Beatrice and Bridget deceived him as they simply wanted to toy with his heart. When he didn't respond to that, I sent him word again for him to come to a friend's place to see the true colours of the Beatrice he wished to wed. I dressed like Beatrice and stood before my friend's house while her brother drew me into his arms and pretended to kiss me just as Lord Northbridge's carriage drew up. Upon seeing him, I fled into the house, and George, as planned, went to plead with him to call off the wedding so he could marry Beatrice; he was to pretend they were in love and her parents wouldn't agree because he wasn't titled. He told Lord Northbridge that Beatrice was only with him because of her parents."

A thick blanket of silence fell over the room after Abigail's confession.

"But why, Abigail? Why would you do such a devious thing?" Beatrice probed when she found her voice.

"Why wouldn't I? I came to London with the sole aim of finding a suitor and getting married. You came here to enjoy yourself. Yet you were the one who was about to marry a Marquess! It was all so unfair. And you didn't even attend the debutante ball! I couldn't stop being jealous and the friend who I made from one of the balls we attended agreed with me and wanted to help."

Edward shook his head. "I'm ashamed of you, Abigail. I cannot believe my sister would do such a hateful thing. Didn't I tell you to be patient and you would find the right person? You have a good dowry; any man would be proud to call you his wife. Yet you had to hurt Beatrice and cause a scandal. Are you happy now?"

Sobbing from a broken heart, Beatrice ran out of the room. How could her own cousin do that to her? Someone her parents had decided to take under their wing and treat her like their own daughter? She had not only soiled their name but cost her the man she loved.

She fell on her bed when she reached her room and sobs shook her slim frame. What had she done to deserve this? Maybe it was punishment for falling in love with the man her sister had been interested in.

She didn't stir when she heard the door open.

"Beatrice?"

She raised her head then. "Why are you here? Have you come to gloat and tell me I got what I deserved? You don't have to. I'm already miserable as it is. That ought to make you happy."

Bridget shook her head sorrowfully and sat on the bed beside her. "I should be happy but I'm not. I don't like seeing you like this. Even though I'm hurt by the turn of events, I'm more hurt that Abigail did this to you."

Beatrice sniffed. "Are you serious or is this a ploy to poke fun at me in secret?"

Bridget shook her head again. "After you left the study and I admonished Abigail for doing such a thing, she called me a hypocrite. After all, I had been saying to her hearing that I wish you would be unhappy and punished for what you did. So, indirectly, I also pushed her into doing what she did. I'm sorry."

Beatrice sniffed. "It's not your fault. I'm sorry for accusing you falsely about being the reason Nicholas cried off."

Bridget nodded. "I deserved it, though, for the way I carried on." She sighed and blinked back tears. "I don't know what got into me. I was so mad and jealous, particularly as I knew you hadn't wanted to forge on with the plan, but I begged you to. I guess I was just looking for a way to let out my frustrations for being abed for two weeks. You know I never did like being ensconced in a place for long."

Beatrice nodded.

"For as long as I can recall, it's the first time I've fallen very sick and I didn't like it much."

"I'm sorry, Bridget. I really didn't mean to steal him from you. I made a lot of mistakes acting like you, so I decided to be myself and then tell you to act like me and when you eventually get him to offer for you, then you could be yourself around him. I didn't know things would turn out this way."

"I understand and I'm sorry for everything. Do you want to know something?"

Beatrice sniffed and nodded.

"I can't even remember what he looks like."

Beatrice's eyes distended. "What? And you made me feel so terrible? Anyway, he's the most handsome man in the whole world."

Bridget laughed. "If you say so. I was only being jealous for nothing. It wasn't like I fell in love with him that night. He just piqued my interest, that's all. And who knows? It might have waned eventually. Am I forgiven for acting like a shrew?"

Beatrice nodded. "Am I forgiven for stealing your first suitor?"

Bridget laughed and they threw their arms around each other in a tight hug. Even though her heart was still broken from the loss of the man she loved, Beatrice was joyous at the truce between her and her sister.

Chapter Ten

"Are you sure we're doing the right thing, Bri?" Beatrice wrinkled her nose as the carriage jostled them across the road in its haste to get to its destination.

"Where is your sense of adventure, Bea? Has love dimmed it? It's the right thing to do," Bridget declared with a wide smile while Abigail groaned beside her.

"Couldn't you have told him the truth without dragging me along?"

Bridget eyed her with annoyance. "You should be happy we're still speaking to you. With that lying mouth of yours, *you* will tell him the devious thing you did."

Beatrice chewed on her bottom lip and looked out of the window. It was two days after Abigail's confession. It had forced Edward to retrieve his proposition of a duel and sent apologies to Nicholas. Her parents had been sorely disappointed in Abigail and only Edward's plea made them not throw her out of their abode.

Beatrice had written a letter to Nicholas explaining everything and begging for his forgiveness, but when he didn't reply to her, she had stayed in her room and wept all day. That morning, she had decided to go on with her original plan of joining Olivia in the colonies. There was no point staying in England any longer when the man she loved no longer cared about her. But Bridget would hear nothing of it. When their mother and Miss Fitzroy had gone upstairs for their afternoon nap and their father was attending to his business partners in his study, Bridget, with the help of their maids, had snuck her and Abigail out of the house into a hired hackney.

"We must see Lord Northbridge ourselves and tell him what happened," she had said on the way to his London townhouse. Beatrice had agreed, but now that they were close to the place, she didn't know what to think anymore. She longed to see him, for she had missed him dearly, but she was afraid he might refuse to see her or give her the cut that would haunt her for a lifetime.

Her heart leapt in her throat when the hackney stopped in front of Nicholas's townhouse on Brown Street. An impressive, overtly large coach belonging to the Duke of Davenshire stood a few inches away.

"We're here," Bridget announced gaily. She paid the driver their fare and helped Beatrice out of the carriage, ignoring the sulking Abigail.

"Good heavens!" Beatrice exclaimed when the thick wooden front door opened and Nicholas, adorning gloves, hurried down the steps. He paused mid-step when he lifted his head and saw the small party, but his eyes focused on Beatrice.

Her breath died in her throat as she expected him to look at her with disdain and then brush past her without acknowledging her presence. Instead, he surprised her by hurrying towards her.

"Beatrice! I was just about to come to you. I arrived back in London only a few minutes ago. My grandfather was unwell, and I had to stay with him until he got better. I only just finished reading your letter."

Beatrice's jaw dropped. So, all this while, when she had thought he had ignored her letter, he hadn't even been in town?

He frowned. "What's this I hear about a duel with your father and cousin?"

If the situation wasn't so dire and dependant on her future happiness, Beatrice would have burst into raucous laughter. So, when her father and Edward had sent the invitation to Nicholas, in their fury, they hadn't even made sure he was in town? He would have been branded a coward had he not shown up that day.

Bridget cleared her throat loudly and jabbed her sister in the ribs who continued gaping at Nicholas.

"Um...pardon me, my Lord, may I introduce my twin sister and my cousin?"

Bridget and Abigail curtsied as they gaped at him, too, and giggled behind their hands.

"You were right, Beatrice. Indeed, he's the most handsome man in the whole world," Bridget said in a loud whisper and Beatrice flushed terribly.

Nicholas grinned. "Before we become even more the cynosure for all eyes, would you ladies please come in? I reckon we have a lot of talking to do."

Beatrice, still believing she must be on her bed dreaming, walked beside Nicholas as they climbed the steps. His musky scent assailed her nostrils and her heart clenched at how much she had missed him. But why was he so welcoming? Something wasn't right.

When they had all settled in his large salon and refreshments were brought by one of his maids, Bridget nodded at Abigail who reluctantly explained the part she played in making Nicholas think Beatrice had betrayed his trust.

When she was done, Nicholas simply nodded and turned to look at Beatrice seated a short distance from him. His grey eyes smiled at her with warmth. "I knew something wasn't right when I received that first letter. I had become so accustomed to you that I refused to believe you could do such a thing. Something smelt fishy and I was determined to find out what it was. But you see," he sighed in a rueful tone, "my grandfather was with me when the second note came, and he maintained on accompanying me. We had only just arrived from Davenshire because he had wished to see you, hence his reason for summoning me in the first place. Unfortunately, he believed every word the man said. He insisted I see him safely back to Davenshire. On the way there, he fell sick and I had to stay with him for some days. I sent word to you of my departure, but I had no idea it didn't reach you because my secretary muddled things up. Unbeknownst to me, my grandfather sent word to his lawyer, and he cancelled our engagement without my consent. It was while I was in Davenshire that I first heard of it. I was sorely displeased by it and told my grandfather so in clear terms. He apologised for his hasty decision and action.

"I worried terribly about what you were thinking because, in my heart, I couldn't believe that was you. If your cousin hadn't sent the first letter, perhaps I would have believed it. But after the second letter, I suspected someone was trying to sabotage our relationship. Alas, I sent a runner to tell you not to worry about the cancelled engagement. But because the weather was so terrible and my coach broke a wheel, he couldn't get here on time. I take it you didn't receive any such letter?"

Beatrice shook her head.

"I have no idea what must have happened. I was unperturbed thinking you had received it. Upon my grandfather's recovery, I returned to London immediately. Imagine my surprise when I received the note about the duel and the apologies, and then yours explaining and begging for a second chance."

Nicholas rose to his feet and Beatrice's heart thumped as he approached her. On a bended knee, he took her hand. "My love, surely you must know that nothing can make me stop loving you. After years spent abroad, I'm not a greenhorn not to know sabotage when I see it. Tis only unfortunate you didn't receive my letter."

Beatrice could hardly believe her ears. She swallowed thickly. "And.... what about the deception part, where I pretended to be my sister at first and then lied about having twin sisters when we were actually the mischievous twins?" She had to know.

A grin spread across his face. "I was disappointed at first that you couldn't confide in me about it as soon as we began to feel something for each other. Then, I wondered how long you wanted to keep the deception when, upon showing my interest in you, my grandfather would have sent people to find out about your family."

"You're not angry?"

He shook his head. "Truth be told, I was initially. But then I remembered you were just being yourself. I do have to plead for one thing though."

"Anything, my love. I will do anything for you."

His eyes gleamed. "Please don't ever do that again to me. You may deceive my grandfather, our servants, and possibly our children. But never me."

"I promise, my Lord. My mischievous ways are behind me."

"I hope not. It will make for a spicy marriage between us."

"We'll give you two some privacy," Bridget said and dragged a reluctant Abigail along with her.

"Am I dreaming? I thought you wouldn't want to see me, given all that has happened."

"That makes two of us. Given the scandal, I thought you wouldn't want to see *me*, and I feared you might have left London already."

"Forgive me?"

He laughed. "There's nothing to forgive, my love. All I ask is for you to come up with a plausible explanation to give the *Ton* as to why we called off our engagement and now want to get married again."

Laughter bubbled from her throat.

He gently drew her to his arms and placed his lips on hers. "I love you, Beatrice. The only twin that has captured my heart."

She smiled merrily. "I love you, too, my scarred Marquess."

Epilogue

"A re you sure you have all you'll need? You won't return to England in a while." Bridget's eyes roamed the trunks beside the bed.

For an answer, Beatrice turned away from the window where she had been watching as Nicholas swiftly got out of his carriage with a smile on his handsome face. She walked over to her sister and threw her arms around her.

"Are you sure you'll be fine without me? We might not get to see each other until next year."

Bridget visibly pushed back her tears. "Dolt! Don't make me cry. Of course, I'll be fine. Please don't worry about me. Enjoy your honeymoon, Marchioness of Northbridge."

Beatrice beamed from ear to ear. She struggled to believe she owned the title after she married Nicholas a few days ago. She had arrived at their London townhouse a few hours ago to pick up the rest of her things for her journey to the colonies with her husband. She and Bridget had never been apart for a long period, and given the circumstances of how she got married, she couldn't help worrying about her twin.

"I'll be fine. Julia wrote to me a few days ago and invited me over. Perhaps I'll call on her when I get too bored without you."

"But the Season isn't over."

"I have already thrown in the towel," she laughed. "Only fat-bellied old men are left seeking for wives."

Beatrice laughed uproariously. "I'm sure you'll find love in the strangest of places, like you always say."

Bridget joined in her laughter. "Please, Beatrice. All of Julia's brothers are married. I dare say she sent for me to help her prepare for her wedding. Who knows?"

"She's betrothed?"

"I think so."

"Well, if you choose to go, please send her my greetings. And have a pleasant time there." Beatrice hugged her again.

"I will," Bridget sniffed. "Be a good Marchioness."

Beatrice smiled. "I will."

Some minutes later, she walked into the salon, where Nicholas awaited her arrival.

"Are you ready, my love?"

Beatrice moved into his embrace. "More than ready." She frowned. "Are you sure you want to go on this trip with me? We could stay back in London or go to Davenshire or one of your residences in the country."

He cupped her chin. "Yes, I'm sure. I look forward to the trip where it will just be the two of us, at last."

She smiled and leaned into his arms, grateful she had found a man who wanted to go on an adventure with her.

He grinned. "I should send my grandfather a special gift for convincing me to attend the ball that evening."

"But we didn't meet at the ball."

"I know. But fate used your sister for us to meet, and I'll forever remain grateful to her."

Beatrice nodded. "Me too."

"Ready to go on a world of adventure, my Marchioness?"

"Yes, I am, my scarred Marquess. And perhaps, you will, at last, tell me how you got that scar."

He groaned. "You won't give me peace about it, will you?"

"Most certainly not."

"It's quite an embarrassing tale. I got inebriated the night I received news about my father's death. I fell down the stairs and got injured."

Although the tale was sad, Beatrice put her hand across her mouth and her shoulders shook with mirth.

"I knew I shouldn't have told you."

"I'm sorry, my love." She stood on tiptoe and kissed the scar. "I love you regardless of it."

"And I love you, too."

The End

Unveiling The Lady

THE LADY SERIES BOOK SIXTEEN

Chapter One

"He's vile, I tell you."

Bridget Blackmore, daughter of the Earl of Keymouth, hid a smile as she sipped her cup of tea in Baron Canbury's drawing room and watched as her friend Julia Wright paced the room in utter distress.

Julia's dark tresses hung across her shoulders in disarray as she combed her fingers through them and stared at the painting above the fireplace. A dark stain from the tea she had spilled on her dress earlier was visible at the helm. Bridget kept her tongue from telling her to change her dress, as that seemed to be the least of her worries at the moment.

Still pacing the carpeted floor with her round face knotted in a frown, Julia carried on with her displeasure. "Father wishes for me to be miserable. That is why he has sold me to such a cruel man."

Amused because she felt her friend was exaggerating, Bridget said, "Oh, please, Julia, don't be so dramatic. How do you know he's cruel? You told me that you have not met him."

Julia whirled around to fix accusing eyes on her. "You do not believe me?"

Bridget shrugged and took another sip from her cup of tea. "I think you're exaggerating because you do not wish to marry now."

Julia gasped and dropped down on the sofa beside Bridget with indignation. "You, of all people, should believe me. We have been friends since we were babies. You know me well. I am not prone to exaggerations." Folding her arms across her chest and her mouth forming a pout, she added, "Beatrice would have believed me."

At the mention of her twin sister, Bridget winced. Julia's words reminded her of how much she missed her twin, who was in the Colonies with her husband at present. They were visiting their older married sister, Olivia, and her husband. They had written to her recently, telling her how much they were enjoying their stay, and wished for her to join them. She was not keen on travelling, so she had graciously refused their offer. Besides, their parents had only agreed for her to come visit Julia because they thought she was still hurting from Beatrice marrying her intended suitor. They had also told her that she still had to find a husband before the Season was over.

With a deep sigh, Bridget replied, "Okay, Julia. Why do you think he is cruel?"

"Everyone knows how unkind he is, Bridget. As a matter of fact, his entire family has been known to be wicked; right from his father to his older brothers. I cannot marry such a despicable fellow."

"Can you mention some of the unkind things he has done?" Bridget questioned, still struggling to believe her friend. Rumours, she knew, could be deceptive.

"Oh, please do not get me started. Lanfolk is only a few miles away, so news filters here all the time. The Earl is the most dreadful man to work for. He is very brutal with his servants. His animals also feel the brunt of his cruelty. Rumour has it that he has a dungeon where he sends his servants who displease him."

Bridget was so appalled that she placed her cup of tea back on the table before her. "Oh, no, you don't say."

Julia went on. "He starves them and has them flogged daily. If a horse dares to try and bite him, it is off with the poor animal's head. He has his horses put down if they so much as snort at him. Unfortunately, because he is wealthy, he replaces them at the drop of a hat," she huffed. "That is the kind of man Father wants me to marry. A devil's spawn."

Bridget frowned. "I do not understand. Is your father aware of how cruel he is?"

"Of course. But he does not care!"

"That is not true."

Both girls turned in their seats towards the door where Lord Canbury stood, leaning heavily on his black cane. So rapt in their discussion had they been that they had not heard him enter the room. Bridget's heart melted at the look of anguish on his face. He limped into the room and sat down on a wing-back chair by the door.

"Julia, my darling, tis not that I do not care about you nor that I have not heard stories about Lord Lanfolk's cruelty. But they are all false."

"How do you know that Father?" Julia demanded testily.

"Because I have had dealings with him. He did not strike me as someone who would heartlessly have his animals killed, especially over a trivial slight like snorting at him."

Julia dropped her arms from her chest and fixed accusing eyes on her father. "How can you say that Father, when he is forcing me into an unwanted marriage with him?"

Her father lowered his head and stared at the carpeted floor for a moment before raising tortured eyes to stare at his daughter. "Because it cannot be helped. I have explained to you before now that I owe his family a considerable sum of money when I was trying to save your dear mother's life, God rest her soul. Repayment is long overdue."

Julia snorted. "And you say he is not cruel? Why can he not give you more time to pay back?"

"I have begged continually for time to pay back. Lord Lanfolk had granted it for years, but his patience has run out." He bowed his head again. "Please understand, Julia. Think about your siblings. If you do not marry the Earl, we will lose everything. And I might end up in debtor's prison."

Bridget's eyes enlarged. She had heard debtor's prison was a terrible place. She looked at her friend with pleading eyes.

Tears glazed Julia's eyes. "So, I am to be the sacrificial lamb for the family?"

Her father lifted his head. "Please understand, Julia. If there was another way, I would gladly take it instead of forcing you into marriage. I suggested several options but the only one he proposed was marrying you. I could hardly say no, given the circumstance."

Julia shot to her feet. "Well, I will *not* marry him. I would rather die a spinster or join a nunnery or runaway than marry such a man."

With that, she gathered her skirts and ran out of the room, not heeding her father's call.

Bridget rose also to go after her friend. She did not understand what Julia was going through, but she felt despair for both father and daughter.

"Please talk to her, Bridget. If there was any other way, I would jump at it. Lord Lanfolk will be here tomorrow to discuss preparations for the nuptials."

Bridget nodded, hiding her shock over the news that affairs had already been set in motion without her friend's agreement. She could only hope that she could convince her friend to marry the Earl for the sake of her family. What a heavy burden on poor Julia's shoulders!

Chapter Two

Dear Bridget,

By the time you read this letter, I will be long gone. I know that this is very selfish of me, but I cannot marry Lord Lanfolk. And so, I have run away. Please do not look for me. I know you will not understand why I have done this. There is another man. He is not a perfect match because he is without a title and money, but I love him. Why don't you marry the Earl in my stead since you do not believe he is wicked, and your parents want you to get married afore the Season is over? You and I look alike, so he will never know the difference. I am sorry for putting you in a tight spot when you were only being a good friend, visiting me in my time of distress. Till we meet again.

Your friend,

Julia.

Bridget blinked repeatedly and read the letter again. Anger surged inside her. How could Julia do this? The disgusting effrontery of her friend to suggest that she marry a man she herself rejected astounded her. How could she do this to her father, who had fallen on hard times because of his late wife's illness and death? It was unfair of her. Julia had no compassion whatsoever for her father and siblings.

Squeezing the letter into a tight ball, Bridget looked around the bed chamber as if she would find her friend hiding beside the bed. What should she do now?

"I must go after her!" She turned to her maid who had woken her up and handed her the letter.

"Alice, we must hurry and go after Julia before she gets far," she said with a note of urgency.

"But my Lady, your clothes are still wet," Alice pointed out.

Bridget gritted her teeth. On the way to Canbury, their carriage had broken an axle; her trunk had fallen off into a ditch and opened, spilling her clothes in the mud. As if that had not been bad enough, the heavens had opened and wet them. Upon their arrival at the manor the day before, Alice had washed and hung them, but they were still damp.

"God's teeth!" Bridget recalled she had even borrowed Julia's nightgown the previous night. "I will have to borrow one of Julia's dresses. Thank goodness we are the same size. Hurry, please!"

A quarter of an hour later, after her hasty ablutions and dressing, Bridget hurried down the stairs and brushed past the drawing room, heading for the front door. She paused and turned around to slowly walk into the drawing room where Lord Canbury and Julia's younger brothers and sister sat at his feet, sobbing. Julia's father held a piece of paper in his hand. He elevated his head, and she saw sorrow in his eyes. He waved the paper.

"Julia has run away. I sent the only footman I have left to go after her, but he could not find her," he told Bridget in a broken voice.

The information did not surprise Bridget. The footman was old enough to be her grandfather and had most likely gone in the wrong direction.

"If Lord Lanfolk arrives and does not see her, I do not know what he will do. I might as well say goodbye to my other children now because I'm sure to go to debtor's prison."

"No, Papa!" his youngest child cried and held on to his leg.

Bridget swallowed back tears at the pitiful sight they made. Tears would solve nothing but delay her from action. She deliberated on what she could do to help the man who had always been kind to her whenever she visited. It was already too late now to ask her father for help, as it would take days for word to reach him, even with a runner.

Why don't you marry the Earl in my stead since you do not believe he is cruel, and your parents want you to get married afore the Season is over? You and I look alike, so he will never know the difference.

Julia's words from the letter came to Bridget's mind. For a second, and only a second, she was tempted to take Julia's place to save her friend's family. But she swiftly shook the thought away. She was not desperate to be married, nor did she think that it was the solution. If the Earl discovered they had deceived him, he was sure to throw her in the rumoured dungeon. Her only option was to go after Julia herself.

"I will bring her back, my Lord. Please make arrangements quickly for a fast horse to be at my disposal."

After reading Julia's letter to her father, which made no mention of the man she was in love with, Bridget surmised that she was on her way to get married in Gretna Green. Canbury was only a few hours away from the border that separated England from Scotland. The footman had indeed gone in the wrong direction.

A short while later, seated on a black mare with her maid behind her, Bridget took the road that led to Scotland. She hoped that she would find her friend before the arrival of Lord Lanfolk.

"Come on, Beauty, we've got to move faster," she urged the mare, enjoying the thrill of the ride as her black tresses flew about in the wind under the bonnet.

Half an hour later, she sighed with relief when she caught sight of a hackney whose wheels appeared to be stuck in the thick mud. A smile lifted her face when she caught sight of the Lady beside the driver, talking loudly and gesticulating with her hands. Two trunks were positioned beside her.

"Just what do we do now? I told you I was in a hurry. Please do something."

"Julia!" Bridget called even before she reached the distraught Lady.

Her friend turned around and horror filled her eyes. "How did you find me?" she asked when Bridget got to her and dismounted from the horse before helping her maid to do the same.

Bridget ignored her question. "You have to come back with me, Julia. Your father and younger ones are in great distress. The Earl will arrive soon, and it will not bode well for your father if he does not see you there."

"Why have you refused to understand, Bridget? I cannot marry that man, not when my heart belongs to another."

"You will come to love the Earl. Please, think of your family."

"My family should think about me! They mean for me to remain in misery for the rest of my life for their sake. It is selfish of me, yes, but it is also unfair I have to be subjected to such a terrible fate."

"Julia, please think about this. Will you be happy when—"

"Oh, no!" Julia suddenly exclaimed and before Bridget could finish her statement, Julia gave her an apologetic look and dashed into the bushes.

"Julia!"

Bridget wondered if her friend had lost her senses. Seconds later, she discovered the reason for her friend's strange behaviour. A red-lacquered chaise with the emblem of the Earl of Lanfolk on the door being drawn by four horses came into view from around the corner of the road. From where she had stood, Julia had sighted the carriage before Bridget.

Bridget gritted her teeth, hoping the Earl would pass by without stopping, for she did not wish to see such an abhorrent man. However, she did not think she had anything to worry about in that regard since he was alleged to be uncaring. So, he would not care to aid a stranded stranger.

Bridget inhaled sharply when not only did the carriage pull to a stop, but the footman also hurried to open the door for a tall, broad-shouldered man who descended from it. Her lips parted company when she craned her neck to look at the square face, deep brown eyes, Roman nose, and chin-strap beard of a man. His dark brown hair was pushed back from his forehead with a few strands hanging on the side. He had on a burgundy coat, a cream shirt, dark brown trousers, and boots. This could not be the Earl. This young, incredibly handsome man in fitted traveling clothes could not be the man that she had thought would be old, wrinkled, and unpleasant looking.

"Miss Wright?"

Tongue-tied, she nodded, still wondering how such a handsome man could be as wicked as believed.

A cold smile curled his lips. "You mean to run away in place of marrying me?"

Bridget's jaw dropped in shock. How had he guessed Julia had been trying to run away? She followed the direction of his gaze and grimaced at the trunks with Julia's initials on their handles.

"You just made the biggest mistake of your life. You should have been long gone before today."

Before Bridget could correct the erroneous assumption, the Earl stepped closer, swept her in his arms, and dumped her unceremoniously in the spacious coach.

"Our marriage will take place, come rain, come shine."

Chapter Three

S till in shock, Bridget gawked as the Earl climbed into the coach after instructing his footman to carry Julia's trunks. Her maid was to ride up front with the coachman.

"What do you think you are doing?!" Bridget questioned when she, at last, found her tongue.

He offered her that wintry smile again and said, "Something I should have done immediately after your father told me you would balk at the news of marrying me."

"But I am not Julia. I am her friend, Bridget Blackmore. I came to Canbury to visit her at her behest."

Thinking of it now, Bridget deduced that Julia had probably planned this all along. Knowing they had similar features, and that her parents wanted her married before the end of the Season, she had invited her over so she might take her place after she ran away.

"How convenient, Miss Wright," Lord Lanfolk simply said and leaned back on the leather seat to stretch his long legs.

"I speak the truth," Bridget insisted, even though she was still concerned about what he might do when he discovered Julia was gone.

"What truth, Miss Wright?" he questioned with a bored tone.

"I am not Julia. I am Lady Bridget Blackmore, the fourth daughter of the Earl of Keymouth."

"Oh, really?" His deep brown eyes searched her face as if trying to peel layers off to see into her soul.

Bridget blushed and looked away.

"Anything else?"

"Yes! I know that the circumstances make it look as though I am lying, but I tell you I am not." She decided being honest with him might be what would save her from the mistaken identity incident. "Truly, Julia ran away, but I went after her and found her. The hackney she hired got stuck in the mud, as you can see. I was trying to convince her to go back home when she beheld your chaise and ran into the bushes."

With an unreadable expression, he remarked, "I grow tired of this game, Miss Wright. The first time I went to your father to discuss... issues with him—"

"I know about the debt."

"Good. I saw you riding across the fields in this same dress and bonnet. I remember the dress vividly because of the many ruffles, I found them hilarious. Preposterous as it was, that was what gave me the idea to marry you in place of the debt. Now cease with this nonsense or I will have you admitted in Bedlam after our wedding," he concluded with a note of finality in his voice.

Bridget groaned inwardly and cursed herself for choosing that particular dress. It was the first her hand had reached, and given that she had been in haste, she had not bothered changing it even though it was not to her taste. "This is not my dress. It belongs to Julia. I merely borrowed it because mine is still wet from the minor accident we had on the way to Canbury."

"How convenient," he repeated in that same uninterested tone.

Bridget had to hold herself from yelling at him to believe her. "Look, I know the circumstances seem damning at the moment, but you have to believe me. The trunks belong to Julia, not me. I know it seems like I am telling a huge fib as everything looks coincidental."

"I suppose it is also a coincidence that you have the same round face, blue eyes, and black hair as my betrothed."

Bridget winced at his words. "Yes. Julia's late mother and my father were cousins. I take after my father."

"How touching."

157

Bridget's face inflamed. "I do not care for your sarcasm."

"I do not care for your lies," he retorted sharply.

"What must I do to convince you that I am not who you think I am?" she yelled.

"Nothing."

"You are as stubborn as a goat!"

Bridget realized the mistake she had made immediately after the insult left her mouth. The Earl's countenance changed completely and then she remembered that Julia had insisted he was a wicked man. Why would she be so unwise as to rile someone like him? His face darkened and his eyes narrowed, but he did not say a word. Instead, he simply tapped on the roof of the coach. Bridget was thrown back against the lavish black leather seat when the carriage lunched forward and started moving.

Not caring for his hard-as-a-rock face, she turned away to look out the window. Hopefully, when they arrived at Lord Canbury's manor, Julia's father would explain everything to him. She could only hope father and daughter were not alike in the sense that to save his neck, Lord Canbury might just claim her as his own daughter.

It was a quarter of an hour later when they passed by rocky terrain that she grasped they were not heading back to Lord Canbury's manor. She had been so aware of his presence and the distinct fragrance of sandalwood that he wore, that she had not been conscious of her surroundings.

"Where are we going?"

"To Scotland, my dear wife-to-be. To be married."

All the colour drained from Bridget's face.

Chapter Four

I f he thinks I will go with him to Scotland and marry him, he must not only be cruel, but addle-brained as well.

Bridget gazed with intense anger at the man who had closed his eyes and promptly went to sleep after delivering his unfavourable message. She had argued until she almost swooned, but he had not said a single word, and not even opened his eyes. He had, however, woken up when she brushed past him and tried to open the door with its shiny silver handle. He had reacted swiftly by putting his arms around her and drawing her back to the seat.

His eyes held a stern warning when he said, "Do not think I will not tie you to your seat if you make any trouble."

She had cursed him to perdition with no avail, but he had not been moved an inch. He had offered her an icy smile and went back to sleep.

Bridget huffed and puffed until she spent her energy and sat back in the opposite seat. She folded her arms across her chest and glared at his sleeping form, annoyed that even in sleep, he was devilishly handsome.

An idea came to her mind, and she craned her neck to stare out the window at the gently sloping hills with riotous colourful wildflowers spread out below them. Her heart lifted when she saw some cottages a short distance away from the hills. Turning her gaze back to the sleeping

Earl, she kicked his booted foot. When he did not rouse but still had his hands positioned on his stomach, she kicked him again.

He opened one eye and peered at her.

"Please tell your coachman to stop the carriage."

He became fully awake. "Why? So, you can make a run for it?"

Forcing a blush on her face, she looked away when she said, "I wish to use the bushes."

When silence greeted her statement, she turned just in time to read the amusement in the depth of his eyes.

"Do you wish for me to wet myself here?" she threw at him when minutes passed, but he said nothing, content with staring at her with humour.

"We will stop at an inn soon. I trust you can hold yourself till then." With that, he promptly went back to sleep.

"Everything that I heard about you is true, is it not? You are as despicable as they say," she tried goading him into letting her out of the carriage so she could bolt across the countryside and ask for help.

He shrugged and, with his eyes still closed, said, "You have said all that already. Can you not think of something new to say or have you run out of insults?"

Her face reddened, for she had hurled all the insults she knew at him when he prevented her from leaving the carriage earlier. "I am not yet done, you suffocating boor. Just you wait. But then again, why will I carry on with name-calling when, most likely, all manner of insults have been thrown at you?"

"Correct."

"Then I will not waste my breath repeating them. For I know you are already aware of what you are."

He shrugged again, further stoking the embers of her fury. She would not bother with throwing more invectives his way. In its place, she would plot how she would escape from him when they arrived at the inn.

She stewed in silence until the carriage finally pulled to a stop. Suddenly, she became a mass of nerves because she planned to bolt for the hills as soon as the footman opened the carriage door. She chanced a glance in the Earl's direction and was glad to see he was still deep in sleep from the rise and fall of his chest. Carefully, she rose to her feet and spread her arms as if trying to keep her balance. Just as she was about to pass by the sleeping man, the carriage suddenly lurched and she found herself thrown against the Earl. His hands instinctively held her to his chest to keep her from sliding to the floor.

His eyes twinkled with humour at the deep flush on her cheeks. "You have a funny way of throwing more insults at me."

Bridget struggled to be free of his arms in a most undignified manner, which brought a deeper flush to her cheeks and a chuckle from him.

"Let me go this minute, oaf!"

He released her abruptly, and she fell on the floor in a heap of satin and ruffles.

"You are the most loathsome man I have ever had the misfortune of meeting!" she flung at him when she rose from the floor. He stared at her with a sardonic smile. Bridget lunged for the door. Immediately, the footman opened it and brought her down the stairs. In her haste, she almost fell flat on her face on the ground.

She caught herself just in time and thrust her chin out, trying to maintain decorum after her state of dishabille, both in the carriage and outside. She noticed an inn behind her, where a robust man and woman waited in front of the old building. She surmised the Earl must have sent his footman ahead to inform them of their impending arrival. She lifted her skirts to flee from the odious Earl who had not yet come out of the carriage, obviously erroneously thinking she would not run away. Her eyes widened when she caught sight of a second carriage with outriders. *How had he managed to arrange for escorts? Had he planned on abducting Julia all along?*

What would happen if she dashed across the road towards the hills? Would the men come after her or would they wait for the Earl to give his command to chase her? She did not waste further time thinking about it. All that was on her mind was flight, and so, she took off in the opposite direction. She cursed because she had not expected her satin slippers to encumber her as she ran, but she went on anyway. When no one chased her, a smile crossed her face. Lord Lanfolk had not told the men to be watchful in case she ran away. A few seconds later, much to her consternation, Bridget understood why the men had not tried to stop her. If she dared to go through the fields towards the hills, she would be caught in a mud bath that she might not get out of without help. The lush grass had deceived her from the carriage window. She swore inwardly at the mud.

Wonderful! Lord Lanfolk was already a bad influence on her. Never in her life had she cursed so much like a drunken sailor the way she had that day.

When she whirled around in disappointment, it was to find the Earl standing beside the chaise with a bored expression on his face. She had expected him to be laughing his head off at her folly.

"Come along now, Miss Wright," he simply called. "Enough of the sightseeing," he added, probably for the benefit of the men gaping at her with masculine appreciation.

Bridget's face contorted into a frown. He could have laughed at her and made it known to everyone what she had tried to do. But he didn't. This did not fit the description of a supposedly harsh man. That is, unless he was into appearances and did not want anyone to think ill of his betrothed or that he could not control her.

Her stomach suddenly rumbled with hunger, reminding her that she had not had anything to eat since the night before and it was almost midday. So, she might as well go with Lord Lanfolk to the inn to dine. With her stomach full, she could think of a better plan. Even though she felt like bursting into uncontrollable tears, she carried herself gracefully to his side. He gave instructions to his footmen as the young lads hurried from behind the inn to take the horses for grooming and feeding.

"Welcome, my Lord. Welcome, my Lady." The elderly man bowed while his wife dipped a curtsy.

Lord Lanfolk gave him a curt nod while Bridget offered them a small smile. "See that my traveling party is attended to and well-fed."

"Yes, my Lord." The woman curtsied again and left.

"Is it ready?"

"Yes, my Lord. This way, please."

Bridget, famished, did not bother to question the look the innkeeper threw her way or what Lord Lanfolk's question meant. She simply followed the men, assuming the Earl had requested a private room. Her eyes widened when they entered a study instead of a secluded parlour.

She turned to Lord Lanfolk. "Why are we here, my Lord?"

"Even though we are engaged to be married, it is improper for us to arrive at my Scotland residence unwed. So, the Vicar here will wed us before we continue our journey."

She glanced at the innkeeper, who doubled as a Vicar before she looked back at the Earl.

"I would not marry you if you were the last man on earth." Anger speedily replaced her shock. His face tightened.

"Give us a minute, Vicar."

The man bowed and left the room.

"How dare you kidnap me and then try to marry me off as if we are some lovesick lovers? It is shameful!"

"You keep on forgetting that we are betrothed. The matter has been settled with your father," he stiffly told her.

"How many times do I have to tell you? I am not Julia Wright!" She stamped her foot on the ground. "God's teeth, I despise obstinate men. I will never marry you."

His face turned to stone. His words were low and harsh. "If you do not, then I will have your father thrown in debtor's prison while I strip your manor of everything in it to have part of his debt paid. Your siblings will be without a home and sustenance."

She gasped. "You would not! That is a heartless thing to do."

"I have been known to do harsher things. Do you think I care about anything other than marrying you?"

"But why? You could have your pick of women. The London Season is still on. Debutantes will fall over one another at your feet in awe. Why me?"

His face softened in a frosty smile. "Why you?"

Bridget flushed, acknowledging her mistake. "I mean, why Julia?"

"Do not carry on with such pretence. It has become wearisome. We will wed here and now. And then, I will take you to my home, where you will become its mistress. You will never lack anything. Your family will be well taken care of. And in case you are concerned about fulfilling your wifely duties, you need not trouble yourself about it. For I want a wife in name only and I do not require an heir."

At that moment, Bridget believed everything Julia told her about the Earl. He was indeed a detestable man, and she had no choice but to marry him because she could not bear to think of Julia's family in penury, even if her friend did not care enough about them to have done the right thing.

What the hateful man did not realize was that their marriage would be null because he was marrying the wrong person. As soon as she could escape, she would report him to the authorities.

"Very well, then. I will marry you," she grudgingly acquiesced.

Chapter Five

Am I truly married?

Bridget questioned herself repeatedly as the carriage turned on a bend. The ceremony, which had not lasted ten minutes seemed surreal. As did the lunch they had afterward. She could not remember what she had eaten, all the while she was conscious of the man who was now her husband. Was he truly her husband? After all, the name on the marriage contract had been Julia Elizabeth. Could she really call herself Lady Lanfolk? But if she was not his wife, then what was she? Fortunately, he had said the marriage would not be consummated — if he was a man of his word. Even though her reputation might be in tatters for travelling with a man she was not married to, she believed she was still very much a spinster.

Bridget rubbed her head, which was aching from thinking so much. Upon re-entering the chaise, Lord Lanfolk had retrieved a case from under his seat and had studied some papers ever since, completely ignoring her. She did not mind, for she was planning her escape. When the entire servants in his manor went to sleep, she would make good her escape. She would feign tiredness from the journey and have her dinner brought up to her room to salvage whatever she could to tide her over for the journey. She had already stolen some rolls from the inn. She would have to make do with them for some days if she could not get more before fleeing.

Bridget turned to look out the window and could not help smiling when her eyes took in a small village surrounded by lush fields and hills. Suddenly, her eyes widened when she looked further and saw an enormous castle covering a wide expanse of land and towering to the sky.

"I see you have caught sight of the magnificence of my castle."

Bridget turned in her seat to cast her stunned eyes upon him. "Your castle?"

"Yes, my Lady." His lips turned up in a sardonic smile. "Your new home."

She turned to look out the window again at the truly splendid building. "How do I escape from such a massive place?" she blurted out before she could stop herself.

"You do not," he curtly said and resumed studying the papers.

Bridget surveyed the building with a mixture of awe and despair. How could she escape from such a building with a tall wall and ten rounded towers bordering the four sides? As the carriage drew closer, the drawbridge lowered.

She itched to ask about the history of the place and how he came to own it, but she bit down on her tongue hard. She would not show any interest in it, lest he assume that he had won her over.

The carriage rode into the massive courtyard and came to a stop before the wide stone steps. Lord Lanfolk put the papers back in the case and glanced at her.

"Shall we?"

Although she was eager to see the castle, she yearned to stay in the carriage and have it take her back to England. She regretted why she had agreed to marry him for the sake of Julia's family. She had thought she could easily escape. But now, seeing the size of the castle that was supposed to be her home, she understood it would be a herculean task.

Without waiting for her reply, he climbed down from the carriage. Reluctantly, she followed, surprised when he did not offer her his hand or wait for her. She watched as he strode up the steps, obviously forgetting he now had a wife, which propriety dictated should be introduced to his servants. As he did not seem to care if she followed or not, she unwillingly trailed him with her maid close behind her.

Bridget's lips parted at the sight of the great hall. Her attention was pulled from the stained-glass windows, the chimney, and portraits on the wall when an older woman descended the stairs with her arms open wide. Bridget gaped with awe as she saw the Earl greet her with a warm smile, which made him even more handsome, as he went to the woman and threw her arms around her.

"My dear boy, you are back. How was your journey?" she kissed both his cheeks loudly.

Bridget turned away at the intimate scene. Julia had said he had no parents, so she wondered who the woman was, who obviously cared a lot about such a beastly man.

"When the runner arrived with word that you were coming here with your bride, I could hardly believe it. I was overjoyed that you finally took my advice."

So, he had planned to bring Julia there? To this prison? Poor Julia. Little wonder she had kept on insisting she would not marry him.

"And this must be your wife. Oh, my, she's beautiful." The woman descended the bottom stair and moved towards Bridget with the same open arms. She enclosed Bridget in a tight hug. Bridget's chest unexpectedly tightened, and tears shimmered in her eyes as she felt genuine love radiating from the woman. She reminded her of her mother, and she missed her.

Lord Lanfolk drew closer, still with that sincere smile. "Mrs. Brown, may I introduce you to my wife Lady *Julia* Tanner, the Countess of Lanfolk. *Darling*, Mrs. Brown was my nanny. She brought me up when my mother died birthing me."

Mrs. Brown curtsied while Bridget stood transfixed for some seconds at the very first information the Earl had divulged about himself. For a reason she could not understand, her heart tugged at the news that he had lost his mother at his birth. Might that be why he had grown up to be such a beast? She had noticed the blatant love between him and his nanny. Had the women not influenced him positively? Or he had been hell-bent on going the way of his father and brothers as Julia claimed.

Bridget did not bother correcting the woman concerning her name. She would not be there long enough for the woman to know her real name.

She presented the woman with a genuine smile. "It is lovely to meet you, Mrs. Brown."

"Welcome to your home, my dear. I had a wedding feast prepared but let me show you to your room first for you to change from your travelling clothes. You must be tired."

Without saying anything further or looking in the Earl's direction, she followed the woman up the stairs, down a passageway, and into a large bed chamber. The huge four-poster bed with its canopy caught her eye, along with a huge dresser, a desk and chair, and a fireplace.

"Come, my dear. I must speak to you before your trunks are brought in," Mrs. Brown softly invited and pointed towards the bed.

It was at the tip of Bridget's tongue to tell her the trunks do not belong to her, but she stayed her words and followed her to the bed.

When they were seated on the gold satin sheets on the bed, the older woman smiled at her.

"Despite the endearment Edmund bestowed on you downstairs, I will not deceive myself to think that your marriage is a love match. But I do want to ask you for a favour."

Bridget wondered about the favour the woman sought from her, but more so that she had left to call the Earl by his forename. This made her understand how close Mrs. Brown and the Earl must be. She found it very strange.

"What is it, ma'am?" she replied when she recognized the woman was waiting for a reply.

"Please, be patient with Edmund. You see, he has had very little love in his life. I tried my best to bring him up the way I would my own son, but his father and brothers got in the way sometimes. Many things have been said about him that are vastly untrue. Despite his brash manner, which he got from his father, he is a superb person. All I ask is for you to give him a chance, get to know him, and you will see he is not the beast everyone thinks him to be."

Bridget itched to ask about Lord Lanfolk's background, but she did not. She would have loved to promise the kind-looking woman anything in the world but certainly not to remain the supposed wife of her ward. The woman had no idea that she did not plan on spending more than a night there before making her escape. The news that a feast had been prepared had gladdened her heart so she could filch as much food as she liked for the journey ahead.

"Very well, ma'am. I shall do as you ask," she fibbed shamelessly.

She knew Mrs. Brown would have talked further, but, thankfully, a knock sounded on the door just then. Two footmen came in carrying Julia's trunks while Alice hovered behind them.

"I will let you rest. We will talk some other time."

With a wistful sigh, Bridget stared as Mrs. Brown left the room. Had the situation been different, she would have loved to become friends with the woman. Alas, that would not be the case because come morning, she would be gone.

Chapter Six

"You are an oaf! The worst kind of fiend ever. I hope you meet your end very soon, so I will be free of you forever," Bridget flung at her husband with a savage bite. Frustration over her three failed attempts to escape from the castle had grossly overshadowed her manners.

Lord Lanfolk laughed and continued climbing the stairs, heading to her bed chamber. If it were not for the fact that he might throw her down the stairs if she wriggled too much, she would have tried to free herself from his muscular arms. Despite her anger, she could not help feeling self-conscious about the proximity between them. Even though his clothes, just like hers, were soaking wet, he did not seem to care. If only she had seen the icy stream from the top of the hill, she would never have ventured in that direction.

Her teeth clattered from the icy water she had fallen into. But she was determined not to show it even though she knew she looked like a sodden bird before him. The Earl, despite his wicked heart, if he even had one, always looked pristine making her feel like a clumsy nitwit.

"You will pay for this, I promise you," she continued, squelching the shivers in her body. "Know you not that my father is one of the wealthiest Earls in the whole of England. You will end up on the gallows for this insult."

He chuckled and she looked away, chagrined at how handsome it made him. "You would love to see your husband on the gallows?"

"Yes, after having rotten tomatoes and vegetables thrown at you in the village square. My father will see to that."

Laughter rumbled from his throat. "I thought by now you would have ceased this fruitless effort of claiming who you are not. Just so you know, I have met the Earl of Keymouth, and I am aware he has five daughters and a son. I sent a messenger to Keymouth to confirm if a certain Bridget was his daughter, and if she was missing. Of course, she is not. The messenger reported that the said Bridget truly exists but is presently in London enjoying her first Season"

"You dolt! I was there but the Season was not successful, hence my reason for visiting Julia. I terribly regret that decision now."

"Dare I guess this vile tongue of yours sent suitors racing in the opposite direction?"

"For your information, I caught the interest of a Marquess but..." she drifted off because he would simply laugh himself sore at the knowledge that the man had chosen her sister over her.

"You opened your mouth and he fled," he concluded with a grin. "You might be the most beautiful Lady I have ever seen, but your foul mouth may be the death of you."

Instantly, Bridget stiffened in his arms and noticed he, too, did the same. She recognized the fact that he had not meant to tell her he found her beautiful. She did not know what to say or how to feel at that.

Silence fell between them until they reached her bed chamber, where he dumped her into the high wooden tub of warm water that he had obviously instructed to be prepared for her before he went in search of her. She came up spluttering and coughing.

"You oaf! Do you mean to drown me?"

He shrugged. "You almost did that all by yourself half an hour ago. Tis fortunate I found you just in time, else you would have frozen to death."

Bridget gritted her teeth at the truthfulness of his words. But she would rather remain silent than thank him for rescuing her just in time. Lowering himself so they were at eye level, he said, "Best you start adjusting to being the mistress of this castle. Word has reached me how you refuse to participate in the activities befitting the mistress of the house."

Bridget stared defiantly at him. Countless times, Mrs. Brown, the housekeeper, and the cook had come to her to take instructions from her as to how the castle should be run now that it had a mistress. But she always told them to carry on with how it had been run before she came. She was still determined to run away even if she was beginning to comprehend the futility of her efforts. From her first night when she had snuck out of her bedroom only to find herself lost in another part of the castle to the time she had tried going through the kitchens and almost fell in the moors; to the most recent attempt when she had successfully left the castle, climbed up the hill, and scraped her hands and knees as she rolled down into the river. Everything had been a disaster.

He straightened. "This ought to teach you that you cannot escape from here. This is the reason I chose to bring you here. If you do not adapt to being my wife here, you will never adapt in Lanfolk Manor or my London townhouse. Believe me, you have it better than your peers. You have wealth at your disposal, and I have never troubled you for your wifely duties and I shant. What more do you want?"

"My freedom."

He smiled, the stony smile she had become accustomed to. "Stop lying about your identity. Accept you are now Lady Julia Tanner, the Countess of Lanfolk and then I might just listen to you. For now, you will be locked in your room until you accept your status."

She gasped in horror. "You cannot keep me a prisoner in here. That is barbaric!"

"You will come to understand I can do whatever I like because I am your Lord and master."

Her eyes smarted with tears. "Never! You are indeed a beast."

His shoulders rose and fell in a nonchalant move, and he strode to the door. "I have never pretended otherwise or denied any of the names you have called me. At least, now those names feel justified."

"Fiend! You will rot in the hottest part of hell for this!" she yelled at him with no avail and her heart clenched when she heard the key turn in its lock after he shut the door.

She placed her hands across her face and wept uncontrollably, her slim shoulders shaking with misery. She missed her twin sister so much that she wished she could conjure her. She missed her entire family.

Alice came out from the curtained alcove to help her undress and bathe.

"If you pardon me being so forward, my Lady, but me thinks you are going about this the wrong way," Alice softly said as she brushed the tangles from her mistress's hair.

Bridget stared at her maid's reflection in the dresser mirror. "What do you mean, Alice?"

"I have been listening to the servants. It is said that his Lordship is not as wicked as people make him. He is strict, yes, but fair. Tis true. In the week we have been here, I have never seen him raise a hand on a servant. He is dark and broody, true, which frightens everyone. But me thinks tis because he does not smile much."

Bridget snorted. "If he is a good man, why did he kidnap me? Even if I were indeed Julia, he has no right to force a Lady to marry him against her will."

"True, my Lady. But me thinks that the only hope to get away from here, to prove you were Lady Blackmore, is to pretend."

Bridget stopped herself from telling her she *was* still Lady Blackmore, given that Lord Lanfolk had married Julia Wright, which she was not. And they had not consummated the marriage. In the entire ordeal, that was the one thing for which she was grateful. Although, she could not deny that she speculated on the thought of him many times. Mayhap he could not father children. Not that it was any of her business.

"Pretend?"

"Yes, my Lady. Let his Lordship think you have agreed to be mistress of this castle and take on its duties. Me thinks he will relent and then you can flee."

When she lay on her bed sometime later, Bridget grasped it might not be a bad idea to pretend and deceive her so-called husband. But she would not give in so easily now for him not to be suspicious. He did strike her as an intelligent man, though a brutal one. Mayhap he would let her go with one last defiance.

"Very well, then. I shall pretend to be the dutiful wife."

Chapter Seven

Bridget's breath caught in her throat the second Lord Lanfolk unlocked the door and strode into her bed chamber in a black jacket, biscuit brown riding breeches, and black knee-length boots. He seemed to favour brown a lot. She guessed it was because it matched his hair colour and deep brown eyes. He was too handsome to be so wicked.

"You wish to speak to me, my Lady."

After staging a "no freedom no food" protest for three days, which elicited no response from him, Bridget was starved to a fragile point. She had given in and accepted to eat. Grateful for so many delicious meals, she had stuffed herself like a pig the previous night. How a man would not care that his wife refused to eat until he granted her freedom was beyond her. She had thought he would be concerned that she was wasting away under his roof and then let her go. What an infuriating man! Now, she wanted to begin her plan of pretending to be a malleable, dutiful wife.

"You win, my Lord. I will become the wife you want."

"Need," he corrected her, hardly showing any triumph at his victory over her. "Again. Call me, Edmund. After all, we are married."

She simply nodded. "Then would you please call me Bridget, not Julia? Please."

He tilted his head to the side for some seconds before nodding. Then he turned away without saying another word. Grasping at straws because she was tired of being locked up in the room, she cleared her throat.

"Mayhap I could go riding with you," she suggested, holding her breath. When he did not respond but continued striding to the door, she rose from her stool. "Please, I beg you. I rode every morning back in Keymouth... em... I mean Canbury."

He paused at the door but did not turn around. She wished she could see his face, for she guessed he would be surprised.

"Very well. Be down at the stables in fifteen minutes or I'll leave without you."

"Alice!" Bridget yelled triumphantly even before he shut the door behind him.

Ten minutes later, garbed in Julia's riding attire, she hurried down the stairs. A footman, instructed by Edmund, led her to the stables. A frown contorted her face when she saw the long stretch of building.

"How many horses are kept here?"

"About twenty, my Lady. His Lordship is a connoisseur of horse-flesh. His friends keep their horses here, hence the number," the man said with pride in his voice.

"His friends?"

"Yes, my Lady. Whenever the London Season is over, his friends come to spend some time at the castle before returning to their homes. They all go riding and hunting at such times. Tis always an enjoyable venture for everyone because there is always so much festivity."

Bridget's frown thickened. "Do you speak the truth?"

The man looked affronted but schooled his features when he obviously recognized whom he was frowning at. "Pardon me, my Lady. I do not have cause to lie. You can ask any of the servants or even the villagers."

Bridget found the man's words puzzling. Had Julia lied and exaggerated the Earl's cruelty so she could get out of marrying him? Or had Edmund instructed the servants to lie to her? She would find out the truth soon. He and the servants can only pretend for so long.

"Julia ... Bridget, this is Bonnie," he introduced a white mare to her when she reached him a short distance away.

Whether he had mentioned Julia's name just to show her he still did not believe her, she did not know. But she ignored it and stared at the lovely mare with its silky white mane.

"She is a beauty," Bridget mentioned with a smile.

Edmund turned away just then but she wondered if she had heard the words *Just like you*.

He helped her up the horse before mounting his own big black stallion he had introduced as Satan; aptly named, just like his master. Bridget, however, did not tell him that.

They rode across the fields in silence for a while. Bridget enjoyed the fresh air that blew across her face and hair. Deciding that drawing him into a conversation to get him to eventually lose his guard was her best option, she glanced in his direction.

"Did you inherit the castle or was it bestowed on you by the King or Prinny?" the question sounded silly even to her ears, but she had to start somewhere.

"I inherited it."

"Do you know how old it is?"

"It was built in the 1400s."

"Do you know the first occupant?"

"The Earl of Wilberforce."

Angered now, she snapped, "Would you please cease with the stilted replies? Is it not apparent that I am trying to strike a conversation with you, so we can converse like married people do?"

He drew his horse to a halt, and she did the same. His brown eyes twinkled with amusement. "Pardon me, my Lady, I did not decipher that was your intention. I am not an authority when it comes to married couples. I did not have the opportunity to experience it since my mother died when I was a baby. My father never remarried, and my brothers did not, before their demise. Everything I ask you to do as mistress of the castle is due to prompting from Mrs. Brown, who was married for many years before her husband died."

His words, although spoken with abruptness were so sad to her that it robbed her of words for some minutes.

"If you want to know about the castle, all you need do is ask."

She nodded. "Okay, my... em... Edmund. Tell me about the castle."

He threw a dazzling smile her way and her heart not only leapt, but her pulse also raced. Her colour deepened, and she looked away across the hills.

"It was built in 1451 but had to be rebuilt in 1510 when a part of it was destroyed by a Duke who laid siege to it and meant to take it by force. If you love reading, there is a book about it in my library."

"Perhaps I will read it later. Please carry on."

By the time they returned to the castle after a refreshing ride, Bridget's thoughts were all over the place. Sometimes Edmund appeared quite forbidding. Other times, he was a different person entirely. She would have to first understand the real Edmund William Tanner, the Earl of Lanfolk, before she could successfully escape.

Chapter Eight

"I believe a contest is in earnest, Edmund."

A chuckle fell from Edmund's lips. "You want a conquest?"

Smiling at him, Bridget replied, "Yes."

"Simply because you can now shoot better than me?"

She placed her hands on her hips and feigned annoyance. "I will have you know that my father taught me how to shoot, and I used to go hunting with him."

"I think we have both established he simply taught you the basics, and I perfected them for you," he replied with a chortle.

Bridget laughed. It was true that he had taught her how to shoot better than what she had learnt from her father when she was ten.

"Well, let us put your expertise to the test," she challenged, eyeing the pistols on the table beside her. "And then we go hunting."

"Hunting?" he cocked his brows. "The only thing you can shoot right now is a rat."

Bridget's shoulders shook with mirth. "Just so you know, I went hunting with my father and brother recently."

His eyes twinkled with humour. "And what animal did you bring back home?"

She shrugged. "It does not matter."

Laughter bubbled from his throat.

Her lips twitched. "I think you are afraid, Edmund that I will best you when it comes to being a crack shot."

Grinning, he reached for one of the loaded pistols. "You have the ability to tempt the devil into repentance. Very well, then, my Lady. A conquest we shall have. And what will be the prize of the victor?"

"That you take me hunting."

"That is if you win. And if you lose?"

"You do not take me hunting."

"Fair enough. Let us begin. What is the target?"

Bridget stared around her at the rolling hills, the valley carpeted with wildflowers, and the huge trees surrounding them.

"It is so beautiful and peaceful here," she remarked, soaking in the loveliness of the countryside.

"Too peaceful to disturb it with gunshots?" he mockingly asked. "If you want to chicken out, we might as well get back."

Bridget hastily shook her head. She did not wish to return to the castle. After agreeing to be a submissive wife two weeks before, she had formed a pattern of daily activities. She would go riding with Edmund in the morning, then they would return to have breakfast. She would oversee the affairs of the castle, and then join Edmund in his study to read while he carried on with his business. They would have lunch together and then go for a long walk in the fields or around the castle grounds before returning to rest and then have dinner. After dinner, she would play the pianoforte and sing as well. Truth be told, she found herself enjoying her stay, and all thoughts of escaping fled from her mind.

Edmund had not only taught her how to shoot properly, but how to fish as well. It had been a pleasurable experience catching Edmund off guard and pushing him into the river. She had run away while he gave her a hot chase. A smile touched her lips at the memory of the event. The servants had put their hands over their mouths to hide their hilarity.

"Someone has developed cold feet," Edmund teased.

"Hand me the gun and I will show you who has cold feet," she bragged and took the gun from him.

Without pausing to aim like how he had taught her, she pointed it at a tree branch and pulled the trigger. She inhaled sharply when she did not even come close to the tree. Her face fell.

Laughing, Edmund reached for another pistol on the table, stood a few paces from her, and fired, hitting a twig off its branch.

With her mouth forming a pout, Bridget shrugged. "I will try again." And she did but did not get to the mark again. She stamped her foot on the ground in frustration.

Edmund cackled. "Let me show you what you are doing wrong." Closing the distance between them, he stood behind her. He gently lifted her hand with the gun, and pointed it at the target. Bridget struggled to breathe as she usually did whenever he was this close to her. Instead of staring at the target, she focused her attention on his strong hand on hers, his broad shoulders enveloping her own.

"Aim and fire." His breath lifted her hair and sent tingles up her body. When she did not do his bidding, he took the gun from her and turned her around to face him, staring at her with concern. "Are you okay? Is anything amiss? It does not matter if you do not make the shot. Giving it a trial shows how brave you are."

Bridget feared that if he did not move away from her soon, she would swoon from the feel of him standing so close. Her lips parted company when he cupped her chin with a gentle caress. For what seemed like minutes on end, her sky-blue eyes held onto the gaze from his deep brown ones. Words did not need to be spoken.

Footsteps coming their way caused him to stiffen and to drop his hand and create some distance between them.

A maid came into sight and curtsied before them. "Pardon me, my Lord, my Lady. Mrs. Brown sent me to inform you that lunch is served."

Bridget presented the maid with a small smile and turned away. She found it hard to look in Edmund's direction because she did not understand her feelings for him these recent days. Over the past four weeks, he had abducted her and brough her to the castle; there were days when he was dark and forbidding. Then, there were days he was lively and like an open book that she could read. She still could not understand the man she married. Was he a friend or a foe?

"Shall we, my Lady?" he invited, evading her face.

"Yes, my Lord."

Throughout lunch, Bridget's thoughts were far away. She wished she could see Beatrice and speak to her about her hot and cold feelings for Edmund and her puzzlement about him. Mrs. Brown had continued to extol his virtues, but she needed to know for herself if he was indeed cruel or kind. Even though he kidnapped her, he had been kind ever since she agreed to be the type of wife he wanted. Was that it? If she was malleable, then he would be kind to her, but if she was not, then he would be wicked? After all, he had locked her in her room when she tried to escape.

"Perhaps a walk might lighten your mood," Edmund said when the meal was over. She had barely touched her food. He must have noticed her pensive mood.

She nodded and hooked her hand in his arm. They took a stroll in the fields.

"Please tell me about your family," she said when they had walked a short distance.

He became rigid beside her. "Could we please talk about something else?"

She shook her head. "Can you not see I am trying to understand the man I married? Before I came here, I heard many slur words against you and added mine if you recall."

"I remember," he said gravely.

She had tried to lighten the mood, but his face was still as cold as a statue. "But getting to know you these past weeks, I have seen a different side of you that has left me confounded. Mrs. Brown has not helped matters by reminding me with every little chance she gets how the sun rises and sets at your feet," she shrugged. "I merely desire to know who you truly are."

He was silent for a long moment; she thought he would not reply to her question. Finally, he made them stop underneath a tree. He removed his dark blue coat and spread it on the tree trunk for her to sit on before sitting beside her. Bridget created a small distance between them so she could listen to what he had to say with rapt attention and not be carried away by their proximity.

"You already know I lost my mother when she brought me to birth," he began, staring straight ahead at the valley.

She nodded.

"What you do not know is that I had the most hateful father and brothers, James and Simon. My father was cruel, and my brothers were just like him. They enjoyed being mean to servants and animals; everyone, in fact. My oldest brother, James, took over from our father in cruelty until he died from a riding accident. My other brother, Simon, became as unkind as our father and oldest brother. And so, the Tanner family became known as wicked men. Their reputation preceded them. Simon died from a gunshot wound from some highwaymen when he refused to give them his purse of coins. Even though I was finally free from them and their despicable ways, my cousin, Benjamin, stepped in. He was my father's brother's son and was as vile as the lot of them. He went about pretending to be me and doing all sorts of abominable things in my name. That is the reason you heard all those things about me. There was nothing I could do about it since we had similar appearances, and I was a recluse. Mrs. Brown always kept me in the nursery, away from the eyes of my father and brothers. That way, I got used to being indoors and did not attend soirees. So no one knew I did not commit all those things."

Bridget's jaw fell open.

"What people did not know was that Mrs. Brown raised me to be a perfect gentleman. She shielded me from my father and brothers and brought me up the way my mother begged her to before she died." He took her hand and caressed it with pleading eyes.

"I am sorry for the way I treated you and for forcing you into marrying me. Believe me when I say I did not want to, but I did not have a choice."

"How so?"

He frowned. "Simon, seeing that I was not like him no matter how much he tried to get me to do evil things, plotted with Benjamin and left a Will. It stated that if I were not married by my twenty-seventh birthday, the title and all that came with it would go to Benjamin. He made it seem like my father willed it, but I later discovered it was all a lie. My father's solicitor told me he would have to enforce it and I had a choice to either ignore it and lose everything or heed it and do the needful. I was desperate to get married to thwart their plans. The servants here are like my family. I couldn't bear to watch them fall under Benjamin's domain. That was why I could not afford to let you go. And also, that is why our marriage has been in name only. All I wanted was a wife to inherit what is rightfully mine and not allow it to go to my despicable cousin. I truly hope you understand."

Bridget nodded, stunned at the revelation. Mrs. Brown was right, in the end. She had known the man she raised was not a brute as alleged. "I understand and I apologize for misjudging you and calling you all those awful names."

He smiled. "I dare say I deserved it. I could not allow myself to feel pity for you, else I would not have gone through with the plan of abducting you and threatening you to marry me. It is the reason I was so aloof."

She smiled. "All is forgiven."

"Splendid!" He jumped to his feet and stretched his hand to hers. "Now, let us carry on with the shooting contest."

Bridget burst into laughter.

Chapter Nine

Love is found in the strangest of places.

Bridget completely believed that now. Who would have thought that when she left London, sad that her Season was a failure and her twin sister was no longer beside her, she would end up with a husband? She had not envisaged that going to visit Julia would be so eventful. She had not also known that she would eventually fall in love with her captor. Not that she could call him that now. Certainly not after that afternoon a week ago when he had talked about his family, and how he came to be known as a beast when he was nothing but a kind-hearted man. Something had changed between them after that. She became more aware of him and sought to spend every minute of the day with him. The thought of leaving him had filled her with so much sorrow. She truly had fallen in love with him. All those times they spent together riding, shooting guns, fishing, reading together, and taking long walks had softened her heart towards him, and she had not recognized it until that afternoon.

After thinking about it long and hard, she had decided she wanted a real marriage. Afore she went to London for her first Season, she had known she was ready to have a husband and children. Now, she was more than sure she wanted that with Edmund.

A knock on the door cut into her musing.

"Enter," she summoned.

A maid came into the room and curtsied. "My Lady, his Lordship wishes to speak with you in his study."

A bright smile crossed her face and she nodded at the maid before heading to the full-length mirror to gaze at the blue muslin morning dress. Edmund was probably wondering what was keeping her as they usually read together in his study after breakfast, or she read while he conducted his business. Although, she must say his behaviour had been strange both when they went riding and at breakfast. She supposed he must be worried about his business as he had had a meeting with his solicitor and accountant the evening before.

Eager to be with him, she hurried out of the room and down the stairs to the library where she knocked briefly before entering. Her smile died on her face when Edmund did not lift his head to acknowledge her presence. He continued scribbling on a piece of paper with the feather dipped repeatedly in a small pot of ink.

"Sit." He nodded at one of the chairs before the desk.

Bridget frowned at his cold tone. Had she done something to annoy him? She knew she had talked ceaselessly that morning, but that was because she had been so glad to see him after a restless night thinking about him.

"Is something wrong?" she could not help asking when he still did not look at her.

Eventually, he raised his head and the aloofness in his eyes alarmed her.

"I have arranged for your departure back to Keymouth."

"What?"

He leaned back in his chair and shrugged. "You have finally got your wish. My carriage is at your disposal. Outriders will follow you there. You do not have to worry yourself about our marriage. I will have it annulled since it was not consummated, and you are not who I thought you were. No one need ever know except the two of us and your maid. My employees are discreet and will keep news of our supposed marriage within the four walls of this castle. So, you can still get married as your reputation has not been ruined. My apologies once again for taking you forcefully from Lord Canbury's home and dragging you to Scotland to compel you to marry me."

Bridget shot to her feet. "You have found out my true identity?"

He nodded and looked away. "Yes. After you told me about your family the other day, I sent a runner to London. He only returned last night after my solicitor and accountant left. I knew then what a terrible mistake I made. Your parents and Lord Canbury have been discreetly looking for you."

Bridget laughed and clapped her hands with glee. The thought of seeing her family again filled her with joy. But then she remembered what he just said.

"All I have to do is write to them about our marriage and have everything sorted out."

Her heart fell when he shook his head. "There is nothing to explain to them, Lady Blackmore."

"Lady Blackmore?" Her eyes narrowed with anger at his obstinate stand and withdrawing emotion from her by not calling her by her forename. "Why do you want to send me away? We can sort it out. My parents are not unreasonable people. All we have to do is to invite them over and explain everything."

He merely shook his head and stared at the paper on his desk. "'Tis best if you leave, Lady Blackmore."

"Call me, Bridget. After all, we are married," she threw his own words at him, and he became rigid. Tears shimmered in her eyes. "I thought ... I thought we have gone past how we met and how I came to be here." The tears spilled down her face. "I thought the last few days..."

Edmund evaded her gaze, and that made Bridget feel even worse. She had erroneously assumed he, too, had fallen in love with her. How foolish of her! He was nothing like his father and brothers. But that did not mean he could love a woman. Perhaps the Tanner men were innately flawed, never to love. It was just her luck that she had fallen in love with a man who was only interested in a marriage of convenience. But she wanted a proper marriage and a family.

Before she could try to convince him why he should let her stay so they could make a genuine marriage of what they already had, a small knock sounded on the door and his butler came in.

"Pardon me, my Lord. There are some men here who wish to speak with you post-haste."

Hardly had the butler finished talking when three men entered the large study. When they saw her, their eyes widened and they looked at each other, nodding with satisfaction.

"Lord Lanfolk?" one of the men asked as he came forward.

"Yes," Edmund answered in an uninterested tone.

"We have an order for your arrest."

Bridget gasped. Edmund sat up in his chair and asked, "For what?"

"For kidnapping Lady Bridget Blackmore."

Bridget hastily shook her head and stepped forward before Edmund could say anything.

"That is untrue."

"What?"

"Ed..." She cleared her throat. "Lord Lanfolk did not kidnap me. I came here with him on my own accord."

The men frowned. "You did?"

"Yes." She turned around and walked to stand beside a stunned Edmund. "Lord Lanfolk and I are married. I escaped with him to Scotland to get married since my parents did not approve of him."

"Are you sure Lady Black ... I mean, Lady Lanfolk? *Your parents* were the ones who made the report and hired us to inconspicuously find you."

Talking with more confidence than she felt, she replied, "They did it so you could bring me back to them. But it is too late. Lord Lanfolk and I are married."

The Earl in question promptly rose to his feet. "Gentlemen, would you please give me and my... Lady... Lanfolk some privacy for a few minutes."

The men nodded and departed from the room. A tense silence followed in their wake. Bridget curved her body in the direction of the window to stare out of it.

"Why did you lie to them?" Edmund asked at last.

"Because I do not want you to go to prison."

"It is what I deserve."

She shook her head and turned to look at his rigid form. "No! You were desperate. That is understandable."

His head bowed. "It still does not excuse what I did."

She held his hand and his head shot up. "It does not matter anymore."

He shook his head and took a step back. "It does. Please go with them."

Her jaw dropped. "What! Why?"

"I want you reunited with your family."

Bridget felt like dropping to her knees and begging him not to send her away, but her pride would not let her do that. She thought about what he said and decided he was being reasonable. She had to go back home to allay her parents' fears and tell them bits of information, and not necessarily the whole truth. They might dislike Edmund even before meeting him, and she did not want that.

She nodded. "Very well. I will go with them to explain everything to my parents and then bring them to meet you."

He turned his back on her and stared out of the windows. "Please do not return."

Bridget drew in a sharp breath. "Do you really mean that? Because if you do, I will go and never come back."

His shoulders slumped, but he avoided her gaze by turning away. "I mean it, Lady Blackmore. Go back home and find a man who will cherish you like you rightly deserve. I am not that man. My apologies once more for everything."

Bridget wanted to yell at him; to tell him he was the man she wanted, but she comprehended that there was no use. He had made up his mind already and rejected her. She would be making a cake of herself if she did.

"All right. I will go and never come back." With her heart breaking into a thousand pieces and tears streaming down her face, she slowly walked away from the room without looking back.

Chapter Ten

"Bridget, you have another letter from Julia," Sarah, Bridget's immediate younger sister, said as she walked into the room.

Lying dejectedly on her bed, Bridget sniffed and wiped away her tears with her handkerchief. Sarah paused at the foot of the bed to position eyes filled with pity for her. "Are you still crying, Bri? Please do not shed a tear for him anymore. Men, I discover, are not worth it."

Bridget frowned and pondered what had happened to her sweet sister. Something was different about Sarah, but since she always kept her cards close to her chest, no one could ever guess what she was thinking or if anything was amiss with her.

"I love him, Sarah. I thought I had found my happily ever after," she argued and sniffed.

"Does that really exist?" Sarah sat beside her on the bed.

"It is existing for our sisters, is it not? Emily, Olivia, and Beatrice are all happily married, are they not?"

Sarah shrugged. "Mayhap it is not for everyone."

Bridget glowered at her. "Thank you for trying to cheer me up."

Sarah blushed. "Forgive me, Bri. I did not mean to add to your sorrows."

"It is fine," she sighed. "I should have known better than to marry a man who wanted a wife in name only."

Sarah patted her sister's hand and gave her Julia's letter. "Everything will turn out fine, I am sure."

Bridget did not think she would be fine, not with her feeling as if someone had wrenched her heart out of her chest. She still could not believe a week ago, Edmund had told her to leave even after she proved her love to him by lying to the Bow Street Runners who had come to arrest him. She had thought he loved her, but now she understood he might be incapable of loving anyone. But he loved Mrs. Brown, did he not? Or was he secretly cruel? Allowing her to fall in love with him so he could break her heart?

With reluctance, Bridget broke the seal of the envelope, knowing what would be in the letter. Julia had sent her several letters since she returned to Keymouth, apologizing for everything.

"Another apology," she informed her sister in a bored tone. She struggled not to sound bitter. Julia was with the man she loved while she was crying over a broken heart. It was not Julia's fault, though. It was all her doing for falling in love with Edmund.

Fortunately, there was no scandal concerning her secret marriage. Her parents and Julia's father had been very discreet in their search for her in the five weeks she was in Scotland with Edmund. Her parents had received the message of her disappearance quite late, hence the reason she had been in Scotland for that long. They had not suspected Edmund abducted her at first until Julia wrote to her father, explaining what happened. They had gone to Lanfolk initially, but when they did not find him and her there, they had gone to his other properties. When all their efforts to find her failed, they had hired Bow Street Runners to search for her and the men had tracked them down to the castle in Scotland.

Her parents, after hugging her and sighing with relief that she was safely back home, had scolded her heavily. They were disappointed in her for running away with Edmund to get married. The Bow Street Runners had sent word ahead, informing them of what she told them. Her parents thought it might be because she was lonely without her twin sister as they had never been apart before. And so, they had forgiven her. Bridget had refused to tell them the truth despite Julia's letter to her father, informing him that Edmund kidnapped her. Only her sisters knew the truth. The only thing Bridget told them was that she and Edmund did not consummate the marriage as they were waiting for the heat of their elopement to die down so they could return to England and marry properly. Consequently, her parents were seeking ways to have the marriage secretly annulled.

She did not bother telling them to stay their hand because Edmund also wanted to have their marriage annulled. She lived in fear of the day she would receive the proclamation that her brief marriage to Edmund, real or not, was over.

Alice rushed into the room just then with excitement written all over her face. "My Lady, a visitor just arrived to see you."

Bridget frowned as she was not in the mood of receiving callers. "Who is the person?" she asked, intending to tell Alice to lie she was ill.

"His Lordship, the Earl of Lanfolk!"

"What?" Bridget and Sarah shared surprised glances.

"He is waiting in the drawing room."

Bridget wondered if she was dreaming. Maybe she had fallen asleep after shedding tears.

"What are you waiting for? Go!" Sarah yelled.

Bridget scrambled from the bed, not caring if her gown was creased or her face had dried streaks of tears. She ran to the door where she hugged her maid in joy and hurried out of the room. Afraid she might stumble on the stairs and hurt herself, she forced her legs to move slowly. At the door of the drawing room, she took in a deep breath and let it out. Suddenly, her palms became clammy, and her heart thundered. What if he had personally come to hand over the missive of their annulled marriage? No. He could not be that unkind, could he?

With her heart in her throat, she threw the doors open and entered the room. Edmund had been pacing the floor by the fireplace. Her heart tightened at the sight of the man she loved so much. Upon sighting her, he strode across the room to cover the distance between them. He yanked her in his arms and his mouth descended to capture hers in a kiss.

"Please forgive me, my love. I should never have let you go," Edmund said immediately after he pulled away.

Stunned, Bridget could not think of anything to say at first. The kiss had blown her away.

"Why did you?" she questioned when she found her voice.

"Guilt."

"Guilt?"

He nodded. "How could I continue to hold the woman I had fallen in love with captive in an unwanted marriage?"

Bridget's heart leapt at his declaration of love.

"I could not do that to you. After you told me about your family and how you had gone to London for your first Season just so you could get a husband and then have children, I knew I had no right to keep you from achieving your dreams."

"Then why are you here?"

He grinned. "Because I realized what a grave mistake I had made letting you go. I can give you your dreams. I love you, and I want us to have a proper marriage and plenty of children to fill the castle."

Tears of joy sprung in her eyes. "I would love that, too."

"I love you, Bridget. I cannot live without you. The past week has been sheer torture for me without you in my life. Please forgive me for asking you to leave."

Before she could say anything, he went down on a bended knee. Her eyes widened.

"Will you marry me for real, Lady Bridget Blackmore, and come back with me to my castle in Scotland?"

"Yes! Yes! I will marry you, my darling oaf."

He rose, laughing, and kissed her again.

Epilogue

"**D**arling, it is morning."

Bridget grumbled and rolled over onto her stomach on the bed. With one open eye, she stared at her new husband. As usual, he looked devastatingly handsome in his riding coat, breeches, and boots.

"I want to sleep some more," she said and closed her eyes.

"Bridget?"

She opened her eyes.

His eyes filled with concern. "Are you well?"

"Why do you ask?"

"You have never refused to go riding with me in place of sleep before. I have cause to be concerned."

"I just do not feel like riding this morning," she quietly replied.

A thick frown covered his face as he drew closer to the bed and sat beside her, pushing aside the canopied curtains. "This is unusual of you."

Bridget sighed inwardly. She should have known she could get nothing past her husband. Love for him rose in her chest and spilled over into her eyes. They got married a month ago at a big public wedding in Lanfolk. Her sisters and their husbands had all attended. At the outset, her parents had balked at her marrying a man she ran away to

Scotland with. But with surprising charm, Edmund had won them over. Well, coupled with her pining away for him.

Even though they knew it was only for the sake of formality, Bridget and Edmund had enjoyed every bit of their wedding. She had also loved Edmund's manor in Lanfolk but had preferred living in his castle. And so, a few days after their wedding, they had made an enjoyable journey to Scotland.

"The only time you did not go riding with me was when you were ill a few days ago. Are you feeling sick again? You refused me calling the doctor, preferring Mrs. Brown to attend to you. But now, I must insist I send for him."

Beaming from ear to ear, Bridget pushed aside the sheets and sat up. "He was here yesterday."

His frown deepened. "When?"

"When you were in a meeting with your business partners," she replied.

"That means you fell sick again?" He took her hand and caressed it; his eyes covered with worry. "Why did you not tell me?"

"Because it is nothing serious."

"Nothing serious? Yet you sent for the doctor?"

To get him out of his apprehension, she laughed softly and said, "That is because it is good news."

"Good news?" He stared at her with perplexed eyes.

"Yes, my love. I am with child."

His eyes enlarged.

"I suspected it. That was the reason I asked for Mrs. Brown that morning instead of a doctor. She confirmed it but then advised I send for a doctor to confirm it as well. Doctor Hemsworth was not in residence when we sent for him until yesterday when he came and congratulated me after examining me."

Laughing joyously, he threw his arms around her in a tight hug and pulled away to kiss her. "I hope it is a girl."

She frowned. "You do not wish for an heir?"

"My family, for three generations, have birthed only sons. For a change, I want daughters and maybe a son, just like your family."

She laughed joyously.

"I cannot thank Miss Wright enough for refusing to marry me and leaving you at my mercy. I would not have so much joy, peace, and contentment in my life right now."

Bridget nodded. "I have written to her to tell her I forgive her and thank her for fleeing that fateful day."

"I love you. I always will. I will never be like my father to you and our children."

"I know. I love you, my darling oaf."

He laughed uproariously and enveloped her in a bear hug.

The End

Saving The Lady

THE LADY SERIES BOOK SEVENTEEN

Chapter One

With the wind on her face and blowing through her blonde hair, Sarah Blackmore nudged her mare with her knees to go faster. This was her favourite time of the day; when she rode as if she did not have a care in the world.

"How delightful. Do you not just love how wonderful this feels, Bonbon?" she asked her horse.

Sarah laughed when the horse snorted, its hoofs sounding loudly on the grass as they crossed the vast fields back to the manor. She wrinkled her nose at the smell of wet grass and smiled.

Spring was her favourite time of the year. She could never tire of gazing at lovely blossoming flowers of various colours. Whenever it rained, she would throw open her windows just to catch the smell of wet sand and sward. Watching raindrops drip from the edges of green leaves to the ground was one of her preferred pastimes.

As she rode closer to the stables, she wished that she could keep riding through the pasture, but she was famished. The fresh country air always gave her a ravenous appetite. Her mother would certainly complain about the large meal that Sarah would devour in the breakfast room, but she would pay her no mind. It was not her fault she was slightly rounded.

"'Tis not that I am portly, Bonbon. Mama does not want me to be voluptuous, which I am not, I must tell you. Papa says I resemble his mother, who had a full figure. They do not realise that I only turned to food for comfort when..."

Sarah shook her head vigorously to push away the sorrowful reason that had made her stuff herself with food until she was sick with it.

"Sarah!"

Thoughts of the lowest time in her life fled at the sound of her name. Sarah groaned when she saw her mother seated regally on a tame mare. Her father, on his black-as-midnight stallion, rode up beside his wife. The Earl and Countess of Keymouth had similar frowns of disapproval on their faces.

"What possessed you to ride bareback and astride?"

Her mother did not wait for her to draw closer before stating her disapproval at the unladylike way her daughter rode her mare. Sarah braced herself for an intense scolding. Her father did not talk much. His scolding came with a few sentences and a frown, but her mother would go on and on until she nearly drove everyone crazy.

Sarah recognised it would be best if she did not say a word in defence of her actions, for her mother would not let her hear the last of it. She had learned at a young age to keep her thoughts and expressions to herself, thanks to her aunt. So, when she pulled her horse's reins to a stop at the sight of her parents, she simply kept silent.

As expected, her mother was not yet done with her tongue-lashing. "Little wonder you declined to attend the coming Season and have refused the interest of a suitor. You enjoy being wild and careless. If any man could see you now; your dress is stained with grass and your hair dishevelled because you did not have the sense and decency to wear a bonnet. He would surely run a thousand miles away from you."

Sarah, as she was wont to do, maintained a passive face, which riled her mother further.

"I do not know what to do with you. Your sisters are happily married with children. But you have chosen to be an old maid. You aim to be on the shelf and be the example for young girls not to emulate."

"Now, now, dear. We can hardly call Sarah an old maid. She is only seven-and-ten."

Sarah lowered her head to hide her smile. Her father, thankfully, always took sides with her when her mother was on the warpath.

"You spoil her so, darling. Tis the reason that she has become so rebellious and no longer heeds my advice. Why a young Lady would refuse to get married is beyond me."

Rebellious? Sarah put a hand across her lips to keep from laughing out loud. In all her seventeen years, she had never spoken back to her mother until a few months ago when she had vehemently told her that she had no desire to get married. Even when a suitor was arranged for her, she had walked out on him when he came calling. The Viscount had shown his displeasure by no longer showing an interest in her and that had embarrassed her parents. Mostly her mother.

"Let us give her a little more time, my dear," her father pleaded, his face softening when his eyes settled upon his daughter.

"More time?" Her mother stared at him with horrified eyes. "Till when she is old and grey? Or maybe when we are in our graves? God forbid it!" She released a heavy sigh after her tirade and shrugged. "Anyway, I will be glad to see you go, knowing that I will have some peace. If Alexander decides to behave himself, that is."

Sarah's head shot up. *Go? To where?* Surely, her parents had not married her off without her consent. They were not so desperate to do away with her, were they?

Her frantic eyes shifted to her father. He stared back at her with resignation. Sarah's heart thundered with fear. Would her father, who had always seen her side of things, allow her mother to force her into an unwanted marriage? She could not blame him, though. Her mother could be quite forceful.

If that is the case, I will run away.

With her mind made up, she thrust her chin out at them and shielded the fear in her eyes by pretending to be nonchalant about the matter.

"What do you mean, Mama?" She congratulated herself inwardly for the steadiness in her voice.

"I wrote to your aunt two weeks ago. She has agreed for you to visit so she can talk some sense into you."

Sarah's heart leapt for joy,but she kept her face from showing euphoria. Aunt Betty was her favourite aunt. She had always been able to confide in her. She had told her things her four sisters were not even aware of. Her father's older sister was the one who had given her a shoulder to cry on when she had felt like wasting away.

"As you wish, Mama," Sarah remarked as she struggled to hide her joy. She would be glad to get out of her mother's hair for a while. Lady Keymouth peered at her as if she wanted to see deep into her daughter's soul. Sarah recognised that she would have to do more to convince her. If her mother caught a whiff of her joy, she would make her stay back and nag her to death.

"In retrospect, being sent to Aunt Betty's is uncalled for. But I shall do your bidding," she added with a frown. *There. That ought to ensure that she sends me.*

"Do not frown. You will get wrinkles that way."

"Yes, Mama. I will return to the house to oversee my packing for the journey. Please excuse me."

As Sarah steered her mare to the stables, a bright smile formed on her face.

Chapter Two

"What do we do now?" Sarah, almost in tears, questioned the coachman.

"We will have to hire a chaise, my Lady," the coachman replied with an apologetic look.

Sarah looked around at the vast grassland spread before her and sighed. She stared at the large coach with its broken axle and frowned. Her stubbornness had led her here. Upon leaving Keymouth earlier in the day, she had instructed the coachman to follow a more scenic route before they met up with outriders who would follow them to Hayward where her aunt lived. Highwaymen had been rumoured to attack unsuspecting passengers on the road to her aunt's house. News of such attacks was few and far between these days, though. So, she was not worried about them at present. But she was worried about arriving late in the day. She did not think that her aunt would have received the letter of her impending arrival to send her servants to be on the lookout for her.

Sarah sighed. How could she have known that the rains had ruined the road and made it so muddy? It was a miracle they had come this far. Her parents did not know about the change of routes and would think all was well.

"My Lady, please retire to the coach. Thomas might tarry if he does not find help," the coachman advised with a small smile.

Sarah looked at the tilted chaise and shook her head. Her head smacked against the door when the accident happened. Besides, it was too hot to sit in there. Her maid had fetched her parasol to shield her from the rays of the sun.

"How far is an inn from here? Do you know?"

The coachman shook his head with regret. "I am sorry, my Lady. I am not familiar with this route."

Guilt rose inside Sarah. They were all in a quagmire because of her and her selfish reasons. She had no one to blame but herself. If she arrived exhausted and looking as though she was dragged on the road by her hair, then so be it.

"My Lady!" her maid Frances suddenly called to draw her attention to the upcoming chaise.

"That was fast, I must say," the coachman said with approval.

Sarah's heart lifted with joy until she realised that the large chaise being drawn by four horses heading their way was not one for hire. Her eyes widened just as every colour drained from her face as the conveyance drew closer.

It cannot be! Surely the gold crest of a breastplate flagged by two horses and a bird could not belong to *him!* But she knew, even before the carriage made its slow descent in her direction, that it belonged to the man she had hoped never to meet again.

Of all the carriages in all of England to come her way, why did it have to be the one owned by the Marquess of Bartondale? It was so unfair that she almost wept.

Any hope that the conveyance might pass by without stopping died when it pulled to a stop directly in front of her and the servants. The footman swiftly stepped down to open the door and place the steps on the muddy ground.

Sarah held her breath as the tall man in a dark blue coat, snowy white shirt, gold brocade vest, dark blue trousers, and black boots stepped down from the carriage. Her heart thumped against her chest as she forced her gaze from his expertly tied cravat to his angular face. Her scrutiny slowly descended from his neatly groomed blonde hair, penetrating amber eyes, pointed nose, and cleft chin.

Time stood still as they stared at each other, oblivious to their servants around them. Tears stung Sarah's eyes as she remembered all the beautiful moments that she had shared with this man who had become even more devilishly handsome than she remembered. Two years ago, she had lost her heart to him. And for a while, he had reciprocated until he had found another Lady with a larger dowry. With the memory of how mercilessly he had broken her heart, her tears dried up instantly, and she glared at him with animosity.

"Lady Blackmore," he said in his rich tones that had sent shivers to her spine years ago but now only annoyed her.

"Lord Bartondale," she replied with a stilted air and refused to curtsy. Her mother would be ashamed of her behaviour but thankfully, she was not there.

"What seems to be the problem?" he questioned, glancing towards her carriage.

"I believe you have eyes to see or has marriage made you blind?" she replied and turned away. She did not care if the servants wondered why she was being rude to the man who might be the solution to her problem.

"Leave us," he instructed his servants and hers and they quickly dispersed to stand a short distance away.

"Lady Blackmore," he snapped, forcing her to look at him. His eyes blazed with suppressed anger. "While I understand that we did not... part on the best of terms, I will not take kindly to you showing me disrespect in the presence of servants."

Smarting from the dressing down, she thrust her chin at him in defiance. "If you are waiting for an apology, then prepare to wait in vain. Hell will freeze over first."

He shook his head. "To think that I assumed you would have outgrown your childishness by now. At seventeen, assuredly, you must know when to put aside hostility for sound reasoning?"

Before she could reply, he nodded in the direction of her broken carriage. "I take it you are heading to your aunt's house. Given the state of your conveyance, you will not get there today, at least not while it is daylight. This road has been known to harbour disreputable men at night. I assure you that it is not an experience you will enjoy."

"Thank you for painting such a gloomy picture to frighten me," she threw at him with a savage bite.

His eyes darkened. "That was not my intention. I merely stated a fact." He curved his body in the direction of his carriage. "Your only option is to come with me. I am travelling in that direction."

Sarah almost said *over my dead body*, but he forestalled her again.

"I will have to take an alternate route, which is slightly longer, but will be relatively safer. Highwaymen do not patrol the area regularly. Upon our arrival, I will send back my coachman and more footmen to have your carriage fixed and sent to your aunt's house."

Everything he said sounded very logical, but she would rather roll in the mud like a pig than accept his offer for help. She wanted nothing to do with him, not even if he was the last man on earth. She would rather take her chances than...

Sarah's lips parted company when all of a sudden as if planned to thwart her resolution, the clouds shifted their position to shield the sun and darken the sky.

"While I admired your stubbornness in the past, I must tell you now is not the time to be pig-headed. It is foolhardy to stay here."

Sarah rubbed the back of her neck, wishing she had not instructed the coachman to come this way. Alas, it was no use crying over spilled milk.

Her decision was made for her when drops of rain fell on her hand. Grudgingly, she agreed.

"You seem to have gotten your way just like you always do," she informed him icily. "I will go with you. But do not try to converse with me, for we have nothing to discuss. Once we get to my aunt's, we will part ways again for good."

"Brilliant!" he simply said and turned away to give his servants instructions.

Memories flooded her as Sarah surveyed the man that she had given her heart to two years ago. She ought to be miles away from him and not about to ride with him. It was left to be seen if she had made yet another mistake coming across Lord Benjamin George Pennington, the Marquess of Bartondale.

Chapter Three

Sarah discerned that by the time she alighted from the carriage, she would have a crick in her neck from staring out the window for so long in one direction. But she would rather have discomfort in her neck than look anywhere near the man she hated most in the world. Even with her maid seated beside her, she still felt as uncomfortable as a cat on a hot tin roof.

Memories of what transpired between them two years ago raced through her mind. She regretted climbing into the coach. How could she be in the same space as the man who had made her feel like she was the most important person in the world and then spun around in the same breath to marry another woman? It was not right.

With despair, she remembered the first time she had met Benjamin, at a birthday party. Her aunt had made her go with her to the party. One look at the tall and handsome man with eyes like fire and she had fallen head over heels for him. He had claimed that when their eyes met across the crowded room, he had felt the same way. And so, she had been fooled into a courtship with him. At that time, her parents had been in London for her older sisters' debut into society. Consequently, her aunt had been assigned to chaperone her. Given that her aunt lived in the countryside and one of Benjamin's residences was close to the area, they had not had a public courtship, albeit they had a wonderful one. And after only a few weeks, Benjamin had announced to her that he would go to London to speak to her father about offering for her. She had been overjoyed until a week after his departure, she had read the news of his impending nuptials with Lady Harriet Weston, daughter of the Duke and Duchess of Clayford. She had waited in vain for Benjamin's return. He never came. Neither had he even the decency to send her a letter to explain. Thus, with her heart shredded beyond repair, she had returned to Keymouth and hated men ever since. When she heard of his wife's demise a year later, she had tried to dredge up pity for him but came up wanting.

And now, she was seated before him in his carriage after accepting his hospitality. Bile rose in her throat at the unfortunate event that had led to her being there.

"Sarah?"

She stiffened in her seat at the gentle way he called her name but refused to look in his direction. "Please refrain from calling me by my forename, Lord Bartondale. I believe we had an agreement for you not to speak to me during the journey."

"I merely wished to ask you if you would like to stop at an inn for a meal... Sarah."

Sarah glanced at him with anger brightening her blue eyes. "I would rather sup with the devil in hell or die from starvation than dine with you."

He chuckled. "That can be arranged."

Incensed by his sarcasm, she turned her red face to him. "Do not dare laugh at me, you despicable, philandering, untrustworthy rake!"

Her maid inhaled sharply, but Sarah beamed with satisfaction when the smile dropped off Benjamin's face. A muscle moved on his chin, drawing her attention to the small divide under his lips. Unexpected tears pricked her eyes as she remembered teasing him lovingly about his cleft chin.

To her dismay, Benjamin tapped on the roof of the coach, indicating for the coachman to stop the carriage. Her tongue dashed across her lips in a fit of nervousness as she stared into his glowing eyes. The rage she saw in the amber depths frightened her a little. She had never seen him like this before. Had she gone too far? But he deserved such harsh words and more for what he did to her.

Immediately, the carriage pulled to a stop. Sarah decided that she would not wait to be dressed down like a child before her maid. When the footman opened the door and positioned the steps on the ground, she rose from the leather seat and dashed for the door. Benjamin did not make any effort to stop her.

"Curse you," she said under her breath to the sky when she saw that the drizzle had stopped. She could feel the moment when Benjamin stepped down from the carriage. She had always been able to feel his presence like the time he came up behind her while she was in her aunt's rose garden.

Why Benjamin? Why did you treat me like dirt when I thought we were a perfect match?

The fact that his presence still affected her so much, unnerved her. Perhaps she should have taken her parents' advice and gone to London for the Season. Then, she would not be stuck with the man she had loved while feeling wretched at the memory of his rejection.

"Sarah!"

She was just about to whirl around to sternly warn him never to call her name again when she saw why he had done it. Heading towards her from the bushes were two men in masks holding guns. Her heart froze.

Highway robbers!

"Sarah! Get inside!"

Sarah was about to do his bidding but when she swivelled around, she saw two other men coming from the opposite direction. The men had probably laid in wait for any unsuspecting victim.

In the confusion of guns blazing, Sarah turned away from the carriage and lifted her dress to flee the violent scene.

"Sarah!"

With all thoughts bent on escape, Sarah did not heed Benjamin's call. When she saw one of the men heading her way, she changed directions, hoping she could hide in the thick bushes. Unfortunately for her, she did not realise that the exact spot she chose to hide was rocky terrain.

A gasp escaped from her lips when, instead of her foot touching the hard ground as she ran, it hung in mid-air. As it was too late for her to pull back, she screamed as she fell and rolled down the hill.

"Sarah!"

Jutting stones scratched her hands and legs as she fell, screaming. Just when she thought that she would finally stop tumbling, her head hit something sharp and sent a bolt of pain racing through her body. Darkness enveloped her.

Chapter Four

Groaning in pain, Sarah frowned as someone touched her aching head. She tried lifting her hand to brush away the hands that kept rubbing her head as if they were searching for something, but she felt too weak to raise it.

She groaned again when the same hands tried to pry her eyes open.

"Cease," she whispered and swallowed painfully through a parched throat.

"Please open your eyes, Sarah. We just want to know you are all right," a strange voice said, causing her frown to deepen.

"Sarah? Who is Sarah?"

She heard a sharp gasp from the person who was forcing her eyes open even though what she wanted to do was sleep. She blinked rapidly as she tried to focus her gaze on the two hazy figures. She closed her eyes again and opened them slowly. A few seconds later, the fogginess cleared. The man closest to her was an elderly man who gazed at her with a kind smile, while the other man was much younger and had a frown across his face. Her eyes lifted to his eyes and her lips parted as her heart suddenly resounded against her chest.

She did not understand why her pulse started racing and her palms became clammy. What was it about this man with expressive eyes that made her feel hot all over? Did she have a fever? Was that the reason she was abed? Unable to bear the unnerving intensity of his gaze, she looked away.

"Water," she whispered. The younger man hastily walked to the bedside table and poured from a pitcher into a cup and took it to her. He supported her head with his hand while he held the cup to her lips as she drank greedily.

"Thank you," she said with a moist throat.

"Are you all right, Sarah?" the younger man asked after placing the cup back on the table. "You gave us quite a fright."

"My head aches and I feel sore all over," she told him in a low tone.

The older man nodded. "It is to be expected. You had quite a nasty fall, but you will be fine in no time. I will give you laudanum for the pain and headaches. All you have to do now is rest."

"I will see that you get the best care, Sarah," the younger man added.

She nodded and winced. "When you say Sarah, are you referring to me?"

The two men exchanged alarming looks that had her terrified. Was she not supposed to have asked the question? She tried to think but her head ached.

"Pardon me, my Lady," the older man began. "What is your name?"

She opened her mouth to say it but then shut it instantly. What was her name? Who was she? Why was she there and who were the men?

Her breath came in sharp gasps when she realised that she could remember nothing.

"Calm down, Sarah," the older man said and placed a hand on her shoulder. "Please do not get agitated. It will do you more harm than good."

"But I do not know who I am." She shifted her confused gaze from one man to the other. "I cannot remember anything."

"Again, that is to be expected, given that you struck your head against a rock."

"A rock? Who am I? Why am I here? How did I hit my head on a rock? Who are you?" she asked spontaneously as she tried sitting up.

The man placed a hand against her shoulder to keep her from rising. The younger man stared at her with a preoccupied gaze.

"Rest easy, my Lady. I am Doctor Fulton. This is Lord Bartondale. He will explain to you how your injury came about."

Sarah removed her gaze from the man who introduced himself as a doctor to stare at the pensive-looking man beside him. She could not tell, but Lord Bartondale did not look as though he would tell her anything.

"Please do not trouble yourself with thoughts about your memory, my Lady. It will come back. All you have to do now is focus on getting better," Doctor Fulton said with a small smile.

"But for how long?" she asked, afraid she might never regain her memory.

He shrugged and frowned. "I really cannot say, my Lady. It might only be for a few days, a week, months—"

"Years?" she tentatively asked.

"I do not think so. You have a small swell at the back of your head. It does not appear to be something we should be worried about. I do not understand the workings of the mind, but I reckon in a few days, you will remember everything."

Hope rose inside of her. "Are you sure?"

He smiled and patted her shoulder. "Rest well, my Lady. Send for me if your headache does not subside in a few days."

"I will see you out," Lord Bartondale finally said and strode to the door with the doctor in his wake.

When she was alone in the room, Sarah again tried to remember something, even if it was only her name. But she ended up wincing from the ache in her head.

Her eyes moved to the door when Lord Bartondale returned to the room. Without saying a word, he walked to the table to pour water from the pitcher into a bowl and placed a small towel in it. He sat beside her, squeezed the towel, and placed it across her forehead. Sarah welcomed the coolness of the water by closing her eyes.

"Does that make your head feel better?"

She opened her eyes and nodded. The towel almost slipped off, but he reached out and positioned it properly.

"I instructed my cook to prepare a chicken broth. You will enjoy it.

After that, I will give you laudanum as prescribed by Doctor Fulton. Hopefully, you will be better by the morrow."

"May I ask you a question?"

He slightly curved his body from her, as if trying to evade her eyes. "You may."

"Em... who am I?" She blushed, not understanding why she felt so self-conscious before him. "I mean, do you know who I am? How did I get hurt? Where am I?"

Still avoiding her gaze, he replied, "Remember what the doctor said. You need to rest without troubling yourself about such thoughts."

"But I have to know," she sighed heavily. "I do not even know what I look like."

He looked at her and her heart stopped beating for a second. His intense scrutiny travelled across her face and made her feel so ill at ease, that she lowered her gaze.

"See your face through my eyes. You are the most beautiful woman I have ever seen. You have the face of a Roman goddess. Eyes that remind me of the sea and hair like the sun."

A tense silence fell upon the room. Sarah could only stare at him as words failed her in trying to reply to his poetic description of her.

He changed the direction of his gaze from her face to the bowl of water. "Forgive me for carrying on so. I do not want you to fret about your appearance. You have a few cuts on your cheeks but not serious. In a few days, your face will return to its perfection."

"Thank you," was all Sarah could say.

He took the towel from her head, put it in the water again, squeezed it, and replaced it on her head.

"Do you not have servants to do this?" she could not help asking.

He smiled. "I do. I wish to take care of you myself. You see, my Lady, I feel somewhat guilty. If I had protected you, you would not have been injured."

"Oh. Could you please tell me what happened? Maybe it might jog my memory. Please."

He sighed. "How can I deny you anything?"

By the time he was done telling her how he, his coachman, and his footmen had subdued the highwaymen and how he had not been able to reach her before she fell, she wished that she had not asked.

"How could I have been so foolish?"

He shook his head. "Please do not say that. Who knows what would have happened? You—"

A knock on the door prevented him from continuing. Upon his summons, a robust woman entered the room with a steamy plate of chicken broth.

Although she was still sore all over and quite self-conscious about Lord Bartondale, she allowed him to spoon-feed her before giving her the bitter medicine. Before she closed her eyes, she smiled with contentment, knowing that this kind man would take good care of her regardless of her memory loss.

Chapter Five

"My! You look bright and cheerful today," Benjamin (as he had insisted Sarah call him) alleged as he strode into the room carrying a breakfast tray.

Sarah blushed and lowered her eyes. The sight of Benjamin, whom she found very handsome, never failed to make her heart skip a beat. She watched as he strode to the bedside table where he placed the tray containing a plate of toast and a cup of tea.

For shame! Eyeing a man from your sick bed.

In the three days that she had woken up to a blinding headache and memory loss, Benjamin had taken very good care of her. Even though he had many servants in the manor, he did not mind coming to the room to make sure that she had her meals and to keep her company. For propriety's sake, a maid always sat in a corner of the room so they would not be alone. Sarah barely noticed her. She had eyes only for Benjamin.

He sat on the chair beside the bed. "How do you feel today? Does your head still ache?"

Seated on the bed in a white muslin dress the maid had helped her to put on that morning after her ablutions, Sarah said, "No. I feel better. Could we please stop with the laudanum? I do not have headaches anymore, and neither do I feel sore all over my body."

He laughed softly. "Very well, then." Unexpectedly, she felt a tenseness in him when he asked, "Have you been able to remember anything?"

She shook her head with sadness. "Sometimes, when it seems as if I am about to reach out and touch a memory, it suddenly fades."

He nodded. "I am sorry about that. I hope you regain your memory soon."

"I hope so, too."

Silence descended between them for a moment until he nodded at the breakfast tray.

"I think it is wise you have your breakfast now before your tea gets cold."

"I will do that on one condition," she answered with a twinkle in her eyes. She smiled when his brows rose in question. "You have told me a little about myself, well, the little that you know— which I am grateful for. But I know nothing about you."

His lips twitched in a smile. "What do you wish to know about me?"

She shrugged as he rose to carry the breakfast tray and place it on the bed beside her. "I do not know. What are your full names? Why have you chosen to take care of me? Are you married or planning to?"

He laughed. "If I answer your questions, do you promise to eat every morsel of your toast?"

Sarah eyed the meal and nodded. She had not had much of an appetite and that had been a source of concern for him. Doctor Filton had told him it was normal, and she would gradually recover it.

"Right. I am Benjamin George Pennington, the Marquess of Bartondale," he cheerfully said with a spark in his eyes.

Sarah reckoned that she had never heard of him. Her memory was selective, as she could not remember some things regarding society. But she knew somehow that his title was a lofty one.

Smiling after taking a sip from her cup of tea, she remarked, "Do you expect me to believe that a Marquess who is supposed to be engaged in serious affairs does not mind ministering to the needs of a commoner?"

Benjamin frowned. "Who says you are a commoner?"

"I think I am."

He shook his head. "I do not think you are a commoner. Despite your ill-health, you carry yourself with a grace that befits a Lady of the peerage."

She laughed, reddening at the faint praise. "Mayhap I learned to mimic my betters."

"I do not think so," he refuted.

"Do not change the topic, my Lord. Why have you deigned to help me recover my health?"

He leaned back in the chair and studied her, making her cheeks turn rosy. "Like I told you earlier. I feel responsible for you. Had I protected you better, you would not have been hurt."

She yearned to counter his statement, but she did not think she would win the argument, so she changed the topic. "Are you betrothed to anyone?" She blushed at the bold question. Was she always so direct? Or was it because he had made her feel so comfortable with him. She felt as though she could ask him anything. "If you do not mind my asking."

A shadow cast over his eyes, making them dull. "I am a widower. I was married for only a year and my wife died a year ago from a riding accident."

Sarah's hand paused in mid-air trying to take a bite of her toast. "Oh. I am so sorry. I should not have asked."

"You do not have to apologize. However insensitive it might sound, I am happy to be free. Her death was unfortunate, but we had a terrible marriage." He bowed his head. "My wife enjoyed favours from other men and was not ashamed of it, no matter how I tried to caution her about it," he shrugged. "Anyway, I cannot say I blame her. Our coming together was not exactly a joyous one in the first place, so I understood her rebellion because I..." He drifted to a stop.

Sarah longed to ask him to continue, but she stilled her tongue. It was not her place to ask. The pain she saw in his eyes when he raised his head tore into her heart. How he must have loved her and suffered when she continuously cheated on him.

"I am so sorry," she whispered.

"Please do not be. The marriage was all for naught, and it was my fault at the end of the day. I..."

Again, he paused and then shrugged. Sarah had an inkling that he was hiding something, but she dare not ask him what it was. Twin red spots stained her cheeks when she found herself yearning to ask him if a Marquess was allowed to marry a commoner. Her memory was foggy in that regard, and she could not be certain whether she had blueblood running through her veins.

But why would I want to know the answer to such a question? Have I taken a fancy to him after just three days of knowing him? Why does it feel as if I have known him for a lifetime?

Sarah chewed on her bottom lip. She did find him very handsome, and her heart fluttered like butterflies whenever he came close to her. She did not know what it meant to be in love or if she had ever been. But she knew that in such a short time, Benjamin had made an impression on her. She could not bear to think about how she would feel when she was well enough to leave his house.

Sadness filled her.

Chapter Six

I wish this would never end.

Positioned side saddle on a mare, Sarah surreptitiously glanced at her riding companion who sat magnificently on his brown stallion. Her heart missed a beat yet again as she marvelled at how handsome he looked in all-black riding clothes.

A week ago, she had known nothing about such a wonderful man. But now, she felt as though she had known him all her life. Although she still did not know who she was, she had regained her health. It was silly, she acknowledged, but she wished she would never recover her memory. She desired to stay in Lord Bartondale's manor for the rest of her life.

It was wishful thinking. But she craved for it to come to pass. He was a widower and she supposed that she was a spinster. So, nothing was stopping them from getting married, was there? Her cheeks turned rosy at her audacious thoughts. How could she be thinking of getting married to a stranger; one who had merely offered her help from the goodness of his heart? Shame filled her from such greedy thoughts. But she could not help how she felt about him. She reckoned that she felt this way because he had taken good care of her and given her his utmost attention. Maybe it was expected of her to feel that way about her rescuer; after all, he was like her knight in shining armour.

The question was whether he fancied her, too. He had not shown any sign that she might have made an impression on him. He treated her with the utmost courtesy and made sure that they were never alone. Even now, a maid rode silently behind them. She had heard of men taking advantage of women when they were alone, stealing kisses and whatnot.

Abruptly, a gasp fell from her lips at a fleeting memory, causing her to tighten the reins of her horse. How did she come about that knowledge? Benjamin promptly turned to her; his amber eyes packed with concern.

"Are you all right, my Lady?"

Sarah nodded. "I do not know, but a thought just came to me. I do not know where it came from, but I just knew it."

Was it her imagination or had he become rigid? It was most likely that her mind was playing tricks on her, for he had asked her daily since the week she came to his house if she could remember anything.

"What did you remember?"

Sarah shifted her gaze to the green fields. "It is nothing important, my Lord."

"Are you certain? Nothing concerning you is unimportant."

And that was one of the reasons why she was losing her heart to him. He told her things that made her feel as if she was the only woman in the world. Could that mean he felt something for her too? Or was he usually this way with everyone? She had not encountered him with anyone other than his servants and the doctor whom he treated with courtesy. So, she could not say.

Her thoughts drifted to his late wife, and she questioned why the woman had cheated on such a caring man. It was beyond reason even though she was aware that she did not have the full picture.

"My Lady?"

"Oh." She had forgotten Benjamin awaited her reply. "Forgive me, my Lord. But it is nothing. It is only a lesson in propriety that I remembered."

He chuckled. "I assure you that you have nothing to worry about in that regard if you are troubled about that."

She hastily shook her head. "Not at all, my Lord. You have been the perfect gentleman."

He muttered something she did not quite catch. Before she could ask him, he inquired, "My Lady, is it a possibility for you to recall whether you play card games?"

She tilted her head to the side and thought for a minute. "I do not reckon I do."

He grinned. "Then I shall endeavour to teach you. It will make a good pastime."

"All right, my Lord. I look forward to it." Her eyes sparkled with mischief. "But be warned. I might not recall anything other than the fact that I am a woman, but I believe I am intellectually sound enough to beat you after a few lessons."

He threw back his head and roared with laughter. Warmth spread through her at the lovely sight of him laughing.

"Laugh now, my Lord, for later you might just regret doing so when you find yourself frowning."

He chortled. "Now I am eager to see how you intend to best me. Know you not that I am considered a master when it comes to card games?"

She smiled. "That is left to be seen, my Lord."

He laughed again. "Why, you cheeky chit. I will just have to make you eat your words."

Before she could reply, her horse unexpectedly neighed loudly and rose on its forelegs. Mortified and afraid of being thrown violently to the ground, Sarah screamed and tightly held on to the reins for dear life.

"Sarah!" Benjamin yelled as the mare, frightened of the snake before it, reared and veered away with speed.

"Benjamin!" Sarah cried as the horse raced on, unheeding the tight pull of the reins and tightening of her knees. She could not differentiate between the horse's hooves thudding on the ground and her thundering heart. Fear raced through every pore of her body.

"Sarah! Do not let go! I am coming!"

She heard Benjamin yell behind her, along with the tremendous sound of his horse chasing after hers. She closed her eyes as the horse continued to jerk her about. Her hair loosened from the bond she had it tied with and it flung about her face and shoulders. Just when she thought she could not hold on any longer, Benjamin drew his horse beside her, reached for her, and swung her into his arms.

Tears of joy and relief that he had saved her before something happened to her flooded her face. Wrapped in his arms and breathing heavily while she felt the thudding of his heart, sobs shook her body.

"Hush, my love. You are safe now. I will never let any harm befall you. Not while I have breath in me."

He pulled his horse to a stop and caressed her hair. When she lifted her head to thank him for rescuing her, he caught her face in his hands. She noted how ashen he looked, and she reckoned that it was because his wife had died in a riding accident. The incident had probably brought back painful memories. She was sorry that she had caused him pain.

"I do not know what I would have done had you been injured, or worse," he whispered fiercely. "I know this might seem too soon, but I cannot bear to be apart from you."

Sarah gawked at Benjamin, hardly able to believe her ears.

"Marry me, Sarah. I will do my best to make you happy."

Happiness engulfed Sarah despite her near brush with death only a short while ago.

Sarah's wet eyes sparkled with joy. "Yes. Yes, Benjamin. I will marry you."

Her wish had finally come to pass.

Chapter Seven

"Say, my Lady, I think we should make the game more interesting," Benjamin inserted two days later as he peered at the cards in his hands.

Sarah giggled. "What do you reckon, my Lord? You have been on a losing streak."

He chortled and stared at her above his raised cards. "Losing streak? You have won only *one* game. I hardly consider that a losing streak on my part."

Leaning back against the red-brocaded armchair in his study, Sarah gazed at him audaciously. "That is because I shall continue winning."

He rubbed a hand across his cleft chin. "I knew it was a big mistake teaching you how to play cards. You will not let me hear the last of it if you win again, will you?"

Sarah's shoulders shook with mirth. "You can count on it. Besides, the honour of being my teacher does not lie with you. My father taught me and my sisters when I was..." Sarah's words hung in the air. An image of her and four other ladies, who held a resemblance to her, with a man standing above them at a large table filled with cards flashed through her mind.

"You have remembered something," Benjamin stiffly said a few seconds later.

With a smile curving her lips, Sarah nodded. "I believe I have four sisters."

Benjamin placed his cards face down on the large oak desk and sat up from his reclined position. "Anything else? Their names?"

Sarah closed her eyes and tried again but after a minute, she gave up. Pockets of memories had been rushing through her mind lately, but she had not been able to piece them together. She had seen images of a woman who she perceived was her mother, one of her brother, another of a maid, an older woman who might be her aunt, and then a carriage. At night, her dreams were filled with a faceless man who usually saved her from falling off a cliff.

Sarah opened her eyes and shook her head with a rueful sigh. "No. The memory is gone again."

With his eyes focused on the cards, Benjamin remarked, "You seem to be recalling a lot lately."

Her face brightened. "Is that not wonderful? I feel as if everything will return to me in a few days."

"It is," he replied, but his tone belied his words.

Sarah's brows arched. She pondered the reason why he was not joyous about her recovering her memory. After asking for her hand in marriage, he most likely was afraid that she would recant his offer and leave after recovering her memory. If only there was a way to assure him other than words.

"Benjamin," she softly called as she raised her head to behold his glowing eyes.

"Yes, Sarah?"

"You do not understand what it means for me to have such memories come and go. Not knowing who I am is like being in a room but unable to find the door."

A tense silence fell between them after her pitiful words. She wished she could make him understand that even though she wished for them to be wed, she also desired to have her memory back, regardless of the consequences of doing so.

Benjamin pushed back his chair and rose. He walked around the desk to drop on a knee beside her. His eyes were shadowed but she could perceive the compassion in him. He took her hand and excitement raced up her body.

"Forgive me, Sarah. I did not mean to be so gloomy at such delightful news. It worries me that you may not want to marry me when you remember everything."

She shook her head energetically, almost unhooking the tortoiseshell comb on her head. "I will not do that. I will marry you, come what may."

Unease rose inside of her when he gave her a sad smile. "Are you sure about that? A lot of things will change and..." He positioned her hand back on her lap and got up to rake his fingers through his blonde hair, mussing it.

"What is it, Benjamin? Surely, you know you can tell me anything," she quietly informed him as she saw his broad shoulders tense and slump.

He opened his mouth to say something, but then he shook his head. "Promise me that when you recover your memory, you will try to be... be objective."

She frowned. "Objective? What do you mean?"

He sighed. "Certain things might be confusing at first, but I would love for you to allow me to explain things to you then."

"Why not explain it to me now?"

"Your foggy mind will not grasp it completely. It will further confuse you, and I cannot do that to you. All I ask is that when you discover who you are, you provide me a listening ear."

Sarah's brows furrowed in a deeper frown. From Benjamin's behaviour and moodiness sometimes, she had always suspected that he was hiding something from her. She had repeatedly questioned what it was but had come up wanting. She wished that he would just come out and say it instead of waiting for her memory to return.

"Benjamin—"

"Please let it go, for now, Sarah. We will revisit the issue some other time." His face softened into a mischievous smile. "Now that I know your stack of cards is a losing hand, could we continue with our game? This time, with a wager."

Sarah wanted to protest but then she laughed at the boyish smile on his face. "A wager?"

He nodded and strode to resume his seat. "If I win, we get married immediately."

Her mouth opened in awe. "And if I win?"

His shoulders rose and dropped in a nonchalant shrug. "Then we do not get married... yet."

Sarah considered the proposition for some minutes. Marrying him would make her the happiest woman in England. But the memories of a family that had filtered through her mind lately made her hesitate. She did not understand, but she sensed that she had always wanted a large wedding with her family in attendance. Could she allow her fate to be decided by a game of chance? Her sense of adventure prompted her into accepting.

Smiling, she stretched forth her hand. "Wager accepted. You have a deal, my Lord."

Benjamin laughed and shook her hand. "No cheating now."

"I believe that is my line, my Lord."

Laughter bubbled from his throat again as he reached for the cards to reshuffle them.

Half an hour later, Sarah smugly placed her cards, a pair of aces, on the table. "I believe I have you beaten, dear Sir."

"Is that so?" Benjamin's eyes twinkled as he ever so carefully laid his cards on the table and slowly turned them over. Three kings.

"You cheated!" she accused as her face mottled with colour.

"Careful now, my Lady," he said with a lazy drawl. "I might tell you to name your second."

The thought of a duel with him was so absurd that Sarah's indignation flew away, and she placed her hand across her lips as laughter shook her body. Benjamin burst into laughter, too.

"I suggest a rematch," she declared, still laughing.

The humour died in Benjamin's eyes all of a sudden. "You do not wish to marry me, do you? Mayhap something deep inside you is the cause of your hesitation."

Sarah raised horror-filled eyes to his dull ones. "You are completely wrong, my Lord. That is not... of course, I want to marry you, but...

but..." She got up and turned her back to him, struggling for the right words to tell him how confused she was. "I do not know who I am. I do not know anything about the family I keep having flashes about. It just does not feel right marrying without them."

She heard Benjamin pull back his chair and then she felt his arms around her as he drew her into a warm embrace.

"Forgive me, Sarah. I did not mean to pressure you into marrying me posthaste. I desire to have you for a wife so badly, that I have lost all sense of reasoning. Pardon me." He gently pulled her away from him to gaze into her eyes. "I love you, Sarah. This might seem too soon for you, but I love you with every fibre of my being and I will cherish you for the rest of my life."

Tears stung Sarah's eyes. "I love you, too, Benjamin. I know it has only been just over a week since we met, but it feels as if I have known you before now and loved you. It has been so easy to fall in love with you. I am mighty glad you found me that day."

Benjamin's eyes held an unreadable expression before he drew her into his arms again. Sarah did not question his change in countenance. She was elated that her love was reciprocated. Now, all she had to do was regain her memory to make everything perfect.

Chapter Eight

"Why do I feel as if I have done this before?" Sarah asked with a frown as she stared at the easel that she had placed on a stand to paint the beautiful scenery before her.

Benjamin muttered something behind her, and she whirled around to look at him with a ready smile on her face. With his back against a tree and seated on a dark blue blanket with baskets filled with picnic treats, he took her breath away.

"What did you say, my Lord?" she questioned.

With his eyes shielded, he replied, "When will you be done?"

She turned around to look at her landscape drawing. "Soon, my love. I find that I have not been able to capture the scenery as efficiently as I desire."

Her eyes moved to her watercolour paints on the table beside her and she chewed on her bottom lip. She swiped her brush on the light blue colour and stroked it across the parchment as she tried to portray the beauty of the sky that lay above her.

"I think I am a little rusty," she sighed when she was not satisfied with what she had done thus far. "Everything in me tells me that I have done this before, much better than this."

"Do not be so hard on yourself, my darling."

Her heart flipped at the knowledge of Benjamin standing directly behind her. She had been so caught up with her painting that she had not even heard him move towards her.

"You have captured the lushness of the fields, the sunlight dancing in the river, and the sky that matches the colour of your mesmerizing eyes. It is beautiful but it does not hold a candle to you."

His bright smile chased away the worry from her eyes. But she protested when he drew her in his arms.

"My apron is stained with paint that might ruin your clothes," she informed him.

"Think you I care about my clothes right now? I want you to see the truth in my eyes and not think that I am merely trying to make you feel better. Your artistic talent is not in doubt. You caught the setting beautifully. I dare say your paintings might grace museums across the world someday. You are exquisite, my love."

Her colour heightened and she beamed from ear to ear. "You say the most uplifting things, Benjamin."

He caught her chin in his hand and made her look into his eyes. "And I mean them. Never doubt my words or my love for you."

She nodded.

"Now come. Watching you paint has left me famished."

"Right." She removed her apron and placed it on the table before washing her hands from the jar of water. She joined him on the blanket and unpacked the baskets of small cakes and biscuits, apple pie, port, and fruits. After serving him, she sat beside him against the huge tree. They sat in companionable silence, devouring their meal.

"I take it no word has been heard from anyone about a missing daughter or niece?" Sarah enquired when they were done eating.

"None."

Sarah rubbed a hand across her neck. It was almost three weeks since she came to be in Benjamin's manor yet no post in the dailies had been made about her. She had thought by now that the family she kept having memories of would be searching for her. It bothered her that she was either a nobody or her mind was simply playing tricks on her by conjuring images of a non-existent family.

Granted, she loved being with Benjamin, but she feared that she may never get her memory back if she did not return to her family. If there even was one to return to.

"What is wrong, my love?"

Sarah forced a smile. "Benjamin, I love you and I look forward to marrying you but there is... I do not know how to explain it for you to understand. Something is missing inside me. I feel incomplete and I know it is because I do not know who I am or where I come from. Oh, if I was whole, I would gladly have married you without a second thought."

Benjamin stared at her thoughtfully for a moment. Then he closed his eyes and released a deep groan. "Sarah? I have something to tell you."

Sarah's chest tightened at the soberness of his countenance. Why did he look so grave? Did he intend to withdraw his proposal?

Before he could reply, a footman ran up to them and bowed. "Pardon me, my Lord. Sir Beecham arrived a few minutes ago. He said it is of the utmost urgency that he speak with you."

Benjamin's face contorted into a scowl. "I left instructions that we were not to be disturbed."

"My apologies, my Lord. He insisted I inform you of his presence. He also threatened fire and brimstone if his order was not carried out."

Sarah gasped in alarm. "My Lord, you must go to him promptly. I cannot bear to think of what would be the cause of his urgency."

Benjamin gave Sarah a rueful grin. "Forgive this disturbance, my love. Sir Beecham is a neighbour known for his theatrics. His outbursts are mostly trivial. I would not be surprised if it has something to do with a missing pot of ink in his study."

Sarah giggled.

"He had once come here accusing his servants of stealing his spectacles. All the while, they were on his head."

A soft gurgle of laughter burst from Sarah's throat. "He sounds like quite a charming fellow."

Rising deftly to his feet, his eyes twinkling with humour, Benjamin replied, "He certainly is not. I will return to you soon, my love."

"Hurry back," she informed him and watched him walk away as if her heart had been wrenched from her chest. An idea came to her, and she placed the bowl of fruits back in the basket and got up to place another parchment on the easel.

By the time Benjamin returned a quarter of an hour later, Sarah had half completed the sketch of his face. While she had sketched, images of the time she had spent with him had swamped her mind and she had come to a decision.

"Who is that ugly man?" Benjamin quizzed with a chuckle when he strode up behind her.

"The man I shall marry on the morrow," she replied and slowly turned around.

His eyes narrowed with confusion.

She nodded with pleasure. "I do not want to wait any longer, my love. God knows when I will get back my memory. What if it is years from now and all I will get are bits and pieces of my past? I love my present as it is, and I know that I will love my future better with you in it. So, yes, Benjamin. I will marry you as soon as it can be arranged."

Benjamin, not minding her paint-stained apron, swung her into his arms and she laughed happily.

Chapter Nine

"Will I do, Edna?" Sarah asked the maid who had tended to her since she arrived at Benjamin's manor.

The maid nodded, beaming from ear to ear. "You are the most beautiful bride I have ever seen, my Lady."

Sarah returned her smile and stared at her reflection in the oval wooden mirror. Yes, the white lace gown with its tight bodice and flared-out skirts made her feel like a bride. The v-shaped neckline made it possible for the pearl necklace Benjamin had given her the day before to be easily noticeable as the pendant dropped towards the deep cut, complementing her earrings. The sleeves were short to accommodate her long gloves, which matched the exquisite chignon at the crown on her head. The maid placed satin slippers before her to complete her ensemble.

Sarah closed her eyes, took in a deep breath, and let it out slowly before opening her eyes. She could hardly believe that three days ago, she had agreed to marry Benjamin without waiting for her memory to return. Since then, he had performed wonders with her wedding trousseau and organised the wedding that required a special license for them to be wed quickly. And he had achieved it all, which had made her fall even more in love with him, given how efficient he was.

Then why am I suddenly a bundle of nerves?

She loved Benjamin and wished to spend the rest of her life with him. So, why the sudden hesitation in her as if she were rushing into it? He was no longer a stranger to her. He had proven time again how much he loved her.

I am doing the right thing.

Ten minutes earlier, Benjamin had sent word to her that the vicar had arrived and so she could come down to his study whenever she was ready. Sarah presumed that if she waited any longer, she might just change her mind. And so, treading carefully because of the long train of the headdress, she crossed the large bedroom to the door. At the landing, she stared down the long flight of stairs, wishing Benjamin was at the bottom to offer her his dashing smile to allay her fears. As he was not there, she gently descended the stairs. She was midway to the bottom when she suddenly remembered that she had left her bouquet in the room. She whirled around to instruct the maid who was carrying the train of her dress. The movement was too sudden for her foot and the veil, and she stumbled. She tried to grasp onto the banister to hold her balance, but it was an exercise in futility as she fell down the rest of the stairs to the bottom where she hit her head. In a split second, the darkness consumed her.

With a low groan, Sarah awoke a quarter of an hour later. She held her head as she tried to rise from the bed, but a pair of hands stopped her.

"Please lie back, Sarah. I have sent for Doctor Fulton."

That voice!

Instantly, Sarah's eyes flickered open. And just as she had hoped, everything came flooding back to her. She held her head in her hands and closed her eyes as old and new memories swirled together, making her head ache. Her memory bank rushed back to the broken carriage and to Benjamin coming along to offer his help. Then, the attack by highwaymen, and waking up at Benjamin's to the loss of her memory.

Her heart tightened with mortification as it dawned on her how Benjamin had sought to charm her and make her think that she was in love with him so he could marry her. He had lied to her about not knowing who she was and made her hang on to his every word for survival. He had portrayed himself as the perfect gentleman when he was nothing but a fiend!

She released a guttural groan at her foolishness.

"Sarah, my love, are you all right?" Benjamin asked with a note of urgency. "Please talk to me."

"Do not touch me!" she yelled and opened her eyes the moment he put his hand on hers.

He shrank back in shock.

"Do not ever lay your hands on me again, you manipulative liar!"

He closed his eyes for a moment as she read the regret on his face. The action made her even angrier. He most likely wished that he had married her before she recollected her memory so she would not be able to leave his manor.

"You despicable lout! How could you?"

He opened his eyes then and placed both palms together in a desperate plea for understanding. "Please listen to me, Sarah. Tis not what you think."

"Not what I think? You lied to me. Everything you told me was a lie."

"Remember, you promised to listen to whatever I had to say when you recovered your memory."

Enraged, she folded her fists on the bed to keep from smacking him. "I do not owe you anything. For the fact that you were willing to marry me even when you knew I would never marry you if you were the last man on earth shows how loathsome a fellow you are."

"Sarah, please, I beg you. Give me a listening ear. I did not mean to deceive you. It was the only way I could get you back into my life."

"By lying, conniving, and scheming?"

He sighed. "Put like that, I know it sounds terrible, but there was no other way. I—"

She flung back the sheets and waited a few seconds for the room to stop twirling. "Save your lies for somebody else. I do not wish to listen to any more falsehood from you." Then she gasped in horror. "Oh, my God. What about my aunt? My parents. How worried they must be! The outriders must have told them I never arrived. What about my maid? And the others? What did you do to them?"

He bowed his head and muttered, "I dispatched the outriders. I sent word to your parents that you arrived safely and also a message to your aunt that you would not visit until next month. Your servants are within the manor. I instructed them to keep away from you to help you heal and get your memory back all by yourself. They have been well-taken care of."

Fighting back tears at how gullible she had been, even though she had not known who she was, she turned away from him after rising from the bed. "I knew how manipulative you could be to get whatever you wanted two years ago, but such deception is supposed to be beneath you. Please send for Frances. I wish to change out of this... this dress and go home."

"Sarah, please, do not leave. At least, not yet. Let me explain everything to you."

She snorted. "Thank you, but I will never listen to you again. Everything you told me was untruth."

"Not everything, my love." He reached for her and whirled her around even though she stiffened in his arms. "Sarah, I did it because I love you."

She scoffed and yanked herself from his reach. "Such love I can do without. Your so-called love means nothing to me. You made me realise that a long time ago."

He swept his fingers through his hair. "Why do you keep on bringing up the past? I gave you a choice. I explained to you what had happened and if you had only responded to my letter, none of this would be happening now."

She eyed him with confusion. "What are you talking about?"

He frowned. "Oh, come now. Do not pretend that you did not receive the letter I wrote to you before I got married."

She shook her head. "I received no such letter." She folded her arms across her chest and gave him a knowing look. "Another one of your lies, no doubt, to exonerate yourself. By the by, I do not care. I wish to be gone from your presence and your house for good. Do not ever come within a foot of me again or else I will report you to the authorities for kidnapping."

"Sarah..." He took a step towards her.

She lifted her hand to stop him and turned her back on him again. "Twice now, you have hurt me terribly. This time is even worse because you preyed on my vulnerability and made me fall... no... made me *think* that I was in love with you when you were only an illusion. Please let me go and never seek me out again."

He was silent for so long that she thought he had left the room. She curved her body a little and saw him staring at her with dull eyes and deflated shoulders. Her heart went out to him, but she quickly shut out any emotion for him other than anger. With his face ashen, he said, "Very well, then. If that is what you want. I shall arrange for you and your servants to go to your aunt's. It is about an hour's ride from here."

With that, he spun on his heel and headed for the door. There, he paused, "I am sorry. I lied to you about every other thing, but I never lied about my late wife and the way I feel about you. I tried to tell you three days ago but I was interrupted by the footman. When I came back to you and you agreed to marry me promptly, it was my greatest wish come true and I did not want to ruin the happy moment by telling you about our unhappy past. God's truth, I meant to tell you tonight after our wedding. Everything I have ever done has been out of love; for my family and you."

Sarah crumpled to the floor when he left and wept her heart out.

Chapter Ten

Dearest Sarah,

My sweet love. I have tried to move mountains to come to you and tell you this in person. Alas, fate seems to be against our meeting. My sister has taken deathly ill. The bridge linking Easterly to other parts of England was washed away by a terrible storm. I must to wait for it to be reconstructed before I can leave. That is if I can leave without having a row with my parents.

Sarah, my darling, the worst has happened. Father has ordered me to marry the daughter of the Duke and Duchess of Clayford, Lady Harriet Weston to save our dwindling finances. He means for me to marry her because not only will she come with a large dowry to revive our dying family business, but he and her father have agreed to commence another business together. Only my marriage to her can seal the deal and strengthen family ties. I have told him, in unequivocal terms, that I do not wish to marry the Duke's daughter because I have fallen in love with you and want to marry you posthaste. All hell has been raised concerning my decision. Prudence, my sister has taken ill because my father threatened to disown me if I did not carry on with his orders. My mother has begged me incessantly to carry out his bidding. If you remember, I told you about my late elder brother, John, who left the family at a young age because he did *not see eye to eye with my father and he disinherited him. Poor John died in penury and my mother fears that will be my own fate. My mother has gone on a hunger strike until I agree, and Prudence is not doing well either.*

I am at loss at what to do, my love. If I do not marry Lady Harriet, we stand to lose everything. Father has not been wise in his business decisions and gambling pastime. But he has quit gambling, only it is too late. And now I must bear the brunt of all his unwise decisions. I love my family and would do anything for them. But in this instance, I love you, too, Sarah. You complete me in ways words cannot explain. I cannot bear to imagine life without you. I lean towards helping my family out of their predicament, but my love, the ball is in your court. If you reply to this letter and tell me not to marry Lady Harriet, I will not, damning the consequences. It does not matter if my father disowns me, for what is the essence of the title of the Dukedom of Easterly without you in my life? But if you do not reply to this letter or tell me to go ahead and marry Harriet for the sake of my family, I will do so reluctantly. I respect your decision squarely. I do not wish to lose you. However, I must receive a reply from you soon because I am at a crossroads to make a decision.

Please, I do hope you understand, my love. My hands are tied, and I wish for you to release me from this burden, to help me decide what to do. We will find a way together to help my family. I do not mind working as a stable lad just to help my family with stipends for survival. All I desire is to be with you. It will be selfish of me to tell you to wait for me pending when I set my family business going and then, whether propriety allows it or not, divorce Harriet and come back for you. Will you wait for me? I do not think it is right, but I can only hope.

I am sending a runner with this letter to be delivered promptly. I await your decision, my love. No matter what you reply, I will never see you as a selfish person, but as the woman I love and will always.

Yours in waiting,

Benjamin.

I love you.

With shaking hands and tears streaming down her face, Sarah unfolded the second letter her aunt had handed her.

My love,

I waited and waited in vain for your reply to my letter but when I did not receive any, it sealed my fate. I had hoped you did not receive it but the runner reported back to me to tell me that you had. I had hoped against hope that you would be selfish and tell me not to marry Harriet. My heart breaks but I understand not hearing from you, it is because you love my family, too, and want the best for them.

Will you wait for me, Sarah no matter how selfish of me it may seem? I love you and I know I will never stop loving you. If I find a way to get out of the marriage after solving my family's finances, will you accept me back, or is it merely wishful thinking on my part? Oh, Sarah. I love you and always will. Forgive me for still longing to be with you even though I am about to be wed today. Forgive me but I cannot help it. I will love you till my dying day.

Yours in misery,

Benjamin.

Sarah raised accusing eyes at her aunt who had been silently sobbing.

"Why are you just giving me these letters, Aunt Betty? It is two years late!" Sarah cried and rose from her wingback chair in her aunt's salon to pace the floor.

She could not believe that her aunt had kept the letters from her that Benjamin wrote to her two years ago. All the while, she had thought Benjamin had merely toyed with her feelings and then went on to marry a Lady with a larger dowry and into a more affluent family. She had not been aware that he had done so for the sake of his family. Oh, how she had misjudged him.

Two days ago, she had arrived at her aunt's house with puffy eyes from crying while leaving Benjamin's manor. Her aunt, although surprised to see her, had welcomed her warmly. Sarah had been hard pressed not to tell her what happened. Aunt Betty had threatened to have Benjamin arrested but Sarah had pleaded with her not to.

Sarah had stayed abed, weeping and regretting why she had not accepted proposals from other men. She would not have been hurt a second time. Her aunt had tried to console her to no avail until she had blurted out that she loved Benjamin and suspected that she had never really stopped. Aunt Betty had invited her to her salon a few minutes ago and given her the letters that she hid from her two years ago.

"Why, Aunt Betty, why? Things would have been different now. I would not have spent the past two years hating him when it was not his fault."

Dabbing at her eyes with her handkerchief, her aunt replied, "I am so sorry, my dear. I was afraid you would follow in my footsteps."

Sarah paused in her pacing and frowned. "Follow in your footsteps?"

She nodded. "Your father did not tell you why I never married?"

Sarah shook her head.

"Come. Sit." Her aunt patted the seat beside her on the sofa. Sarah reluctantly went to sit beside her.

"I, too, fell in love with a dashing Earl at a young age. Oh, he was everything I desired in a man. He promised to marry me, but then his father forced him into an unwanted marriage with a Duke's daughter. He begged me to wait for him and I foolishly did. Men came my way, but I did not accept their proposals. My guardian, your father, did all he could to get *me* married, but when I threatened to waste away by taking something poisonous, he left me to my fate.

I waited in vain for Charles, but he never came back to me. I wrote him countless letters, but he stopped replying after he got an heir and became wealthy and powerful from the union. Like a fool, I kept on waiting for him, thinking he would come back to me. His wife died and I am ashamed to say I was overjoyed, but Charles never returned to me. I sought him out one day, and he told me too much water had passed under the bridge for us to be together again. He lived only for his children, no one else. Heartbroken, I returned home, but alas it was too late for anyone to look my way. Your father bequeathed this house to me, and here I have been ever since; society's definition of an old maid."

Her aunt sniffed and held Sarah's hand. "I did not want that for you, my dear. I saw how much you loved Lord Bartondale when you were courting. I feared that you would make the same mistake. So, I thought it was kinder to hide his letters, so you could find someone else to fall in love with and marry, rather than to pine away for him; and live an empty life.

Please forgive me, my darling. I was clearly mistaken. Benjamin has undoubtedly shown that he is nothing at all like Charles. I will never forgive myself if I have ruined your chance at happiness."

Sobbing, Sarah threw her arms around her aunt. Pity for what the old woman went through stung her. Even though she did not approve, she understood why her aunt had done it. Her aunt had always seen her as the daughter she never had. After her mother birthed her younger brother, Lady Keymouth had fallen sick. It was Aunt Betty who had taken care of Sarah and taught her how to keep her emotions at bay.

Hopefully, it was not too late for her to rectify the mistake her aunt had made in trying to protect her.

"Aunt Betty, I must go to him. I must explain to him that I did not get his correspondence. Even if I did, I would not have married him. Maybe I would have waited for him, but I would not have allowed him to abandon his family for my sake."

Aunt Betty nodded with approval. "You do that, Sarah, and tell him how sorry I am for interfering in your love story."

"I will." Sarah swiftly rose and hurried to the door. Just as she opened it to step out, she bumped into a rock-like form. Her eyes enlarged when she took a step back and saw it was the man she desired.

"Pardon me, my Lady. I had no idea you sought to leave the room," he immediately said and held her hand. "Your aunt's butler is nowhere to be found. I heard voices and came this way to make my presence known. I know you asked me never to come near you again, but I cannot do that. I have a lot of explaining to do—"

"As do I," Sarah quickly interjected.

His forehead creased. Sarah turned away. "Aunt Betty, with your permission, could we go for a walk in the garden?"

Aunt Betty nodded and Sarah almost laughed when Benjamin's eyes widened, having only just realised her aunt was there. He exchanged pleasantries with the older woman before leading Sarah through the side door to the garden. They walked around the flower-laden gazebo bathed with sunlight for some minutes before Benjamin spoke. Sarah had not known where to begin.

"I must say that I am pleasantly surprised that you have chosen to give me a listening ear, Sarah. I half feared you would have me thrown out on my rear."

Sarah giggled. "Tis because I owe you an apology, my Lord."

"You do?"

She nodded and with fast words, she relayed what her aunt just told her.

"I knew it!" Benjamin grounded to a halt. "I suspected you did not receive the letters."

"Yes. My aunt also told the runner to tell you I did. I am so sorry for judging you harshly all this while. If it is any consolation to you, I would never have agreed for you to abandon your family in their time of need. But I wish I had known your reason for marrying Lady Harriet before now. Even though I would have still been heartbroken about you marrying another woman, it would have saved me from hating you and all other men."

Benjamin caressed her chin. "Will you forgive me for the way I misled you? I could think of no other way to spend time with you again. Having keeping track of you for over a year now, I was desperate not to lose you."

"What?"

He smiled ruefully. "Yes, my love. After Harriet's death, I have been trying to find a way to win you back. When I found out you were coming to visit your aunt from your brother—my secret accomplice—I knew it was my chance to meet with you again. As fate would have it, I came to your rescue." He sighed. "I did not mean to deceive you. After living a miserable life with Harriet who was only interested in attending soirees and cavorting with whichever man was available, I knew my happiness lay with you. I poured myself into the family business and tripled its fortune, but it never gave me joy. I lived in the fear that someday, I would receive news that you were to be wed. When Harriet died riding with an unknown man she sneaked to the countryside with, I knew I had to find you and prove to you that I never stopped loving you. Sarah, will you take me back? Not a day has passed since we parted that you have not crossed my mind and made me wish things were different. I love you."

Sarah pushed back tears of joy. "I love you, too, Benjamin. I never stopped loving you, no matter how hard I tried to pretend otherwise. Why else was it so easy to fall in love with you all over again, even when I thought you were a stranger?"

"Oh, my love." He gathered her into his arms and kissed her lingeringly. "Our love is forever and always."

Epilogue

A month later

Five women, garbed in finery, were seated on a huge bed in their father's house, laughing and teasing one another. The Blackmore sisters had gathered together to converse after the wedding of the youngest sister.

"For shame! To think none of us wanted to get married. But here we are with our husbands and children," Olivia, the second daughter of the Blackmore family, said with a short laugh.

Emily, the first daughter shook her head. "I never said I did not want to marry. I was not interested in whoever Papa and Mama chose for me."

"I am not ashamed to say that I did not want to get married. At least not when I did, but Nicholas swept me off my feet and well..." Beatrice, the third daughter put in with a shrug and they all laughed.

Bridget, the fourth daughter, raised her hand. "Everyone knows I was ready to get married. Only not the way I did."

They all guffawed.

"Sarah," Olivia began. "I must confess that I never thought you would get married. I do not think anyone of us here ever knows what you are thinking. Fudge, we did not even know you had a whirlwind romance with Lord Bartondale."

Sarah blushed to the roots of her hair. "Aunt Betty knew all about it."

"You have always been closer to her than any of us," Bridget grumbled.

Olivia nodded. "I reckon that she taught you how to hide your feelings."

Sarah laughed. "Tis true. Truly, we find love in the least expected places."

They all concurred with her with nods and smiles.

Emily reached for Olivia's hand and nodded at the rest seated on the bed to hold each other's hands.

"Things have turned out beautifully for all of us, have they not?"

"They have," they all agreed.

"I am thankful we all found our happily ever after," Bridget inserted.

Beatrice's head bubbled. "With a Gentleman, a Viscount, a Marquess, an Earl, and another Marquess. I say, the Blackmore sisters have done very well for themselves."

"Here. Here," they chorused.

"I reckon that we will be back here for Alexander's wedding," Olivia snorted.

Sarah snorted as well. She was closer to their only brother than the others since they were closer in age. "Do not count on it. He is hell-bent on being a libertine, a rake. He told me so himself."

"We shall not allow it!" Olivia announced. "Mama will definitely nag him into changing his ways."

Emily shrugged. "Tis too early to worry about it. He is only ten-and-four. There is hope for him yet."

"Why not meet at my husband's castle for Christmas? It is more than enough to house us all," Bridget suggested.

The other sisters agreed and nodded. Sarah glanced surreptitiously at the clock. Although she enjoyed the reunion with her sisters at her wedding, she longed to be with her husband for their honeymoon trip to Paris.

"I know that look," Beatrice mentioned and laughed. "Come on. Let us get you ready to find honey on the moon."

An hour later, having said a teary goodbye to her parents, Aunt Betty, her sisters, and her brother, she promised to write and to go to Scotland for the Christmas holidays. At last, snuggled in the coach, Sarah turned to her husband with loving eyes.

Laughing a little, she reached out to trace his cleft chin with her finger. He caught her hand and kissed it.

"It is still like a dream to me that we are married at last."

"Believe it, my love. You are mine and mine forever."

Her lips twitched. "I love the sound of that."

The End

Did you enjoy *The Blackmore Collection*?

Please consider rating it on Goodreads, Bookbub or your favorite retailer. Reviews help me reach new readers.

Read ***The Norrington Collection*** the next collection in The Lady Series.

Join my Newsletter for updates, sales and giveaways!

www.ingramcontent.com/pod-product-compliance
Lightning Source LLC
Chambersburg PA
CBHW031226020726
47499CB00002B/658